▼▼

The Ferrik house was a shambles, as Amber had said. Someone has searched for something. Carver stepped into Ferrik's sculpture studio. Big bare beams, tall sloping windows.

An immense larger-than-life abstract figure stood in the middle of the room. Apparently a work in progress. The materials of Ferrik's art were strewn about. Carver noticed that one window had a bullet hole in it, the glass glittering on the floor. He turned and looked back at the statue. Sure enough, a bullet hole. He'd let the cops dig the slug out.

Where was Ferrik? So far there was nothing that suggested where he might have gone. Carver started back toward the front room—and stopped.

In the entrance hall a man stood aiming a short-barreled pump-shotgun at Carver. "When is it?" the man asked. The vicious-looking weapon didn't waver. . . .

**Another Fawcett Book
by Kenn Davis:**

WORDS CAN KILL

MELTING POINT

Kenn Davis

FAWCETT GOLD MEDAL • NEW YORK

A Fawcett Gold Medal Book
Published by Ballantine Books
Copyright © 1986 by Kenn Davis

Library of Congress Catalog Card Number: 86-91080

ISBN 0-449-12901-2

Manufactured in the United States of America

First Edition: May 1986

*This one is for
Zekial Marko,
with gratitude*

PROLOGUE

"Look, Roy, look at that," the young black man said. "On the sidewalk."

"Yeah, I sure see that," Roy said. "Blood spots."

"Come from that little white girl just passed us." He slowly fanned his face with a folded newspaper. "Maybe she was knifed?"

"None a our business, Leonard. Looks like she knows where she's goin'. An' it's too goddamn hot to make it our business."

Amber Ferrik, eleven years old, clutched her shoulder where the bullet had hit. Blood stained her yellow dress. She fought back the pain, walking stiffly down Fillmore Street, repeating a particular address fixed in her mind. Small spatters of blood dripped like molten metal onto the hot concrete.

ONE

Rose Weinbaum leaned listlessly in the open doorway between Carver Bascombe's office and her own secretarial domain. She fanned herself with a limp hand and licked salty droplets from her upper lip.

Where, oh, where, she asked herself again, was the fog we're so famous for? Natural air-conditioning? Hell with that.

The windows were wide open in the third-floor office. The air was stifling. The incoming light filled the room with an eye-squinting glare. The heat was a killer. A noisy table fan whirred in a corner, stirring dust particles on a battered old desk. Vivaldi's *The Four Seasons* played softly on a stereo set. The music competed with the clattering of the fan.

Carver Bascombe sat behind the desk, slowly rubbing one stockinged foot over the other. He exhaled, more in exasperation, and wiped the sheen of moisture from his brow. His movements were conscious and slow.

On the desk was an icy bottle of Anchor Steam beer. Carver lifted it to his lips and drank slowly, savoring the chill, tangy brew. He looked at his office door and sighed. More exasperation. He had stared at that door many times in the past few days.

He looked at Rose, still fanning herself, still listless. He nodded once at the beer, a gesture of invitation, and Rose shook her head. He looked around the office. Metal filing cabinets, a television set, a small refrigerator, bookshelves. The fan. The stereo. The lettering on the open windows threw a stark shadow on the floor that read:

PRIVATE INVESTIGATIONS
CARVER BASCOMBE
CIVIL—INDUSTRIAL

On Carver's right was a door that opened to his small apartment. A bedroom, kitchenette, and a bathroom. Office and apartment combined.

Rose had often strongly suggested that he rent a bigger apartment; his books were crowding him out. Surrounding the bed were rows of brick-and-board shelves with books on law and criminology, sharing space with volumes on painting and poetry, ballet and opera. All the arts. Unmatched editions of Dickens, Chekhov, Wright, Simenon, Felix Kuttnur, and others mingled with books on the Renaissance and impressionism.

Carver looked again at the closed office door, at the mail slot. Rose shook her head at him.

"It's still not here," she said.

"What's not?" Carver asked.

"The letter."

"Oh," he said sheepishly.

"The letter from the State Bar Association will get here," Rose continued, "when it gets here." She exhaled slowly, almost a sigh, as though the effort exhausted her. "Staring at the door isn't going to make the mail from Sacramento move any faster."

4

He averted his eyes from the door and took a pull from the beer bottle. Had he passed the state bar examination? Was he a legally qualified lawyer? Or would he have to take the test over?

"I'm nervous," he said, and tugged at the lightweight, open-necked shirt that stuck to his skin.

"No, boss, you're apprehensive."

"Is that what it is?"

"Sure."

Rose Weinbaum had the most sexual, erotic voice Carver had ever heard. On the telephone, her words, courteous, everyday, businesslike words, dripped with unintentional suggestiveness. It was one of Mother Nature's little whims that matched an erotic voice with a plain, somewhat thin woman.

She was the widow of Bernie Weinbaum, a private detective who had been gunned down while working on a case with Carver. A taint of guilt over Bernie's death still tickled at the corners of Carver Bascombe's mind. Particularly since Rose had never blamed him, not one particle.

Rose had showed her practical self when she offered to come into Carver's business for a one-third split of the profits. If any. She was willing to take that chance. She also threw in a steady backlog of Bernie's clients. With a little coaxing, she had convinced Carver to expand the office, to create a secretary's office for herself, complete with leather couch and chairs, telephone, and a very good secondhand top-of-the-line electric typewriter.

"Rose, I'm still not used to this sitting and waiting," Carver said. "No more law classes to attend. No clients. I don't like waiting. Not like this, anyway, not in this heat. The other students who pass the exams will be looking for jobs in big legal firms. Not me. I already have a business. Or do I? Don't we have anything on the line? Anything at all?"

"None whatsoever. Nothing to get your mind off that letter. Or the heat. You recovered that painting for whatsisname, and you don't have to deal with the electronic security on

Moseby's Gallery for another week. Checkups on the other galleries and shops aren't due for a fortnight."

"A what?"

"Two weeks. English style."

"You say these things just to aggravate me."

"Sure."

A single knock on the outer door caught Rose's attention. Two more feeble knocks were heard as she went into her office. Carver heard the door open and then Rose gasped harshly.

"Carver! Quick!"

He hurriedly joined her in the outer office.

A young girl knelt at the entrance, one blood-smeared hand clutching the door frame. The shoulder of her yellow dress was sodden with blood. A matching purse, which hung from her other shoulder, had a few small red dots. He swore under his breath. He knelt beside the girl and thought he heard her whisper "Daddy," but he wasn't sure. He slipped loose the shoulder of her dress.

"How bad?" Rose asked.

"She's been shot," Carver said, his words clipped, urgent. "The bullet nicked her. Call an ambulance, Rose, and get the police."

"Are you Mr. Bascombe?" the girl asked faintly.

"Yes, I am."

"Oh, good," she said, and closed her eyes. She folded over.

He lifted the girl gently, carried her into his bedroom, and laid her on the bed. He opened the gold-colored purse and removed a wallet. He looked at its contents. The girl fluttered her eyelids and looked at the tall man kneeling beside her. Carver smiled at her.

He waited, feeling her pulse. Rose came in and dampened a face cloth in the bathroom and got some disinfectant from the medicine cabinet. She handed them to Carver.

"The ambulance and the cops are on the way," Rose said.

"Are you strong enough?" Carver asked the girl. "Strong enough to answer questions?"

"Yes," she said faintly. "I think so."

"Who are you?" he asked.

"I like your color," the girl said. "It's a very handsome brown."

"Thank you, but who are you?"

"I'm Amber Ferrik," she replied, shutting her eyes and clenching her teeth. "I'm eleven years old."

"Are you in pain, Amber?"

"Of course," she said as though she could hardly believe anyone would ask such a silly question. "Yes, it hurts."

Carver grinned. As he sat beside her and cleaned around the wound, Carver studied the girl. Amber Ferrik was slender, with dark-yellow hair that fell just past her shoulders. Her eyes were the brown of rusted metal. Long lashes cast shadows over her cheeks. Her mouth was set in a thin line. When she spoke, her lips were full but pale. Under normal circumstances, they would be moist and pink.

"Why did you come here, Amber?" Carver asked.

Her voice was faint, as though it had been whittled down from a larger specimen. She looked around the bedroom, at the books, and then at the kitchenette.

"Do you live here?"

"Yes, I do."

"My daddy would find that interesting, I'll bet. You live where you work, and he works where he lives. Where we live."

"Any idea why she came here?" Rose asked Carver.

"Not yet." He turned to Amber. "This lady is Rose. She's my secretary. And friend. Rose, this is Amber."

"Hello, Miss Rose," Amber said.

"Who is your mommy and daddy, Amber?" Rose asked.

"Just my daddy. My mommy doesn't live with us anymore."

"What's your daddy's name, Amber?"

"Tom. Tom Ferrik. And he's lost." She looked at Carver. "Would you find my daddy, Mr. Bascombe?"

"If I can. I'll sure try."

"Carver," Rose asked, "do you know her father?"

"No. The name does sound familiar." He held out the wallet from Amber's purse. "She lives over in Berkeley. Somehow she got all this way." He turned to Amber. "Who shot you, Amber? Do you know?"

"No, Mr. Bascombe. I—I didn't see anyone."

"Do you know why anyone would shoot at you?"

"No, not really. I don't know why. But my daddy said I should look for you. I had your address. It's in my purse. My daddy is missing. I haven't seen him since yesterday when I went to school."

"Easy now," Carver said.

He had been holding the girl's wrist, checking her pulse. She seemed to be in good condition despite the bloody wound. As far as he could tell, the wound was superficial; shock was the real danger, but Amber seemed strong and able. Who would shoot an eleven-year-old kid? And why?

"Did you tell anyone else?" he asked.

"About my daddy, Mr. Bascombe?"

"Yes, that, and about your coming here."

"Do you think I'm dumb?"

"No," Carver replied.

"Then I wouldn't tell anyone, would I?"

"No, I don't think so."

"I didn't tell anyone. I know better."

"You seem like a very self-reliant person, Amber. Tell me everything, if you can."

"Of course I can. I'm not dead. I have a good memory. An exceptional memory, my daddy said. And this didn't happen last year, did it?"

"Hardly," Carver said with a grin.

"I came home from school yesterday, and the whole house was a mess—"

"As though it had been searched?"

"Yes, that's it. Like the television cops-and-robbers shows. And there was a broken window in Daddy's studio. I was scared, real scared."

"What did you do then?"

"Then the phone rang. It was Daddy, and he said he had to go away and that I was to see you. He made me repeat what he said. Then he hung up. I was afraid. I spent the night at a girl friend's house. This morning I made believe I was going to school, but I really took the subway across the bay and came looking for you. Like my daddy said I should do."

"Tell me about the shooting."

"I was getting off the bus when I was shot. Only a few blocks from here."

"Did you hear the shot?"

"No, I didn't."

"And no one helped you?"

"No. I didn't feel anything at first, just as if someone had pushed me hard. I didn't even know I was bleeding until I had walked about a half a block. Then I just held on to my shoulder, looking for your address that Daddy had once given me."

From the office came a clatter of sound, and seconds later a young doctor stepped into Carver's apartment. He was followed by two ambulance attendants carrying a stretcher. The doctor wore white and looked like a high-school valedictorian.

Unruffled, seemingly unaffected by the heat, the young doctor was brisk and soothing, smiling quickly and genuinely at Amber. He checked her over, rolling her eyelids back, shining a light into her pupils. He cleaned the wound, then injected a painkiller and antibiotics. Carver and Rose quickly gave an explanation of the situation to the doctor.

Two perspiring uniformed cops came in, followed by a

middle-aged plainclothes detective. The detective took off his jacket and rolled a handkerchief around the back of his neck. Carver talked briefly with them in his office, which was getting crowded; body heat was raising the temperature.

The older uniformed cop had graying, grizzled hair under his cap. He wiped beads of sweat from his thick upper lip. Both policemen were in short-sleeved blue uniforms, but their bulky equipment of guns, radios, batons, and cuffs made them seem excessively hot and weary. The other cop was younger, in his midtwenties, Carver guessed. The young officer looked around the office, his eyes settling frequently on the bottle of beer on the desk. He licked his lips.

Carver opened the door of the office refrigerator and took out three cola bottles. He handed them to the detective and the two cops.

The detective's eyes glittered, and he licked his lips. He unscrewed the top and drank down a third. He seemed more interested in something frosty than in what had happened to a little girl. And so far he was nameless. As Carver slipped into his shoes, he asked the detective's name.

"Stein," the detective said, drawing the word out as though it might fill itself with ice-cold draft beer.

Detective Stein sighed and used one hand to pull out a notebook. He took another pull from the bottle. Almost empty. He put the bottle down on Carver's desk and then used a wet exhalation to blow the pages over. He breathed laboriously and carefully searched for a pen.

Stein was only an inch or so under Carver's six-two. He was over forty, going into an early grave from heat prostration. At least that's what he had told himself at least five times since getting out of bed. Hard rolls of fat strained his shirt and greased his armpits in blobby crescent shapes. There was little doubt that a lot of weight loss would improve his life expectancy.

He found a pen and poised it over a damp page of his

notebook; he waited as the doctor had Carver Bascombe sign some papers. God, what a job, Stein said to himself. He finished the soda pop. Wasn't there nuttin' he could do to cool off? He'd already had two beers since breakfast. And a bottle of pop, full a sugar, too.

The young doctor told the two attendants to carry Amber out.

"Wait," Carver asked the stretcher bearers. He leaned over and spoke to Amber Ferrik. Her wound wasn't serious, Carver told her, but she was going to a hospital. The doctor didn't want to take chances.

"Are you going to come with us?" Amber asked him.

"Rose will go with you." He looked at Rose, and she nodded. He looked at Amber. "I'm going to Berkeley, to your house. You want me to find your daddy, don't you?"

"Oh, yes. That's the most important of anything."

"Then I need to know what he looks like. Give me a description of your daddy, Amber."

"Oh, he's tall, almost as tall as you, Mr. Bascombe," Tom Ferrik was also an old man, much older than Carver, about thirty-eight, or so, Amber told him. Daddy had often said funny things about turning forty in a couple of years. And he had light brown hair, which he wore long in back and tied off with a rubber band. And he had a nice laugh, and he smelled like different kinds of wood 'cause he carved a lot of wood. Was that enough? Amber asked.

"Plenty," Carver said, and pressed her small hand. She squeezed back, smiling at him. He opened her purse and removed a key. "This is your house key?"

Amber nodded, and Carver put the key in his pocket.

Following the doctor and the stretcher, Rose closed the door behind her.

"Okay, let's have it official, Mr. Bascombe," Stein said.

As Carver related the details of Amber's visit, the other

two cops stood near the open windows. Just breathing air, drinking soda pop.

"Okay," Stein said. "No idea why the little girl came here, Mr. Bascombe?"

"She said her daddy told her to come here. If she was in trouble."

"Yeah? What kind of trouble?"

"I haven't the faintest idea."

"Who's her father?"

"Tom Ferrik. He must be a sculptor. I've heard the name or read it in an art review."

"An artist, huh?"

"Yeah," Carver said.

"You're a private detective, huh?" the young cop asked.

"Yeah."

"Never met one before."

"Consider it a privilege," Carver said. He looked at Stein. "If there's anything more, I'll come down to the station and give a more complete version, but there's not much else."

"You in a hurry?" Stein asked.

"Sure. I've got to find the girl's father."

"You taking her on as a client?"

"Why not?"

"No retainer?" the young cop asked. His question had an edge. "I thought all you guys worked for money."

"Oh, you can be sure I'll collect a fee. When I see the girl at the hospital." He stood in the doorway, a lightweight jacket folded over his arm. "Anything else?"

Stein shook his head. The three officers followed Carver down the stairs. The cops gabbed with each other: where they were going to eat lunch and wouldn't an ice-cold beer just taste great? Stein said nothing but rolled his tongue over his lips. Carver noticed the blood spots on the stair steps. Amber's trail. A few smeared handprints. Didn't the cops notice?

On the street, a few bystanders still milled about. Carver

could just make out the city ambulance hustling down Fillmore Street. A black-and-white police car was parked in front of a fire hydrant. An unmarked green sedan was parked nearby. The cops climbed into the black-and-white. Stein shambled across the sidewalk and got into his sedan. As the two cars pulled away, Carver wiped a film of perspiration from his forehead. He nodded to himself; he was hot and sweaty just walking down three flights.

Oh, yeah. It was going to be one scorcher, all right. And he had a couple of blocks to walk to the Hi-Valu service station where his car was stored and serviced. Carver made a mental note to stock up on beer when he returned.

He looked at the sidewalk; the crowd had smeared most of the blood spots. Carver followed the rust-colored spots up Fillmore. At the Hi-Valu service station, he was greeted by his good friend Jimmy Bowman.

"Need the Jag, Cahva?"

"Yeah, Jimmy."

"I've kept it in the shade, outta the sun."

"Thanks, Jimmy."

"You won't burn your ass on the seats."

"I'm going for a walk up the street, Jimmy. Have it ready in ten or fifteen minutes?"

"Sure, Cahva. That car is almost becoming a classic. Why don' you sell it? To me?"

Carver smiled and shook his head. They'd been around this buy-the-car routine a few times.

"It must cost a helluva lot just in insurance premiums," Bowman said. "You oughtta get you'se'f something with better gas mileage, one of them Japanese cricket cars. This Jag-u-ar eats gas. Some kinda child in candyland, is what it is at the gas pumps. You know, I'd take real good care of it, if I owned it."

"Same pitch—same answer, Jimmy," Carver replied.

Bowman shook his head regretfully. He was a darker shade

of brown than Carver. Chocolate-chip-colored freckles were spotted over his face. He thrust his arms out, exorcising his regrets, and then grinned. Oh, sure, he knew he was never going to own that beautiful car, but he had to try now and again. Carver understood. Gambling fever. The Hi-Valu wasn't only a gas station. It was a permanent floating crap game at night. Sure.

Jimmy waved his friend away.

Carver moved on, following Amber's trail. Damn, it was hot! The sidewalk practically shimmered. He put on a pair of sunglasses. The spatters of blood looked black, like tiny jagged pits that had opened up in the concrete. The few pedestrians walked on the shady eastern side of the street. But they walked slowly, as though it were a terrible effort to move down the slight slope. There was a smell in the air, the smell of a city frying.

A block past the Clay Theater, Carver stopped on the north side of Washington Street. This is where it happened. He looked over the territory. The bus . . . It would stop about here, and the passengers would get off about here. Yeah, there're the first blood spots. Now where would a sniper hide? The sniper couldn't have known where Amber was going, unless she had told someone. She had said that she had told no one. Which means that he—or she—had to have been following the bus in a car.

He wondered where the sniper had picked up Amber's trail. In Berkeley? At the girl's house? If so, why hadn't he shot her then? Or had he—or she—somehow known that she would take BART into the city? But had not known her destination? A lot of questions. Yeah. A lot.

Yeah, if he were the sniper, Carver figured, he would have driven behind the bus, watching who got off, keeping about a half block behind. Maybe stopped on the other side of the intersection, parked for a few moments illegally, in front of that fire hydrant, maybe. Then what? Take a rifle—maybe a cut-down varmint rifle. Maybe.

A green sedan pulled into the curb. Sergeant Stein climbed out. He looked at Carver and nodded without saying one word. He looked at the blood spots and walked slowly to the intersection. He looked up and down the streets. A few notes were written into the notebook. Again Stein nodded, more to himself this time. He exhaled noisily, wiped sweat from his neck, and then climbed back into his car and drove off.

Carver watched, then went back into his own thoughts. Back to the basic question: Why? To stop Amber from seeing Carver? How would the would-be assassin know where she was going? Did the shooter simply take advantage of Amber finally being on foot? Amber had said she had taken the rapid-transit train. Which meant that the sniper had to have had some means of following her underground. Had he been with her on the train? Then when did he pick up the car?

Carver returned to the Hi-Valu station and climbed into his Jaguar. He checked the car's burglar alarm system and then pulled into traffic and took the quickest route to the freeway. He followed the signs east to Berkeley across the bay. The hot wind blew against his face.

A case, he thought. Certainly more interesting than sitting around a hot, stuffy office. And there were all these fascinating questions. Little morsels to chew on. Did Amber's father leave her a note? Apparently not—unless she overlooked it. That would be one thing he would search for in the Ferrik house.

Why hadn't he taken her with him? Had he been in that much of a hurry? Could he have known that someone might try to shoot her? It didn't seem probable. Surely he loved her and would do almost anything to protect her. Wouldn't he? Some parents didn't. And where was Tom Ferrik?

*   *   *

Sgt. Ernie Ludlow squinted against the glare reflecting off the rippling water of the Vaillancourt Fountain. He slid a pair of sunglasses over his eyes. Much easier to see the corpse that floated in the water.

The nearby Embarcadero hummed with heat and traffic. The bay was a taut-stretched skin of plastic wrap. The nearby high-rise buildings of the Golden Gateway seemed to twinkle with heat, throwing bald-sky reflections from hundreds of windows. The hilly streets seemed to be made of taffy, warping and flowing in a gauzy, lung-choking inferno.

The fountain was a series of giant slab-sided ducts that crisscrossed overhead, spreading over a vast pond like a skinned beast. Water flowed through and over the ducts, creating waterfalls and spillways that passed over walkways. The spot was an oasis, a cooling trickle, a splashing pond, reminding wilting citizens of balmier times past. (Would the heat ever break?) The fountain was for the public's amusement and enjoyment; they could saunter around and under the cool, trickling ducts. Even in the glaring daylight, the water spilling from the Vaillancourt Fountain reflected the rotating red Mars lights from the nearby police cars.

The dead man floated gently in the fountain's water.

A crowd of curious bystanders were kept back by police officers. An ambulance was parked nearby, with several attendants ready to retrieve the body at the command of the medical examiner. The M.E. stood a few feet from Sergeant Ludlow.

"Who found the body?" Ludlow asked.

A cop pointed to a bystander. Ludlow gestured for the man to step forward.

Ernie Ludlow was a large man, built like a block of lignum vitae. He was the color of old iron, almost solid black. He wore a hat in any weather, and today the sweatband was stained almost as dark as his skin. He wore a lightweight gray suit, carrying the jacket over one arm. At his hip was a .357 Smith & Wesson with a two-inch barrel.

The man who had found the body was nervous; he was white and seemed to be ill at ease as he faced the black city detective. Ludlow was used to the reaction; he took great pains to cultivate it. He had little liking for white civilians. For that matter, he didn't like many of the white cops and detectives. Going a step further, he didn't care for much of humanity. White or black.

But he was a good cop, a tough cop, and he knew his job. He removed his hat, wiped the sweat from the band, pulled the sunglasses off, and smiled at the witness. The smile was like the grin that a shark might have before chomping a swimmer in half. Ludlow knew about public relations. He'd been told about it by his superiors hundreds of times.

"So, you found the body?" Ludlow asked.

"Ah, nosir, not exactly. I just noticed it. He'd been there for some time."

"Okay, Jack, back up a bit." Ludlow pulled a notebook from his pocket and poised a pen over a blank page. "From the beginning. Your name, where you work, your immediate supervisor, your home address, telephone number, and some sort of identification."

"Ah, yessir," the man said, clearing his throat and wiping the sheen of sweat from his forehead.

He handed Ludlow his wallet. His name was Jack Esse, and please no jokes. He was twenty-six years old and worked for an advertising agency as a copywriter, and then gave all the other particulars. Ludlow returned the wallet.

"It was a hot day, and, ah, I volunteered to take some papers for my boss over to his accountant. I sort of took it easy, you know, sort of goofing off, and figured I might take a stroll around the fountain. You know, cool off a bit. Then maybe buy a cold beer."

"That's when you found the body?"

"Not the way it is now. See, I was walking under one of the waterfalls and I noticed this man sitting on the edge of the poolside. He had his pants rolled up to his knees and his feet in the water. I thought to myself, now there's a good idea. I wondered if I could take a few minutes and soak my feet. Then I noticed something odd."

"Yeah?"

"His head was down on his chest and he had his coat draped over his shoulders. Goddamn hot for a coat, I said to myself. And he hadn't moved in the few minutes I had seen him. Maybe he was sick or something. Maybe a heart attack. You know, a hot day, and suddenly your feet get into cold water, that might be a shock for some people."

Ah, Christ, Ludlow thought to himself, hurry it up, Jack. He didn't have all goddamn day.

"So I went over to him," the man continued, "and asked him if he was okay. He didn't say anything, and I put my hand on his shoulder. I'll never forget it as long as I live." Esse shook his head and wiped his mouth with the back of his hand. "Yeah, the guy just sort of toppled over, went face-down into the pool. I still had hold of the guy's coat. And then I saw the two holes in his back and the water getting kind of red, sort of pink. I just knew it was blood. Knew he'd been shot."

Ludlow nodded, and after a few minutes he had all the information he was going to get from the man. He took the dead man's coat from Jack Esse and dismissed him, telling him that he'd probably be called as a witness. Then Ludlow turned to the M.E., Dr. Wolfram.

"Okay, Doc, you might as well pull him in, check him over. Tell me what you can."

As Dr. Wolfram motioned for the ambulance attendants to get the body, Ludlow checked the coat. An off-the-rack job from a chain department store, he noted silently. Nothing in the side pockets. Looks like a bit of clay on the elbows and a smear of the same stuff on one collar point. Jesus. Ludlow wrinkled his nose. The guy hadn't taken a bath very recently and sure hadn't had the coat cleaned often; the lining almost rotted out around the armpits. Let's see—the wallet. I'll be damned. Intact, no credit cards stolen and over eighty bucks inside. First guess, an execution. Not a robbery. But let's not get ahead of ourselves.

"Shot twice," Dr. Wolfram said, coming up alongside Sergeant Ludlow. "Close range. There's a definite aureole of gunpowder around each entrance wound."

"Yeah?" Ludlow replied. "Any exit holes?"

"None. The slugs are still inside."

"Any guess as to what caliber of weapon?"

"Nothing heavy, but I don't think it was a twenty-two. Not that kind of an execution."

"Don't try to read my mind." Ludlow grunted.

"What was the man's name?" Dr. Wolfram asked, pointing to the open wallet in Ludlow's hand.

"Ferrik," Ludlow said, "Thomas Ferrik."

TWO

The main room was as Carver had imagined: two-story ceiling, natural wood paneling, and tall windows facing west. The closed-in heat almost sucked the air from his lungs. Carver shrugged off his jacket, folding it over one arm. He left the front door open and then opened sliding glass doors that led onto a prow-shaped deck. He fanned himself as a hot draft sluggishly moved the heated air.

He had looked over the Ferrik house from the outside and had noted the shingled sidings and the steep roof. The house was on a slope, with small pines, shrubbery, and a well-kept lawn in front. The scents of many flowers rose like liquid in the hot air. Violets. Rhododendron. He had checked the mailbox before entering. It was empty.

The front room was furnished with soft leather couches and chairs. The place was a shambles, as Amber had said. Someone had searched for something. Off to the left he could see into a spacious kitchen. The large house seemed comfortable and well-lived-in. He could imagine Amber romping from room to room, throwing her clothes and schoolbooks any which way, scattering papers, crayons, and toys wherever she used them.

Or was she one of those neat children?

Couldn't tell from the tossing.

Carver moved through the house, absorbing the impressions of the father and daughter who lived there. Along the walls were niches where small, prized sculptures were placed: some Eskimo carvings and several nice African masks—a Dogon *Kanaga* (Hand of God) mask and a mask from the Baule tribe of the Ivory Coast.

Carver liked the masks from the Dogon and Baule tribes; they showed the natives' intellectual curiosity and awareness of other African tribes, and even of white Europeans. Yeah, they were originals, all right. Masks were protection for the wearer rather than disguises to hide behind. Did Ferrik have some other reason for owning them—other than their monetary worth?

Other statues were a knobbly Giacometti figure, a stainless-steel Battenberg. On one wall was a large Fletcher Benton; powered by tiny electric motors, its multicolored panes still moved and shifted.

Eclectic gathering, Carver thought, but all revealing an appreciation of quality modern work. No imitation stuff, no replicas, no junk. That said something about Tom Ferrik.

Why hadn't the statues been stolen? Valuable stuff.

Carver stepped into Ferrik's sculpture studio. Big bare beams and a block-and-tackle to lift heavy materials. Tall, sloping windows let in northern light. Hundreds of art books filled the bookshelves. Carver gazed at them with a touch of envy.

An immense, larger-than-life abstract figure stood in the middle of the room. Apparently a work in progress. Several mallets, chisels, drills, and drill bits were scattered over the dropcloth-covered floor. The materials of Ferrik's art were strewn about: stone and wood cutting tools, clay figures, armatures, and large slabs of marble and wood.

One window had a bullet hole in it, the glass glittering on the floor. Obviously fired from outside. Before hitting the glass, the bullet would had to have passed between two bushes.

He turned, then walked over to the statue. Sure enough, a bullet hole. He'd let the cops dig out the slug.

Carver went into the kitchen and took a can of beer from the refrigerator. He popped the top and drank. He sighed and rubbed the chilled can against his temples. Yeah, it was hot. Trite but godawful true. Stinking hot.

Where was Ferrik? So far there was nothing that suggested where he might have gone. Maybe Carver might have better luck in the bedrooms.

He started back toward the front room—and stopped. In the entrance hall a man stood aiming a short-barreled pump-shotgun at Carver. His face was distorted by a woman's stocking pulled tight over his head. The vicious-looking weapon didn't waver from Carver's chest.

"When is it?" the man asked. His voice was low but carried well; it had a gruff, self-conscious timbre, as though the man were an actor reading a part.

"When?" Carver asked slowly. Buying time. "What do you mean, when?"

He slowly raised the beer can and sipped. Try and act natural. What kind of a question was "When"? The guy didn't ask "Who are you" or "What are you doing here?" Nothing like that. Just "When?" Oh, the nutsos come from the woodwork out.

Stepping into the room, the man motioned with the shotgun, the gesture telling Carver to back off. Arrogance and self-assurance described the man's attitude, and they fitted his movements. He held his head erect on a thick-veined neck. A trickle of sweat slid from under the stocking, down his neck, and stained his pale yellow polo shirt. The sweat didn't come from nervousness.

"You know what I mean," the man said. "When is it. Ferrik knows, and I think Argent knows. And if he does, you probably know."

"You're making a mistake. I don't know, because I don't know any Argent—whoever he is. And I don't know Tom Ferrik."

"Sure," the man said sarcastically.

"I'm looking for him," Carver explained.

"Sure," the man repeated. The word was as snide as before.

"I'm a private detective—"

"I don't give a shit who you are," the man interrupted harshly. "I only want to know one thing—"

"Yeah, I know . . . 'When?' "

"You got it."

"Tom Ferrik is missing, and I'm looking for him."

"Sure."

The man had a fondness for the word. Probably only knew one way to use it.

"You can check my identification," Carver suggested. "It's in my wallet."

"Okay," the man said, and stepped closer, holding out one hand for Carver's ID card.

Carver cursed himself later. He should have seen it coming. The guy was almost too casual.

As Carver reached into his coat, the man swung the shotgun. Carver sensed the sudden movement and snapped his head to one side. The steel barrel glanced off his head, but Carver staggered. His feet skidded out from under him and he fell. Beer splattered from the can, soaking his dropped jacket. For a brief moment, he was close to blacking out. He shook his head, trying to clear it. Roll! he yelled inside his mind. Move it!

The man kicked him. Carver forced himself back from a gray cloud that clotted his mind. He shook his head—that was another mistake. A surge of nausea flashed up from his stomach. He blinked his eyes and turned over.

The man with the stockinged face was searching his coat. Looked at his license in the ID wallet. Glanced at Carver. Shook his head slowly. The man threw the coat onto the floor and then the wallet. He looked around the room, then strode through the sliding doors and onto the deck. In another second he was gone. Just walked away.

Carver forced himself erect. He stood weakly on two blubbery stumps of gelatin. Now what? Well, the first thing would be to call the police. No, he didn't like that. Well, then, how about chasing the guy? Better.

Carver stepped outside. The deck overlooked gardens strewn with bright-colored flowers. The sunlight was almost painful. Carver moved to the side of the deck and found a wooden ladder. He went over the railing, then moved through the garden and quickly found a trail. Which way? Up or down the trail? Much easier to go down. Carver loped downhill. The trail took a slight bend, and as Carver followed the curve, a sudden explosion made him jump. A rhododendron bush disintegrated! Carver heard the rattle of shotgun pellets blasting through the leaves and branches.

To hell with it.

That much noise would surely have the neighbors calling the police. Carver waited for a full minute, listening to his own breathing. And damned glad to be able to do so. Some distance away, an automobile started and shrieked away, tires squealing. If the guy wanted to go, fine, let him go. Carver knew a nasty message when he heard one. He walked back to Ferrik's house.

In the kitchen Carver cleaned the blood from his temple. In another part of the house he found several bedrooms, one of which was apparently Amber's. In the master bedroom he

searched for an indication of where Tom Ferrik might have
gone. Not a damn thing, he thought to himself. Nothing in
the closets, but on the dresser were two photographs of a
lovely young woman. She was black, with large eyes, prominent cheekbones, a mouth that smiled generously, and long,
fluffy hair. The photos had signed inscriptions: To Tom, with
love, Sharon. Nice handwriting.

Other photographs were of Amber—and none of an older
man, no Tom Ferrik, and none of any woman who might
have been Amber's mother. He rummaged further in the
dresser and found an address book. Carver turned the pages
and under "A" he read the name Sharon Argent. With an
address on Bernal Heights. There was no other Sharon in the
book. No other Argent.

Other than the address book, nothing. Nothing in the dresser,
nothing among the papers in the study. He put the address
book in his pocket.

He looked in Amber's bedroom and selected a pair of
yellow pajamas and a red robe. Carver figured the girl would
need them. He headed for the front door. And stopped.

A man stood near the entrance. He was a dark silhouette
framed by the glare of the open front door behind him.

Carver cursed silently.

"Yeah," the man said. "Just don't move, Jack."

Carver recognized the voice and let out a breath of air.

"Bascombe," the man said, "what the fuck are you doing
here?"

Sgt. Ernest Ludlow. Carver sighed. Well, it was certainly
better than the gunfighter coming back. Right? Right.

A uniformed Berkeley policeman stepped into the entrance-
way. Sergeant Ludlow told him to stay. Keep the door open.

"You vouch for him?" the cop asked, indicating Carver
Bascombe.

"Fuck, no," Ludlow said. "But I know the bastard. Just a

private cop. What the hell, Bascombe, just what the hell are you doing here?''

"I'm on a job," Carver explained, holding out the clothing. "Just picking up some things a client might need."

"Oh, yes, what is he, a midget?" Ludlow looked around the room. "And I suppose you just like to throw coats and beer around. You often treat your clients' homes like your own?''

"She's a little girl," Carver said, ignoring Ludlow's last question. "You know, Amber Ferrik."

"Why would I know her?" Ludlow asked.

"Isn't that why you're here? Because she was shot only a little while ago?''

"No," Ludlow said.

"No?''

"You heard me," Ludlow said. "I don't know anyone named Amber Ferrik.''

He walked into the room, surveying it. Carver followed and picked up his coat and placed the beer can on a coffee table. He watched the black detective, realizing that Ludlow was probably making a mental inventory. Sergeant Ludlow, the man with the incredible memory, almost a photographic eye, a filing-cabinet mind.

"With the permission of the Berkeley police," Ludlow said, then grunted, "I'm just checking on the man of the house.''

"Tom Ferrik?''

"You know him?''

"No, I don't," Carver said, and gave a brief version of Amber coming to his office. And that he was looking for her father. He fingered his temple. "That's how I got this." He told Ludlow about the intruder with the shotgun.

Ludlow scanned the room. "He toss the house?" he asked.

"I don't know.''

Ludlow completed his circuit of the house, scanning the

studio, the kitchen, the bedrooms. He looked at the photos of Amber and Sharon Argent. Carver could almost hear Ludlow's mind clicking and filing.

"Jesus," Ludlow muttered, "another nigger lover. Ferrik." He looked at Carver, an evil, satisfied glint in his eyes. "Well, Jack, you can stop looking for the father. We found him. He's dead. He was fished out of the Vaillancourt Fountain less than an hour ago."

A painful jolt seemed to hit Carver's chest. Droplets of sweat broke out on his brow. He wiped them off. Damn. Damn. This was getting out of control.

"How did he die?" Carver asked, his heart sinking, realizing that he would have to tell Amber the bad news.

"Shot. A couple of times in the back. The killer had some ghoulish sense of humor—managed to plant Ferrik at the pond like he was soaking his dogs."

He looked quizzically at Carver. Something was wrong, and Ludlow didn't like it when he smelled something putrid. Fuck, no. Especially when this black asshole Bascombe was mixed up in it. Nosir, he didn't like the stink of this one. Not with a white guy taking up with a black woman. People should stay with their own kind. Yeah, it smelled. And there was something Bascombe wasn't telling him.

"This intruder," Ludlow said, "this guy who you say attacked you, you know something about him, don't you?"

"I do?"

"Goddammit! Don't play cute with me, Bascombe. You've done it in the past and all it does is get you into big trouble. Did you recognize him?"

"I told you—he wore a stocking mask. He was white, he was tall, six feet, about two-twenty. A big guy." Carver had held back the man's odd question—"When is it?"—and he wondered if it was smart to tell Ludlow.

"You're thinking, Bascombe," Ludlow said, "I can see it in your face. Come on, let's have it."

Reluctantly Carver told him.

"When, huh? That means he wanted to know when something was about to happen."

"That's what I figured," Carver said flatly. He didn't like Ludlow's attitude, so he withheld the knowledge that the guy had mentioned the name Argent and that the photos in the bedroom were of a woman named Sharon Argent. The cops would get to her in their own time.

"Any idea what he meant?"

Before Carver could answer, they were interrupted by the hurried entrance of two Berkeley cops. Two young men with revolvers drawn, waving the handguns this way and that. The neighbors' report of gunfire had brought them running, and what the hell—two black guys are standing there with fire coming out of their eyes. What the hell is this?

"Easy, fellas," said the cop who had accompanied Sergeant Ludlow. He gave them a rundown. They looked at Ludlow's shield and then dubiously at Carver's ID. Would Ludlow vouch for the private detective? Nah. For all Ludlow knew, Carver was making everything up.

The two officers looked at one another; the only civilian in the house was the P.I.—and the cops had to go by the book. Bascombe had to give a statement at Berkeley headquarters. Bascombe agreed even though he wanted desperately to see Amber Ferrik at the hospital.

"Tell you what, Bascombe," Ludlow said, his tone more of a command than a request, "after you get through with these guys, I want to hear all of this story in detail. I'll be at the morgue. You meet me there."

"Now wait, Sergeant," Carver said irritably, "I told you—I never met Ferrik. I can't identify the dead man. Amber told me what her father looked like, but it wasn't much. I was hoping to find a photograph of the man."

"Okay, Jack, so I'll settle for a temporary identification. I want to hear more about this guy who jumped you—want to

28

think about that question he asked. Doesn't make much sense, not yet it doesn't. We'll talk at the morgue.''

Was there a choice for Carver? Not with Ludlow. He knew the homicide detective too well. He agreed to meet with Ludlow after he had given his statement to the Berkeley cops. Ludlow agreed but gave Carver a time limit. Ninety minutes, or there'd be trouble.

Carver parked near Seventh and Bryant streets and went through the automatic routine of turning on the car's burglar alarm. For some time now, he had kept in the trunk of the Jaguar a 35mm single-lens-reflex Nikon, a first-aid kit, a flashlight, and several walkie-talkies. And in a locked, custom-built compartment, he had concealed one of his Colt Python revolvers.

On Seventh was the Hall of Justice, a six-story gray building. Crossing the intersection, Carver glanced at a jumble of twisted gray metal pipes at the corner of the building, a large sculpture that looked to him like plumbing that had been clumsily stacked by some demented giant plumber. He crossed the police parking lot behind the Hall of Justice and followed a covered walkway to the morgue. Inside, he found Sergeant Ludlow waiting for him.

''Come on,'' Ludlow ordered, and began walking through several swinging doors.

''What's the rush?'' Carver asked.

Ludlow didn't answer. He pushed open the doors to the white-tiled morgue and Carver followed. An attendant went ahead of them and pulled open a drawer with a corpse inside. The sheet was pulled back.

''Well?'' Ludlow asked bluntly.

''Like I told you . . .'' Carver started to say, then paused. ''This isn't Ferrik.''

''Yeah? You said you'd never met him,'' Ludlow said.

''Right. I don't know him, but I know this guy.''

A wave of relief washed over Carver. He wouldn't have to tell Amber that her father was dead.

"If he isn't Ferrik," Ludlow asked, "who is he?"

"He's a would-be sculptor by the name of Lou Piombo. A guy I met a couple of times. Myron Moseby knows him."

"Moseby? Oh, yeah, your faggot pal who owns the fancy art gallery on Stutter Street."

"He prefers the word 'gay,' " Carver said tightly.

"Oh, certainly. Let's not rub the cocksucker's feelings the wrong way. I really get a bellyful of you sometimes. The people you know—the ones you call friends. Shit!"

"Ludlow, you've been riding me a long time," Carver said, his words clipped and hard.

"From the very beginning, asshole. Running around with that white chick and always sucking up to the white establishment. Guys like you make me sick."

Carver slowly uncurled his balled fists. Ludlow breathed hard as he watched Carver's eyes. There was an invisible crackling of heat and danger between the two men.

"Go ahead, Bascombe," Ludlow muttered. "Go ahead. Just do it." He looked Carver dead straight in the eyes. "Nah, you haven't got the guts. Like I've said, you don't know what's going on out there. I bet you don't even know why those Berkeley cops were nervous when they came in?"

Carver said nothing. He shoved both hands into his pockets. Let Ludlow shoot his mouth off. Carver wasn't going to give him the satisfaction. He knew there was a war on. A couple of miles from Ferrik's house was a street war, a drug war that went on day after day, terrifying the neighborhoods. One of the worst drug wars outside of Harlem. Of course the cops were edgy. Over fifty people had been killed in the last year.

"Don't push," Carver grated. "The important thing is, this man is not Tom Ferrik."

"Yeah, Jack." Ludlow waved the words away. He nodded

to the attendant, who then shut the drawer. He narrowed his eyes at Carver. "What did Moseby tell you about him?"

"That Piombo was a small-time crook, liked to peddle phony pre-Columbian statues. Among other scams and swindles. Apparently he had enough talent to get by. Liked to hang around with sculptors and painters. Enjoyed the social scene of gallery openings."

"What kind of a connection would he have with Ferrik?"

"I don't know," Carver said. "Why should there be any connection? Because of the identification?"

"Yeah, the guy was found in a coat with Ferrik's wallet in the inside pocket."

Carver turned with Ludlow and they left the morgue. A familiar feeling stirred inside Carver. He knew what it was— the old itch, the ghostly, hollow sound of the hunting horn. His own personal demon. Questions fluttered through his mind, questions that he could not ignore. That old feeling. Itching and crawling under his skin. The huntsman, the inner person whom he knew so well. That old friend who showed up from time to time, the heartbeat racing. It was going to be that kind of a case! All the signs were there.

A neutral expression masking his excitement, Carver took a detour in his conversation with Sergeant Ludlow.

"I haven't seen Lieutenant De Anza in quite a while," Carver said. "How is he?"

"He's okay. Like all of us, Raphael is just older. He's up for a promotion."

"I didn't know that."

"Keep it under your hat. Yeah, Raphael is up for captain of detectives."

Several years back, Carver had first met both Raphael De Anza and Ernie Ludlow, and their paths had crossed a number of times after that. The first time, Carver had just opened his one-man office and was trying to locate a missing teenage boy. The boy had been found murdered, and De Anza and Ludlow had been on the case.

"There couldn't be a better choice," Carver said. "I didn't know he had the seniority."

"He doesn't, but the others don't want the job. They're too close to retirement, I guess, and don't want the aggravation."

"Raphael will make a good captain."

"If he gets it."

"Sure he will. He has the qualifications. He's the best man for the job."

"What does that have to do with anything?"

"It stands to reason," Carver said.

Ludlow stopped and lit a cigarette. His look was a dubious one, tinged with a sneer.

"Bascombe, sometimes I think you haven't learned nothin'. So what if De Anza is the best man? There's a lot of office politics, infighting like you wouldn't believe. And besides De Anza is a Mex. You think the top brass wants tamales heading the detectives? Not on your ass."

"Times have changed," Carver said.

"Fuck that." Ludlow said the words slowly, with exasperation. As though he were talking to a dumb student. "You're too soft. That's what comes from all that stupid artsy-fartsy shit you like. Makes you soft—"

"I can handle myself."

"You go to those art galleries and symphonies—I never hear you talk about football or baseball, nothin' like that. That's what happens when you hang around with fags like Moseby. Man, that's an infection. Good thing I know you're all the time hoppin' in the sack with broads or I'd suspect you of being a queer yourself. Christalmighty, what kind of nigger are you?"

"Not your kind."

The heat. Had to be the heat, Carver decided. Ludlow was worse than usual. Damned if Carver would succumb to temptation. He'd just stop the verbal fighting. A no-win situation. Nothing could ever change Ludlow's thinking.

They stopped at the outer door of the morgue. Ludlow was going to stay for the autopsy; he wanted to get the bullets from the dead man over to Ballistics.

"Sergeant," Carver said, changing his tone of voice, "you said you wanted to know more about the guy who attacked me."

"Yeah." A long pause. Ludlow dragged on the cigarette. Yeah, let's change the subject. "The guy said 'when'? Let's take it from there. He had to be looking for Ferrik. You say Ferrik is missing. Voluntarily? We don't know that. He might've been kidnapped. That might explain why the girl had no calls from him. Or he's laying doggo, even not calling his own daughter. Does any of that make any sense?"

"That depends on what kind of man he is."

"And I suppose you're going to find out?"

"If I'm looking for him, I'll be talking to people who know him. I might learn a few things."

"I doubt it," Ludlow said, implying not now or ever.

"We'll see."

"Yeah? Okay, Jack, you know the rules. And you know mine. Don't get in my way. You learn anything, you get word to me."

"And if you learn anything, you don't tell me."

"Yeah, right, Jack," Ludlow said, grinning. He stomped the cigarette out under his foot.

Amber Ferrik sat upright on the hospital bed. She smiled at Carver as he gave her the yellow pajamas and red robe. She was in a busy emergency room at the hospital, with nurses and doctors passing through every few minutes.

A white curtain had been drawn around the bed. A doctor stood next to her and introduced himself: Dr. Stone. Rose had explained Amber's circumstances to him.

"I want you to see this, Mr. Bascombe," Dr. Stone said. He turned to Amber. "I'm sorry, dear, but I really must."

"I don't like it," Amber said. "It was a long time ago."

Dr. Stone shook his head and rolled Amber onto her stomach. He loosened the hospital gown and exposed her back.

"Oh, my God," Rose said in a harsh undertone.

Carver clamped his lips tight. Some things he could never get used to. Maybe Ludlow was right. But this, this—

Scars crisscrossed Amber's back and shoulders. Not just two or three, but over a dozen. Faint lines, but ugly nevertheless.

"Who did this, Amber?" Carver asked as she faced them. The doctor tied up the gown. "Was it your father?"

"No, of course not," she said. "My daddy has never hit me."

The doctor finished tying Amber's gown. He had a grim look.

"The scars are well over a year old, and my guess is that some of them are even older. Eventually most of them will disappear, but for now, to see this kind of abuse—well . . ." He shrugged, but there was anger in the gesture.

"My mother," Amber said. "She used to hit me. That's why she doesn't live with me and daddy anymore."

"I'm taking her with me," Rose said. "I have plenty of room in the house."

Carver agreed that that was the best idea. Unless someone objected, but he couldn't see who would.

"I'll love having you, Amber," Rose said. "I live just across the street from Golden Gate Park. I think you'll like it."

"And I won't be any trouble, Rose. I think it sounds like fun." Amber turned to Carver. "Did you find anything that would tell you where to find my daddy?"

Carver told her that it was too early to tell, that he had found little that would give him a lead. Besides, there was something very important that had to done. Something official.

"I need to be paid a fee, and that makes you legally a client, with all the legal safeguards."

"How much, Mr. Bascombe?" Amber asked as she looked into her purse.

"What have you got?" Carver asked.

"Three quarters and a dime and a dollar."

"I'll take a quarter."

With a solemn expression, Amber handed him a quarter, and Rose wrote out a receipt. Dr. Stone shook his head.

"Now it's official. You're my client, and you are my boss. I do whatever you say and I report to you every day. But sometimes I might have to ask you questions and you might not like them. But that's my job."

"Oh, I understand, Mr. Bascombe."

"Call me Carver." He turned to the doctor. "Okay if I ask her a few more questions?"

"Of course," the doctor replied. "She can leave the hospital as soon as she gets dressed. I'd like to see her tomorrow, but first she should get a good night's sleep, and a nap this afternoon would do wonders. I'll write a prescription for a few antibiotics and then she's free to go."

Carver handed Amber her pajamas and robe. He motioned to Rose to join him outside as Amber dressed. He told Rose in great detail about what had happened at the house and his run-in with Sergeant Ludlow.

"Anything I can do?" Rose asked.

"Call a taxi for you and Amber," Carver said. "I'm going to see Sharon Argent. She might know something about Tom Ferrik or where he might be. I want to get a line on Amber's mother, and Sharon might know where the ex–Mrs. Ferrik lives now. As for the rest, I've got to stay out of Ludlow's way. He's getting very ugly in his old age."

Carver returned to the room. Amber was dressed in the pajamas and robe. Carver picked up the bundle of bloody dress and shoes. He looked at Amber Ferrik with a serious expression on his face.

"Amber, who is Sharon Argent?"

"Oh, she's my daddy's friend."

"A good friend?"

"The best. My daddy and Sharon are supposed to get married. Wouldn't that be interesting? I'd have a black mother."

"You'd like that?"

"Oh, yes. Sharon is a wonderful lady. She is lots of fun, and she likes me. We've been to the zoo, and she likes movies, like I do. And she likes my daddy. And I think that's the most important thing. Don't you?"

"Yes," Carver said, "I do. Now, Amber, there are a few more questions, and then you can leave the hospital."

"All right," Amber said.

"Do you know where your mother lives now? Or what name she uses now—maybe her maiden name?"

Amber didn't know, and Carver didn't force the issue.

"You had my business card, Amber," he said, "and your daddy gave it to you. When did he give it to you?"

"Oh, a long time ago. Last year. I kept it and showed it to my friends at school, to show them my daddy knew a real private detective."

"I see," Carver said. "But I don't know your daddy. Who gave him the card?"

"I don't know that, Carver. Daddy knows a lot of people."

A nurse brought a wheelchair for Amber. Carver pushed her outside where Rose stood next to a taxi at the curb. Carver shook hands with Amber and told Rose he'd phone later. He watched as the taxi pulled into the traffic, then he climbed into his Jaguar. Carver headed to the address he had for Sharon Argent on Bernal Heights.

THREE

Like a hammer, the heat poured from the dead-bone-colored sky. Carver wiped the sweat from his face and parked on the shady side of the street. The address for Sharon Argent was opposite, one of many houses baking in the afternoon sunlight. The type of house was common on Bernal Heights—old and wooden, with an apartment on each side and a central corridor. One single door led into the interior.

He got out, took off his sunglasses, and put them in his shirt pocket. He climbed the steps and rang the bell. He heard shuffling steps and then a harsh voice spoke through the closed door.

"Whatta you want?"

"I want to see Sharon Argent," Carver said affably. "It's important."

The bolt and chain drew back and the door opened. The woman was a robust fiftyish, with amazingly black hair, which contrasted with gray eyebrows. An orchid-printed dress flowed like a breeze around the woman's ample body. One beefy fist held a cigarette, on which she dragged roughly.

"Who're you? You her brother?"

"No. I'm an investigator, and Miss Argent could clear up some items in a case."

"Don't give me that. Was I born last month? You ain't with the police. You'd show me your shield and all that shit."

Carver admitted that he wasn't a city policeman and showed her his ID.

"A private cop, hey?"

"Is she home?" Carver asked.

"Of course not, buster."

"Are you a tenant or the landlady?"

"Nosy son of a bitch, ain'tcha? You got the hots to know, I own this dump." She dug out a crushed pack of cigarettes from a deep pocket in the dress and used the butt to light a fresh one. The motions were fluid and well practiced. "She's in trouble, huh?"

"Not that I know of," Carver said.

The big woman looked Carver up and down, measuring him as a liar. Hell, all men were. For that matter, all women. The whole son-of-a-bitchin' human race were liars and crooks. And a fuckin' lot worse. But at least this guy gave her a break in the day, somethin' different, somethin' she could gossip about with her neighbors, not that they're worth a morning's cough and a piss.

"She's workin'," the woman said finally. "Down at the foundry. You can find her there."

"Where is it?" Carver asked.

She told him the address, and Carver gave her a business card. If he missed Sharon Argent, she could give him a call. He thanked the woman, and minutes later he was tooling north on Portrero Avenue, heading for the light industrial area south of Market. He turned off on Townsend and parked in an alley, switching on the burglar alarm.

Carver walked over unused train tracks and passed old, rusted warehouses and machine shops. He carried his jacket. His shirt was clinging to his back, and his slacks were shapeless. His feet squelched in his shoes. One thing he desired—a cool shower and a change of clothes. But right now he'd settle for something cold to drink.

The largest building had a faded sign over open truck-sized, corrugated-metal double doors. The sign read: HUTTE AND SON—METAL FOUNDRY—CASTING AND FABRICATION.

Carver stepped inside.

He threw his arms in front of his face. Goddamn! Carver felt as if his eyebrows had been singed off. The white-hot air came in waves. Slowly he lowered his arms and let his eyes get accustomed to the dim interior. The smells of molten metal tickled Carver's nose. Massive beams, black with age and soot, crossed the high ceiling. Pools of orange and phosphorescent green light glowed from liquid metals in black, encrusted cauldrons. Feeble overhead lights barely lit the walls; shafts of sunlight streamed in from narrow clerestory windows.

The shouts of the workers mixed with the chatter of winches, the high whine of cables, and the sizzling din of pouring metal. The darkness went deep, punctuated with sparks and glows.

Steep stairs led to a catwalk around two sides of the foundry. On this shadowed mezzanine, Carver saw offices with dusty, windowed doors.

Workmen with bulging muscles, wearing thick leather aprons over bare torsos and goggles over their eyes, moved cauldrons that hung from blocks and tackles. Sparks flew as crucibles were tipped by the workmen using pouring shanks. The molten metal hissed into gigantic molds.

Carver walked farther into the inferno, his shirt dripping.

He wiped his face. The floor was made of packed clay and sand, which gritted underfoot. On the mezzanine, a door opened and a figure hurried down the stairs. The sound of his heavy footsteps clattered over the raucous foundry sounds.

"Hah, you!" the man shouted. "*Schwarzer!* Yes, you!" he yelled, pointing at Carver Bascombe. "What do you want here? I do not know you!" He spoke with a heavy Teutonic accent.

The man reached the bottom of the steps and strode purposefully toward Carver. He was medium height but large, wearing corduroy pants with a heavy belt and buckle encircling a thick body. He oozed strength, and his face was round and hard like a Black Forest boar's head. Fingers like blunt bolts with knuckles like rivets hung curled at his side. Bands of ancient leather encircled both wrists. Gray, grizzled hair curled around small thick ears.

"What do you want?" the man said loudly, accustomed to speaking over the shouts of the workmen and the blast sounds of pouring steel and bronze and copper.

"I'm looking for Sharon Argent," Carver said loudly.

"Ah, I cannot help you," the man said, waving his beefy hands, dismissing the black man.

"I understand she works here?"

"Hah! Here?" He turned and gestured at the heavy-duty activity in the foundry. "Do you see a woman here? Never! Never will you see a woman here. Not in my foundry. And not a *schwarzer*. *Nein*. I hire who I want. No women. No *schwarzers*. No Spanish. Go away!"

A man carrying a clipboard walked over to Carver and the heavyset man.

"I'm sorry, mister," the man said. "I have to apologize for my dad."

Carver saw the resemblance, but the son was not as heavyset. He was taller than his father, with a weightlifter's build. Broad shoulders and a narrow waist were evident under the leather apron and pants. Well-defined muscles rippled under a skin-tight T-shirt darkened with sweat. He didn't carry one ounce of fat. His features were benign, like a Rodin bronze bust, with chiseled lines radiating from the eyes. Carver didn't think he'd want to go against either father or son.

"What can we do for you?" the man asked.

"Bah!" the older man said, and stomped away, muttering loudly. "The world is insane. I will kill myself someday."

"Please forgive him," the son said. "So what can—"

"I'm looking for Sharon Argent. I understand she works here."

"Are you her brother?"

"No, I'm not. She does work here then?"

"No, Dad's right on that, she doesn't work here, but we rent her space for a studio. It's next door, but you can go through that connecting door under the stairs."

"Thanks," Carver said, and introduced himself, shaking hands.

"I'm Bob Hutte, and that, I'm afraid, was my father, Karl. I guess he's never quite got used to the way things are in the United States. Democracy and tolerance aren't his long suit. He resents getting old, I guess—and me taking over the foundry. Again, I apologize for his rudeness."

"I've forgotten it," Carver said, and thanked the man.

He picked his way through the foundry and found the door that Bob Hutte had indicated. On the other side was a narrow alley and another door. He went in.

The studio was large, with skylights letting in glaring light. Bent sheets of metal were propped along the walls, and several drawing tables were against a far wall. Large sheets with drawings were tacked to the walls, and in the middle of the studio space was a massive metal sculpture, all angles, twisted curves, and spiky outgrowths. The piece had to be ten feet tall, and it had a grotesque plantlike quality, a suggestion of alien flora or an ugly tropical flower that had swallowed an animal whole.

In front of the thing was a person in overalls, a hooded welder's mask covering the face, and large asbestos gloves. Cascades of sparks blasted in front of the welder as an acetylene torch cut into the metal.

Carver moved close and caught the attention of the welder. The safety shield of the mask went up—and Carver stared. Sharon Argent. She was easily recognizable from the photographs in Ferrik's bedroom.

But the photographs hardly did her justice. Not that photos lie, they just don't tell everything. A sin of omission. Then Carver realized that he had been staring at her. God, look at those eyes! Deep, purple-black, with thick lashes, and lips that were sensual yet strong.

Sharon Argent tilted her head and looked at Carver. She turned off the flaming gas-jet and wiped her face with a large bandanna.

"What do you think?" she said, bobbing her head at the tall metal sculpture. "Do you like it?"

"Ah, it's . . . it's . . ." Carver said, grasping for something to say, perhaps something diplomatic. He was still thrilled by the quality of her voice: sensual, firm, direct, and wonderfully musical. "Well, it's too soon for me. It's something you'd have to look at for a while."

"You mean it doesn't immediately take your breath away?"

"I'll cop out and say it's too hot for that. I lost my breath just walking through the foundry."

"Oh?" she said. "Looking for someone?"

"You're Sharon Argent?" Carver asked, trying to keep his voice neutral. But he also felt foolish asking since he knew who she was. She said she was, and Carver pulled out his wallet, which slipped from his sweat-slick fingers and fell to the floor. He bent and picked it up, silently cursing his own clumsiness. He dusted off specks of clay and sand and took out his ID. He showed it to Sharon.

"You're a private detective?" she said. "Really?"

"Yes, really. My name is Bascombe, Carver Bascombe."
So far everything he had said sounded idiotic.

"I thought maybe, just maybe, you were an art dealer."

"No. Sorry. I'm looking for Tom Ferrik."

"Why? Isn't Tom at home?"

"No, he isn't. I understand you're a friend and I hoped you
might know where he is."

"I'm afraid I don't understand."

"When was the last time you heard from him?"

Puzzled but friendly, Sharon hung the cutting torch over
the acetylene tank. She told Carver she had talked to Tom
Ferrik on the telephone just the other day. And they had a
date for dinner this evening. He was going to pick her up at
home as soon as she showered and changed.

"Has something happened?" Sharon asked. She stood
next to the metal structure she had been working on, one hand
on a spiky metal projection, the other in a pocket of her
coveralls.

Carver could not help but notice that she was bare under
the work clothes. Lovely brown skin, like hand-rubbed, hand-
oiled mahogany. A statue of grace and fluid loveliness.

"I don't know," Carver replied after a few silent moments. "At least nothing I can be sure of."

He told her of Amber's visit to his office but did not
mention the shooting. He admitted that the little girl was now
his client and that Tom Ferrik was missing. Sharon was
visibly shaken.

"My God, my God," she repeated several times during
Carver's narration. "How utterly bizarre."

She paced away from him. She trembled, her eyes downcast, and then she turned and faced Carver. Was there anything else Bascombe could tell her? He shook his head. She
stared at him, her arms folded tightly against herself, as
though this would hold in the tremors.

"This is terrible. You come to my studio and tell me a

frightening story—I don't know what to think. And where is Amber? What the hell is going on?''

"Ferrik seems to be the key. As for Amber, she's safe with a friend of mine. An older woman."

"I want her with me," Sharon said. "Tom would want it that way."

Carver shrugged.

Then the studio door opened and Bob Hutte entered.

"Everything okay, Sharon?" he asked.

"Oh, Bob, come in," she said, and introduced Carver. "This is Bob Hutte, Karl Hutte's son. They own this foundry."

"We've met," Carver admitted.

"Bob, Mr. Bascombe is a private detective. There seems to be some foul-up with Tom."

"Oh?" Hutte said. He eyed Carver, his gaze taking in the tall, sweat-dripping black man. "What's the problem with Tom?"

"He seems to be missing," Sharon said, and laughed quietly, hoping to deaden her own anxieties. The laugh was a nervous one. "But I'm sure he'll turn up, Mr. Bascombe. He wouldn't leave his daughter to run around loose. I would like to see her—and to take her home with me."

Carver shook his head. He wasn't about to explain that Amber had been shot and that he had been attacked by a man with a shotgun. Letting others know too much could be dangerous.

"We'll have to see about that, Miss Argent," he said. "What I need now is information. What kind of a man is Tom Ferrik?"

"Tom? Oh, he's a fine person . . ." she began, but there was a catch in her throat. A tremble went through her. "I really don't feel up to this, Mr. Bascombe."

"Call me Carver, Sharon. All right, I'll get in touch later. But would you happen to know the ex–Mrs. Ferrik, Amber's mother?"

"Yes, I do. As a matter of fact," she said defensively, "she's been here a couple of times. To warn me off seeing Tom. If you think Tom is seeing her, you're wrong. He wants nothing to do with her."

"I just want to talk to her. Does she go by her maiden name?"

"As a matter of fact, she does. Barbara Stahl. She lives out of town, but not far. In Sharp Park." Sharon gave him the address.

"Is that enough, Bascombe?" Bob Hutte asked, barely masking his annoyance.

Why was this guy being so protective of Sharon Argent? Carver wondered about that. He stalled for more time, enjoying each second he could look at her. Oh, she was lovely, with a wonderful voice and bright intelligent eyes. A woman with inner strength and a spark of toughness.

"We're concerned, Mr. Bascombe," Bob Hutte added, "because we know Tom. He's had many of his pieces cast here at the foundry."

"I didn't know that," Carver said.

"You've never seen a sculpture cast before? No? When you have time, I'd like to show you how we do it."

Carver thanked him for the invitation and asked Sharon for her telephone number.

"Would you," she asked, her voice catching, "would you keep me informed? You know, let me know if you find Tom? And, please, don't forget I'd like to take care of Amber."

Carver nodded noncommittally, doing a very good job of concealing an emotion peeking around the edges of his heart. Jealousy? Envy? Of Tom Ferrik? Carver idly wondered if he should stall the hunt for Ferrik. As he wrote Sharon's telephone number in his notebook, he whisked the thought away. He thanked her, then left the studio.

Choices, choices. Should he first see the ex–Mrs. Ferrik or stop for something to eat? God, no, it was too hot to eat. All those calories added heat. But how about a cold beer? Ex–Mrs. Ferrik or a cold beer?

The beer won.

Ah. Carver sighed as the ice-cold brew trickled down his throat. Besides, sitting in a bar was a good place to write down questions, getting them into a logical sequence.

Only a few hours ago he had been bored, hot, and sweaty, listening to Vivaldi and wishing for anything to get his mind off the results of the bar exams. Had he passed the bar? Was he a lawyer or not? That letter from Sacramento was traveling by U.S. Snail.

Get his mind off that. Think about the lovely Sharon. And her white boyfriend. If Carver took his time looking for Ferrik, then he'd have more time with Sharon Argent—and who knew where that might lead?

The more he thought about it, the more the images of Tom Ferrik intruded. Whatever possessed Sharon to get engaged to Ferrik? She was so young. Had she really thought about what she was getting into? And if Ferrik wasn't found for a while, then perhaps she would see that the marriage wouldn't work.

No, those thoughts were unfair. Carver hardly believed he was thinking like that. Unlike him. That's more like Ludlow. Carver didn't care about people's color. Or did he? His thoughts were in a turmoil.

Do something! Sitting around a bar wasn't getting the job done. Besides, the bar wasn't air-conditioned and the big floor fan made more noise than his office fan. To hell with it. Let's see Barbara Stahl.

By the time he drove to Sharp Park, the sun was touching the horizon. Before making the trip, he had gone to his office, showered, and changed his clothes. He felt better in dry slacks and a lightweight tropical shirt. The air was still coming from an open oven.

Next to the Pacific Ocean, Sharp Park was part of the

bedroom community of Pacifica. Mostly lower-income shabby homes and seedy apartments. Carver parked at the address Sharon Argent had given him and walked across the brown, splotchy lawn. Even before the heat wave, the lawn hadn't been green in months. The house was small, what used to be called a junior five, with dusty windows, paint peeling from the front door, and gravel shingles missing from the roof. A television aerial leaned precariously, tied by wires to the brick chimney.

Carver rang the bell but didn't hear a sound. Out of order. He knocked, and moments later a woman opened the door.

"Yes?" she asked pleasantly.

"Barbara Stahl?"

"Yes. What can I do for you?"

Carver introduced himself and went through the routine of showing his ID.

"Won't you come in, please."

She stood aside and then followed him into the front room. The light from the setting sun streamed in through a picture window that faced the ocean. Carver looked over the plain furnishings, noting three framed fashion magazine covers on the walls, all featuring a younger Barbara Stahl in glamorous poses.

Barbara Stahl stood in the middle of the room, arms held tight against herself. She looked at Carver.

"The probation department didn't tell me they were sending—"

"Excuse me," Carver interrupted, "but I'm not from the probation department."

"What? Then I don't . . ." she said, her words faltering. A shade of concern crossed her face. She had let a stranger into her house. A faint tremor passed through her lips.

"Please look at my identification again," Carver said, sensing her fear. This woman had been pushed around by the system, and she was afraid of anyone who smelled of authority. He could take advantage of that—or not. "I'm a private investigator, but I'm not employed by any probation department, city, county, or state."

He handed her the license and she read it carefully. He studied her—a woman in her early thirties, he guessed. A plain housedress, worn shoes, and no stockings didn't hide her beauty. The sunlight behind her made her blond hair glow like a nimbus from a radiant dandelion. Her skin seemed to be made of pale English porcelain. He was fascinated by her large brown eyes, the color of autumn acorns.

Barbara Stahl handed back his ID and then sat on the sofa. She trembled slightly, then took a cigarette from a case on the coffee table and lit it with a table lighter. She stared at Carver.

"I really don't understand . . ."

"I'll make a bargain with you. Let me ask some questions, and I'll tell you what this is about—as much as I can."

Barbara thought about that and then nodded.

"Agreed then," Carver said. "Have you seen your ex-husband recently?"

"I haven't seen Tom in many, many months."

"He's missing," Carver said bluntly.

"What do you mean, missing? Did that bastard run off and—" She stopped and clamped her mouth shut. After a few seconds of hard breathing, she had regained her composure. "I'm sorry. My therapist has done wonders for me, but once in a while old habits flare up. Now, what is this about Tom being missing? Is Amber with him? And why are you involved, Mr. Bascombe?"

"Amber is not with him. A friend of mine is taking care of her. And I'm involved"—he decided to bend the truth—"because an acquaintance of Tom's is worried and doesn't want this reported to Missing Persons. Not yet, at any rate."

"Must be that black bitch—" She stopped, embarrassed, and avoided looking directly at Carver. "I'm sorry, I apologize. My emotions are still too close to the surface. My therapist says . . . Well, that's another story.''

''I know something about your problems, Miss Stahl,'' Carver said sympathetically. ''I know about Amber's whippings.''

''Tom did those!'' she said angrily. ''Not me!'' She stubbed out her cigarette, biting her lips. She breathed hard and then once again regained control. She lowered her eyes. ''Once again I have to apologize. It's not true. Tom never hit . . . my baby. My therapist—a wonderful woman—says if I tell the truth to myself—and to others—I'll feel better about myself, that I'll be able to face the past honestly. Getting rid of guilt.''

''Yes, I can understand. You don't have to talk—''

''But I do,'' she said firmly. ''I—I must . . . I should. Yes, I used to hit Amber. With a—with a strap. She was . . .'' Barbara paused, taking a deep breath. ''She was an abused child. And I was the cause.''

''How long were you married?''

''I was young—twenty—when we got married. Thirteen years ago. Tom was six years older, and I was a model making very good money. Not a top model making big bucks but getting there.''

''You were the main financial support?''

''That's the way it was. Tom wasn't making enough money to buy cigarettes.''

''Did you resent that?''

''Not then. I modeled for catalogues, newspaper ads, a few national ads, and I had my eye on an acting career.''

''What kind of a man was Tom?''

''Strong and . . . opinionated. He has an enormous ego, and he thinks he knows everything there is to know about the arts. Talk about sculpture, and he knows it all. That was one of the things that used to drive me up the wall. He had to be

49

right all the time. Nobody else's ideas or opinions were worth a damn. He felt he was so damned superior.''

"Then why did you marry him?''

"He . . . had a way of hiding his attitudes. He made jokes as though he didn't take art all that seriously. But he did, and he spoke like a scholar. He really has a personality that is charming and overpowering. He could devastate your ideas with a few chosen words. But he had another side. He loved the outdoors and camping out. The mystery of nature—you can see it in his sculptures. He tried to get me to go camping, but I always had some excuse—the sun would ruin my complexion, the dirt would take days to wash out, my nails would split—that sort of thing. Tom went by himself. He said he needed to get away, to commune with nature.''

"And then Amber was born?''

"Yes, and I had to cut my jobs. Tom helped out, one of the first househusbands, I suppose. But—''

"It wasn't easy.''

"No. You've probably heard this before. My parents . . . .''

"You were beaten as a child,'' Carver guessed, "an abused child.''

"Yes, an old story. Amber . . . she loved the woods, the mountains. Tom took her many times. Maybe she just wanted to get away from me. I don't know. I never asked her. I guess—I guess I was never as close to my own baby as I should've been.''

"You continued modeling, didn't you?''

"Those jobs, the goods ones, got fewer, and Tom was taking any kind of sculpturing job—did you know he was a window decorator? He used to design those fancy Christmas windows for some of those Maiden Lane shops. Very chic, very expensive shops, and they paid him practically nothing.'' Barbara lit another cigarette and gazed out the window at the evening light. "I was home much of the time but still trying to keep my career going . . . and a crying child, frustrations, changing diapers, feeding her . . . Well, it was just too much for me. I took my fears and resentments out on her. Ugly, very ugly.''

"Eventually you and Tom were divorced," Carver said, keeping his tone neutral. It was difficult not to judge, not to sound moralistic. He detested child-beaters.

"Yes, several years ago," Barbara said slowly, painful memories delaying her responses. "And I lost custody of Amber. An unfit mother, the courts said. God, she was such a sweet child. I truly hope she doesn't carry mental scars with her like I do."

"She seems all right."

"I'd hate to think I might be responsible for a future grandchild being an abused child. But you know, that's what my therapist says happens. How many generations back does it go? Apparently all the way, as far as we can see." She looked at Carver. "Horrible, isn't it? When they gave custody to Tom, they said this is how we stop the chain of abuse." She dragged on the cigarette, the smoke curling around her face. "I hope so."

"Do you harbor a grudge against your ex?"

"At first. Hated him. For a long time. But the courts made me see a therapist as part of my probation. Otherwise I'd have ended up in the county jail."

"You seem to be doing okay now."

"I hope so. I'm seeing a very fine man, and I'm getting my modeling career going again. But the competition, all those young women . . ." She looked at Carver, pleading in her brown eyes. "I would like to take care of Amber—just until Tom shows up."

Carver said nothing.

"Please, Mr. Bascombe," she pleaded, "just to talk with her?"

Despite the woman's candid words, Carver felt there was

more to her story. But he had more than he needed; further probing seemed unnecessary.

As he had promised, he told her of Amber's morning visit to his office, of looking for Tom Ferrik, and of talking with Sharon Argent. Barbara was deeply interested in the narration, nodding several times. Despite the divorce, she was still tied to the past. Barbara wrung her hands as Carver told the story. He did not tell her that someone had wounded Amber.

Could Tom Ferrik be hiding in the mountains? Possible, but Barbara didn't remember the location. Just somewhere in the Sierras. She couldn't help Carver; she had no idea where Tom Ferrik might have disappeared to. She agreed to call Carver if her ex-husband should get in touch with her. And Carver would see what he could do about Amber visiting her mother.

"Couple more questions. Ever hear of a man named Piombo?"

"No," she said, shaking her head, "I've never heard the name. Is it important?"

"Check the newscast tonight. It'll be on it. If anything about the man should occur to you—"

"Call you?"

"No, call the police," he said, a slow grin spreading over his face. "So there's only one last thing: Do you have a photo of Tom Ferrik?"

"Yes, I do. Several."

He waited at the front door until she returned with a glossy four-by-five photo. He thanked her and left. In the growing darkness, stars were coming out. Sitting in his car and using a flashlight, he wrote his notes. He wanted to get to his office, telephone Rose, and see how Amber was doing.

He had eaten little during the day and realized how hungry he was. A chilled seafood salad appealed to him. There must be some tuna or crab in his refrigerator. He had to sort out questions and plan the next day's activities. He had to check out the murdered man.

Searching Piombo's apartment meant stepping on the tender toes of the police, and that meant Sergeant Ludlow. Unless . . . Sure, he'd see if Raphael De Anza could help him.

FOUR

"Good night, Frank," the night dispatcher called out.

The slender black man turned and waved at the night man. He did not call him by name since he didn't know it. Frank Argent kept to himself; he was a solitary man, given to long silences, with others and with himself. He often thought of himself as a man waiting for something to happen—and nothing ever did.

Until recently. Frank Argent didn't want to think about it.

As he walked out onto Townsend Street, he blanched at the heat. Coming from an air-conditioned office into the oven-hot evening made him dizzy. He gathered his strength and looked for a taxi. The thought of jamming into a city bus crowded with people, everyone sweaty, made him nauseated.

Turning the corner at Townsend near Fourth Street, Frank Argent bumped into Ed Zinn.

"The car is over there," Zinn said, pushing a revolver into Argent's stomach. "Move it, handsome. Get in."

"I don't know why the hell you're doing this, Ed," Argent

said, pausing at the open rear door of a dark sedan. "I told you I don't have the—"

"Sure," Zinn said. He pushed the gun hard, shutting off Argent's flow of words.

"Damn, Ed," Argent muttered, rubbing his stomach, "that hurt."

"Sure. Supposed to."

The driver looked at Argent and grinned, his mouth wide like a toad's. Argent got in the back and Ed Zinn slid in beside him, closing the door. The driver gunned the engine, wheeling the car into the traffic. The driver looked into the rearview mirror at Frank Argent, enjoying the black man's fear; a small grin puckered his fat lips. He caught a glimpse of Ed Zinn's eyes.

"Cholly, you pig fucker," Zinn said quietly, "don't look, just drive."

Cholly Lehm flicked his eyes to the front and drove with one hand. With the other, he picked at his nose. He gave a quick look at the tiny glop on the end of his finger and then licked it off.

"You booger-eater," Zinn said, "pay attention to the driving." He turned to Argent. "Okay, Frank, when is it?"

"Goddammit, Ed," the black man blurted, "if I've told you once, I've told you plenty of times—I just don't know. I don't work there anymore, and it's tough for me to find out stuff like that. It's secret, and they keep it that way."

"Double bullshit. It's getting close. I know, I can smell it. Time—it's running out." He turned to the driver. "Cholly, take the next street. To the left. Frank, I want to know the time of shipment. I don't want to find out afterwards. You understand that, don't you? Frank?"

"Yes, yes, I know. Look, Ed, I'm not forgetting anything, not one damned thing. We agreed. I can use the money. But if I can't find out when, then I just can't."

"Sure. You mean you haven't been able to find out. Yet."

"Uh, yes, sure, Ed, that's what I meant."

"So we understand each other. You got a mind of your own, a brain, the IQ of a Globetrotters' score. Not like Cholly. He doesn't have a lotta dimes in his automat, but he's a good mule."

Argent chuckled nervously.

"So," Zinn said, "what happened to Piombo?"

"I don't get you. What about Piombo?"

Up in front, Cholly's laugh sounded like tinfoil crinkling.

"Shut up, Cholly. So what's the matter, Frank, you don't read newspapers?"

"Well," Argent said nervously, "I haven't had a chance today."

"Sure. Sure, Frank. What about the radio, you didn't listen to any newscasts?"

"No, I don't have time for that either. But what about Lou?"

"He's dead, Frank. Shot. Killed. And you tell me you don't know nothin' about it."

"Oh, God, no, Ed, I swear."

"Sure," Ed Zinn said, wrinkling his nose at the odor of fear that Argent was giving off. "Whatever you say."

The car turned another corner, south on Guerrero. After several minutes, Cholly parked the car in front of an old frame house. They all got out, with Zinn prodding Argent.

"Cholly," Ed said, "bring in the shotgun and, for God's sake, wrap it up. All the neighbors are sitting on their stoops and leaning out the windows. Don't wave the goddamn thing around."

Cholly nodded, then opened the trunk. He wrapped the shotgun in an old blanket and stuffed a coil of rope and several woman's stockings into his pockets. He followed the other two men up the stairs. Argent was reluctant to go in. Zinn cocked the gun and the sound in the hot air made Argent wince. He unlocked the door and they went in. Argent reached for a light switch, but Zinn hit his wrist lightly with the gun barrel.

"Open the windows, Cholly," Zinn ordered. "God, it's hot and stuffy in here. Frank, you really shut this place up tight when you go to work." He uncocked the gun, lowering the hammer down carefully. "Lessee, let's you and me and Cholly go into the bedroom. Yeah, that's a good place to start."

"To start what?" Argent asked worriedly.

"A lesson in—in trust. Sorta like 'Truth or Consequences.' Ever hear that old radio show? My folks used to listen to it. Thought it was swell. I didn't like it much, but I sure came to appreciate it later. Truth—or consequences."

Zinn smashed the gun into Argent's head and he collapsed across the bed. Zinn hummed tunelessly as he looked around the bedroom. He moved a chair alongside the bed.

"Oh, yeah," he said to the unconscious man. "Truth or consequences, a good game."

"Hey, Ed," Cholly said, coming into the dark bedroom. "Did you know there was a town used to be called that?"

"Called what, Cholly?"

"Truth or Consequences. They named a city after that show. Somewhere in Arizona or New Mexico, one a those places."

"Ever been there, Cholly?"

"Me? Nah. Never been outta the state."

"Then shut up, Cholly. Tie him up."

"Sure, Ed," Cholly said, and took the rope from his pocket. He wiped the sweat from his face and pushed Frank Argent into the chair next to the bed. He propped Argent's feet onto the bedspread. Grunting a few times, he tied Argent's wrists and then lashed the upraised feet. He removed Argent's shoes and socks.

He stood back and admired his work. He snaked a finger into a nostril and dug around, poking this way and that.

"For God's sake, stop eating boogers. You hungry, go into the kitchen and see what's there."

Cholly nodded happily and trundled into the kitchen. Zinn heard the refrigerator door open and slam shut, then Cholly returned.

"Found a couple cold hot dogs. Want one?"

"No, I don't want one," he replied, mimicking the big man. "You leave fingerprints on the fridge?"

"Ah, no, Ed," Cholly said, pushing the words around his mouth full of meat, "whatta you think? I'm some kinda amateur?"

"Wake him up," Zinn ordered, pointing to Argent.

Cholly waddled into the bathroom and returned with a glass of water, a sponge, and a washcloth. He splashed water onto Argent's face with the sponge.

"That's fine," Zinn said as Argent spluttered to consciousness. "That's very good. Now the rest, Cholly."

A table lamp was rigged with a powerful bulb and aimed directly at Argent' face. Ed Zinn stood over Argent.

"Believe me, Frank," Zinn said, "this is necessary."

Argent stared at him.

"You have to be convinced that we are not playing. Understand that, Frank? We are not playing games. . . ."

Suddenly the telephone rang in the front room. Zinn and Cholly waited for it to stop. It rang over twenty times. Cholly counted the rings, his lips moving with each number. Then it stopped, and Zinn looked at Argent.

"Now, Frank, Frank, we could ask questions, and you could keep saying no, no, over and over. I don't care if you talk or not. Not at first. I want to muck up that handsome face of yours. I imagine all the ladies just fall at your feet, a fine-looking young man like you. Not like ugly Cholly here. He has to pay whores double to get screwed. Can you imagine? Sure you can. Once for the screwing and once for having

58

to look at him. Did you know that Cholly drools when he humps? The women don't like that very much.''

Zinn bent close and used a handkerchief to wipe the sweat from Argent's face.

"Now, you know I respect and admire you. You got a terrific imagination. You came up with a terrific scheme. We just want to work with you on it.''

He looked benignly at Argent.

"So, Frank, I want you to think about three answers.'' He held up one finger. "First, who was your black friend at Ferrik's house this afternoon?'' Another finger. "Where is Tom Ferrik? And last . . .'' The third finger. "Who killed Piombo? The poor guy, he just didn't have a chance, did he? Anyway, think about those questions for a few seconds. The other questions—when and where—will come later.''

Zinn stood back and waited, his arms crossed in front.

"I swear to you, Ed . . .''

Zinn shook his head and pointed to his forehead, then to Argent's head. He waited. Frank Argent sweated. Zinn mopped his face once again.

"I think that's enough time, Frank," Zinn said. "You ready to answer? How about number one? Who was the black man at Ferrik's?''

"I swear, swear to God, Ed," he mumbled thickly, "I don't know who you're talking about.''

"Sure, Frank. He said he was a private detective. Real tall, looks kinda like that guy on that old Jack Benny show. Rochester? Only thinner. He's gotta index finger bent sorta funny.''

"I don't know anybody like that, don't know any private detectives.'' The words were said haltingly, with difficulty.

"I said that's what he told me. I didn't believe him for a second.''

"Eddy Anderson," Cholly said.

"What?" Zinn asked.

"The name of the nigger on that Benny show."

"Don't say 'nigger,' Cholly. Have some respect for Frank."

"I don't know him." Argent sobbed, tears trickling down his face. "Honest to God, I don't."

"Hear that, Ed," Cholly said, "he don't know Eddy Anderson."

"Of course not, asshole. He was talking about . . . God-damn you, Cholly, you're screwing me up. Go pick your nose. In the other room."

Cholly Lehm grunted porcinely and returned to the kitchen. Zinn focused on Frank Argent.

"And you don't know who killed Piombo?"

Argent shook his head, and cried and sobbed his denials at each question Zinn put to him. He swore he didn't know where Tom Ferrik was hiding. Honest, honest, honest to God.

"I'm sorry for you, Frank, honest to God, I am." He called out to the overweight man in the kitchen. "Cholly, get your booger face in here."

Scraps of meat, probably a frankfurter, dangled from Cholly's mouth. Zinn looked disgusted. He pointed to Argent.

"Cholly. Do it," he said, and left the bedroom, closing the door.

He stood by the open windows, wishing for a cool breeze. Behind him he heard soft thuds as Cholly used padded fists to work over Argent. He looked at his wristwatch and waited for two minutes to pass.

Ed Zinn looked at the apartment. Not bad, he decided. Not a lot of stuff but interesting.

On one wall was an African mask with two short spears crossed beneath. The furniture consisted of leather chairs and a velour sofa. Rattan end tables. A pretty nice painting of a lion over the sofa. Zinn didn't think it was an original. But the small statue near the bookcase was. One of Tom Ferrik's pieces. A nice smooth piece of marble, an abstraction of a female figure. A white woman. Apparently not modeled after Argent's sister.

The phone rang again, a long time. Zinn waited. Someone wanted to talk to Frank real bad. He wondered who it was. He was tempted to pick it up, but . . . No, don't tempt fate. But whoever it was might decide to come for a visit.

He looked at his watch. Time's up. He returned to the bedroom.

Argent's nose had been split open, and blood made parentheses around his mouth. One eye was bruised and swollen. An eyetooth was missing. Blood spilled down his chin. The front of his shirt was splotchy with red stains.

The room was furnished with the large bed and a bedside table with a lamp. Several hardcover books lay there. The walls were painted a light tan with a darker brown trim. Several feet from Argent's head, the wall was spattered with many droplets of blood. Several spots were large enough to trickle.

"A good start," Zinn said. "Very good. You all right, Frank? We don't want you drowning in your own blood. Frank? Frank?"

Zinn looked into blank eyes. He reached out and touched Frank Argent's face; the head lolled. Zinn jerked his hand away, and then he turned to Cholly Lehm.

"Cholly. Cholly, you stupid shit—you've killed him."

"Ah, crap," Cholly said.

Zinn turned back to the dead man. Now what could he do? It meant that he'd have to restart his search from another direction.

"Ah, Frank," Zinn said, "now you really don't know anything. You can't help me. But maybe it's not all lost. Maybe there is someone—someone who can help me."

"Ed?" Cholly said.

"Yeah?"

"You're talkin' to a dead man."

"Sure. Shut up, Cholly," Zinn said without anger, and looked at the body of Frank Argent. "Yeah, Frank. Your sister."

FIVE

Smoke and sweat and beer and liquor smells mingled in the air. Carver stood inside the doors of The Bench and looked for one familiar face in the crowded bar. Men and a few women were elbow to elbow, laughing, telling yarns, loudly ordering drinks from the bartender and the waitresses. The Bench was a favorite hangout of cops and lawyers and bail bondsmen. Bondspersons. The bar was down an alley, a half block from the Hall of Justice.

Carver pushed his way through the crowd, scanning the length of the bar, peering into every booth and at every table. Again his shirt was damp, clinging to his ribs. He squinted his eyes against the nicotine smoke and rubbed his nose, as though that would keep the boozy smell out. Fat chance. Where was De Anza? He pushed and muttered his excuses as he made his way past loud customers.

"Carver," a voice called.

Carver turned and made his way to a booth in a corner.

"Good to see you," Lt. Raphael De Anza said. "Have a

seat. Take a load off, and, believe me, *compadre,* you look like a man with a load.''

De Anza slid over, pushing against the woman seated next to him. Carver sat down, part of his butt off the leather seat.

Whatever a cop, a detective, should look like, Lt. Raphael De Anza did not fit the picture. The other detectives said he looked like a shoe salesman in a shopping mall. In his middle forties, he had thinning hair, a stocky build, eyes set close together. De Anza was proud of his black bandit's mustache, which he flicked with the back of a finger from time to time. He and Carver Bascombe had been friends for many years.

''We're celebrating,'' said De Anza, snapping his fingers to get the attention of a waitress.

''What's the occasion?'' Carver asked.

''My promotion,'' De Anza said with a grin, and told the waitress to bring over . . . what? He tilted his head at Carver.

''Anchor Steam, ice-cold,'' Carver said.

''That's the only way our beer comes, sonny,'' the waitress replied. She waited while De Anza made a circling motion: the same again, all around. She went off, a woman in her forties, maybe married, maybe with kids, with a helluva future in the waiting-on-tables business.

De Anza introduced Carver to the others: a policewoman named Joyce; two detectives, Hugo and Barney; two motorcycle cops, Orville and Ben. Nobody paid much attention.

''Everybody in here celebrating?'' Carver asked De Anza, pointing at the crowd in the bar.

''What, am I made of money? No, just the people here at the booth and others sucking around for a free drink.''

''I heard you might get the job,'' Carver said.

''Oh, damn right, I'll get it,'' De Anza said, nodding to himself, a self-satisfied grin wandering over his face. ''Old Satan Kennedy, finally giving it up. Retiring. Seat open . . . watch the rush! But I got the credit, I got the seniority, the best man for the job.''

Almost twenty years in the police department. Four years a cop in uniform. The rest with Vice, Burglary, and the last ten years in Homicide. De Anza was just at the right level to qualify in those days. Now it was easy. Easier. But a cadet, man or woman, had to be just as strong, just as good.

A few years short of fifty, De Anza would be the youngest captain of detectives in the department's history. He rubbed a finger over his thick black mustache and grinned crookedly at Carver.

"You don't think," Carver asked slowly, "you're being a bit premature? The promotion?"

"Nah, 'cause there isn't anyone better. The older guys, they don't want the gaff, the shit, the politics. Me, I don't mind. And I got the record, the best busts, the best convictions. And I got to thank you for a couple a those. Yeah, I sure do. A couple a days . . . Captain De Anza. Nice sound, huh?"

The waitress brought the drinks, and De Anza threw a large bill on her tray and told her to "keep 'em coming and keep the change."

"Just a minute of your time," Carver said, tilting the bottle to his lips and swigging down a third of the beer.

"The body in the fountain. Yeah, Ludlow told me about it, and about your identification. Whoa, Jesus Christo, was he burned. The wrong ID." De Anza chuckled boozily.

"I want to look at Piombo's rooms tomorrow."

"Oh, yeah? Think you're goin' to find somethin' we didn't?"

"It's been known to happen."

"Listen, Carver, this case belongs to Sergeant Ludlow. He's a good cop and he won't stand you getting in his way."

"I don't get in his way. He gets in my way."

"Now, dammit, that's the sort of thing I mean. Steer clear if you see him coming."

"Does that mean I get in?"

"Huh? Oh, you mean Piombo's? I suppose so. Why the fuck not."

"I've been talking to a couple of people—and the cops're going to find them sooner or later, but I'll save them some time—"

"God, not now. I'll never remember their names, and I don't want to take the time to write anything down. Call me in the morning, okay? Give me the names and addresses then."

"Right," Carver agreed.

"You're good at your job. I'll say that. The D.A. might not. Remember, you owe us. Plenty of times the D.A.'s been all over Captain Kennedy's ass to pull your license."

"That's crap, Raf. They never said that. You know that."

"Shit, yes, I know that, but it sounds good. Anyway, Kennedy has gone to bat for you—and so have I. Don't fuck up this one. Call me in the morning, tell me your addresses, and I'll give you Piombo's address. And I'll alert the on-duty cops."

Finishing his beer, Carver asked De Anza to remember him to his wife, Laura, and to his son.

"Oh, Antonio. Know what Tony's majoring in? He's a junior, you know. Political science. Poli sci, he calls it. Lots of ideals. Wants to change the world. Maybe he got his eye on being president. How about that? A Mexican in the White House. Could happen, you know." He drank off his gin and tonic, then snapped his fingers at the waitress.

Carver left the bar. In twenty minutes he had parked the Jaguar at the Hi-Valu service station, and in another five he was in his office. The windows were still open and the fan still clattered.

He clicked on the desk lamp and turned on the stereo, and moments later Respighi's *The Birds* poured out from the loudspeakers. He went into his apartment. What was in the fridge? Something cool. A cold salad sounded good. He pushed a few cans and packages around and found a can of crab. He opened a bottle of chilled gewurztraminer and poured a glass. Then he cut up a head of lettuce, some tomatoes, cucumbers, onions, and put everything in a bowl. He mixed in mayonnaise and took the salad and the wine into his office.

He sat behind his desk and slid off his shoes. Ah, very nice. He opened his notebook and looked at the questions he had written. Any answers? Nothing came to mind. He ate some salad, then moved over to a corkboard on the opposite wall. He took out the photo of Tom Ferrik and pinned it to the board.

Okay, Tom, where are you? Hiding out in the mountains? Maybe. Was there anything at Piombo's that would tell him, something the police overlooked? Tomorrow would tell.

He wrote a few names on three-by-five cards and pinned them to the board. Behind the desk he looked at the display. Not much, but then it was early yet.

Calling Rose Weinbaum, he learned that Amber was watching TV. The girl and Rose got along just fine. Rose had called Amber's school and explained some of the situation; Amber didn't have to attend classes for a few days. After they had left the hospital, Rose figured Amber had to get her mind off things. She had bought her a new toy, a green frog puppet; Amber loved it.

Carver thought that was a good idea. He told her his schedule for the next day: seeing De Anza about Piombo, then checking Piombo's rooms, then he would be out to see Rose and Amber. The girl just might know where her father liked to go camping.

Then Carver gave Rose a rundown on his day's activities, with capsule evaluations on everyone he had met.

"Any of them telling the truth?" Rose asked.

"Probably not," Carver replied. "Wouldn't know the truth if I heard it. Too damn hot."

"I did a lot of checking on the wife. Got the information from court records—including her current address. But you found that out. She was into more than just child-beating. She was into booze and drugs. Not heavy, but enough to tilt the world in her head."

"Anything else?" Carver asked, enjoying Rose's sexy voice.

"Of course. Do you think I spend my time out in the hot sun chasing down suspects? I stay inside where it's cool and let my fingers do the walking."

"Okay," Carver said with a laugh. "What else?"

"Did she mention she's seeing another man?"

"Yeah, she did, but didn't elaborate."

"Another sculptor. Did she tell you that?"

"No. I must be getting stale."

"Got this from that guy we know, writes the art reviews for the newspaper. Her sculptor friend is Hermano Grabar. Mean anything?"

"No."

"He got into a fight with one of the art commissioners a year or so ago, had a real knock-down-drag-out slugfest with him. Alex Marteau. Grabar beat the daylights out of him for saying that his statue was a piece of junk and that the commission wasn't going to approve of it to be placed at Aquatic Park. Grabar broke his jaw, knocked out a mess of teeth, and broke Marteau's arm."

"All that in a fistfight?"

"You should see what this guy looks like. He's got arms like Popeye. But handsome, with a Clark Gable mustache. I had a photo sent to the office by messenger from the newspaper." She paused. "You didn't say anything about Stahl's alibi."

"What alibi?"

"For the time that Piombo was shot, or when Amber was shot."

"I'm paid to look for Ferrik, not chase down killers. I'll leave that to the cops."

"You're going to let Ludlow get there first?"

"Why not? It's his job."

"Bullshit."

"All right, Rose," Carver said, suppressing a yawn. "I'll see you in the morning, at your place. No sense in your coming to the office."

"You're the boss."

"Yeah, so you say. Take care of Amber. Anything else?"

Rose said there wasn't and hung up the receiver. She returned to the living room, where Amber was snuggled down in an overstuffed easy chair watching television. She nuzzled her new toy.

"I'd say it was your bedtime, Amber," Rose said quietly.

"I suppose so," the girl replied. She sounded tired but willing to argue the point with Rose. "I would like to finish this program—and then I'll go to bed."

"No fuss?"

"No, I won't kick up a fuss. My daddy lets me stay up sometimes until almost ten o'clock. But someday . . . What I really would like to do is to stay up and see midnight."

"There isn't much to see."

"That's because you're grown up. But I've never seen it, and that's what makes it interesting. Midnight . . ." She gave the word a mysterious quality, as though twelve o'clock had all of the trolls, goblins, fairies, and witches of times past. "It's the witching hour, you know," she said.

"Yes, I was told that, too. When I was little."

"Rose," Amber said slowly, one eye on the TV screen, "don't you have a husband?"

"I used to, Amber."

"Why don't you have one now? Are you divorced?"

"No. He—he died. Some time ago. His name was Bernie."

"You sound sad. He must have been a nice man."

Rose didn't reply. She gazed idly at the TV screen. Yes, that would describe him. Bernie Weinbaum had been a good man. He had been a good private detective. He had liked to help people, and seldom made moral judgments. He had liked working with other P.I.'s. And with Carver Bascombe. Rose sighed, remembering. She had tried to put herself in Carver's mind, to feel what he felt about Bernie's death, but it had been a futile task. There was no way she could know how he felt, just as he couldn't know how she felt.

Mistaken identity? Sort of. The killers had thought that they were gunning down Carver Bascombe, but it had been Bernie, who had been asked by Carver to be there at that particular place. Carver had been doing something else. No way for him to know that a bullet would tear into Bernie's head and kill him.

One thing Rose and Bernie had agreed upon: Vengeance never compensates. It never takes the bitter taste away; never dries the tears. Oh, she didn't blame Carver, but still it took a while to see him for what he was: a victim also. Just like everybody else.

She had come up with the idea of coming in as a partner, a junior partner, for one third of the profits—but Carver didn't have to accept the offer. Rose knew he had because he felt guilty. Maybe it hadn't been nice to play on his guilt, but it had been a case of her survival. What else could she do? The house on Fulton seemed empty, and just how many times could she watch reruns of *Gunsmoke*? How could she get interested in the artificial troubles of puppet people in soap operas?

She jerked herself from her thoughts. The TV was running a commercial. She leaned over and spoke softly to Amber, then realized the girl had fallen asleep. Rose picked her up and carried her to the bedroom. She put her into bed, gently pulling the sheets to her chin. Rose put the green frog in Amber's arms and put out the lights.

*   *   *

Carver leaned back in his chair, enjoying the semidarkness and the music. A vision, more a memory really, of Sharon Argent pushed into his mind. What a lovely woman. He remembered her curves, the way the coveralls seemed a strange type of outfit for her. What was she like in a gown or some sporty, short-skirted thing?

Did she like music, his kind of music, or was she part of the crowd, into rock or jazz or blues? Her sculpture told him that she had an imagination, one of a strange and perilous nature.

What was this? Thinking of love? He didn't believe in love at first sight. But maybe that's because it had never happened to him.

Sipping his wine, Carver Bascombe realized that he had the beginnings of an erection. A distraction was needed. He looked around the office and then stepped into Rose's office. He found a manila envelope on the floor where the messenger had slid it under the door. He opened it and looked at the photo of an athletic-looking man. He turned it over and read the inked-in name. Hermano Grabar. Barbara Stahl's man. He pinned the photo next to Tom Ferrik's and went back to his desk.

He drank more wine and finished off the salad. He turned off the stereo and the lamp and then . . . He paused.

Footsteps. Coming up the stairway . . . and then down the hall. He waited. After all, there were more offices on the third floor than his. A travel agency, a couple of accountants who mostly argued during the day, an artist who designed greeting cards, and two mail-order outfits (one of which was a front for a local small-time numbers game).

And every one of them was closed after 5:30 P.M. The only office anyone might come to at night was the detective agency. And Carver was not expecting anyone. He looked at the filing cabinet where he kept one of his .357 Pythons. On the street outside, a MUNI bus blurted out a few exhaust remarks.

The frosted glass showed the gray silhouette of a figure. A woman. And something tightened across Carver's chest. Hunch time in the old coconut.

SIX

He opened the door.

"Oh, Mr. Bascombe," Sharon Argent said.

"Call me Carver, please," Carver said, his tongue almost stumbling over the words, "so I can call you Sharon. Come in, please."

"Thank you. No, don't turn on the lights. That little lamp is plenty. I'm afraid I've been letting loose a few tears."

Carver sat on the edge of the desk. Sharon sat in the straight-back chair facing him. He offered her a cigarette from a case he fished out of the desk.

"No, I don't smoke. Go ahead if you want."

Carver shook his head and returned the case to the drawer. He liked the change of dress. Instead of grimy coveralls, Sharon wore a dress of sheer yellow and orange fabric and a cool-looking pearl-gray blouse. She was quite unaware of the effect she had. She was too disturbed for that. He braced his hands against the edge of the desk. The difficult part was keeping his thoughts clear. Questions had to be asked. She had come for a reason, not just to let Carver Bascombe stare like a slack-jawed teenager at some silver-screen goddess.

"So," he said, "what brings you here? Something about Tom Ferrik?"

"Yes. I've been asking myself questions, where would he go and why didn't he tell me. The second question I have no answers for, but the first, maybe there is something . . . Tom liked to go into the Sierras—"

"He liked camping. I know."

"Oh."

"I've already talked to Barbara. That's where I got that photo." He pointed to the corkboard. "That is Tom, isn't it?"

She looked at the photo, at the man with the lean face, the pulled-back hair, the deep widow's peak, the hard, omniscient-looking eyes.

"Yes, that's Tom. Didn't you think it was? Or didn't you trust Barbara to give you the right photograph?"

"Check and double-check. That's my business."

"I'm not sure I like that kind of business." She pointed to the other photo. "Who's that?"

"Just a man."

"He looks mean. Who is he?"

"Hermano Grabar," Carver said, enjoying the conversation. It could go on for hours as far as he was concerned. "Do you know him?"

"No, I've never seen him before. Does he have anything to do with Tom's disappearance?"

Carver shrugged.

"I don't think your profession is good for the soul," Sharon said. She turned away from Carver and looked out the windows. "Not to trust people. I think it would destroy something inside yourself." She turned again and looked at Carver. "Do you think everyone lies to you?"

"I'll take the Fifth Amendment on that," he said. "And now let's get back to Tom. Barbara didn't know the place where he liked to camp."

"Tom told me she wasn't interested in that part of his life. But that's the reason I've come here—"

"You know where he liked to camp?"

"No, I never went either. Not that I didn't want to, but . . . anyway, that's something else. I believe you're right, thinking he might have gone into the Sierras. It was one place he went for solitude, for inspiration, for thinking things out. And the person who might know the location is my brother, Frank. Have you met him yet?"

"No. I don't know where he lives."

"That's why I'm here."

She looked directly into his face, the desk lamp throwing irregular shadows onto his lean brown face. Sharon's brown eyes were soft, like molten chocolate drops. Carver squirmed under such a direct stare. Did he still have an erection? He closed his eyes. No, not fully erect. Did she notice? He hoped not.

"I want you to drive me to his apartment," she said. "And, please, no questions until we're on the way."

"No," Carver said. "No. Just a couple of questions. You're worried. Why?"

"Frank doesn't answer his phone. After you left, the police came and questioned me. That's when I began to realize that this is getting serious."

"A man named Ludlow?"

"Yes, that was his name. You know him?"

"Yeah," Carver said noncommittally. "Go on."

"He asked me a lot of questions—he seemed particularly interested in where I was this morning. I told him I'd been working in the studio. He didn't seem to believe me."

"Yeah, I know."

"After he left, I tried to call Frank to let him know about Tom and to see if he might have heard from him—they were getting to be good friends. He didn't answer. . . ." She stopped talking and wiped her eyes with a handkerchief.

"The phone was okay? Not out of order?"

"I let it ring twenty times. Twice."

"Does he have a girl friend?"

"There are a few women that he sees, but almost always on weekends. He seldom goes out on weeknights. He likes to cook and doesn't like paying restaurant prices. He should have answered the telephone. Please, Carver, I am worried."

Carver felt a tingling sensation. He hadn't told her about Amber getting shot. If he told her the truth, then she would be even more concerned, and even more involved. He would see more of her. Carver liked that. He liked her and wanted to see more of her, be with her. He did not resist the temptation.

"There's more to this, Sharon," he said. He walked to the window and looked out. The night air was cooler by only a few degrees. At least his shirt wasn't sticking to his back. He turned to her. "Before coming to my office this morning Amber was shot and wounded."

Sharon stared at him. Her eyes grew large, and she plucked at the cuff of her blouse. He told her the rest of the story; what Amber told him, his going to Tom's house, the white man who slugged him and fired a shotgun at him. He left out only his theories and conceptions, which were minimal and fuzzy at best.

"So," Carver said, "let's go see your brother."

He took her arm—and felt his own hand tremble for a moment. Did she notice? Carver locked the office door, and they walked to the Hi-Valu station. Minutes later they were driving across town, following Sharon's directions. Carver asked her to go on with her story.

"Why would your brother know where Tom might be hiding?"

"He went fishing with Tom several times. He was very excited too, since he'd never gone fishing in his entire life. The outdoors was different. He grew up in the city . . . we both did. Frank is your basic home person. He doesn't like roughing it. That's what he liked about camping with Tom. They lived in a cabin, next to a river. All the creature comforts, Frank said. Including a VCR hooked up to a television and lots of videotapes."

Sharon pointed to a house, and Carver parked half a block away. After turning on the car's alarm, he followed her to the front door and waited while she rang the bell.

From habit and experience, Carver scanned the neighborhood. Most of the house and apartment lights were on. One streetlight was out. Up the street two people sat chatting on the front stoop. Two pedestrians walked on the sidewalk opposite, and one on this side. He took note of many of the parked cars. The front windows of Frank Argent's apartment were open.

"He doesn't answer," Sharon said.

"There's a window open," Carver said. "Why don't you crawl in and unlock the front door."

"Me? Why don't you do it?"

"It's illegal, which doesn't mean I wouldn't, but you're a relative. I'll give you a boost."

She thought about that for a few seconds and then agreed. Carver went down the stairs and stood under the window, and Sharon stepped over the railing onto his shoulders. He steadied her, and she climbed into the window. She opened the front door and Carver joined her inside. He clicked on the lights.

The apartment was quiet. Carver went into the kitchen and then into the bedroom. Sharon followed. She stopped and choked back a strangled gasp.

Frank Argent sat tied to a chair, his legs propped on the

bed. His face was turned to one side. The wall he seemed to be staring at was spattered with long streaks and small spots of blood. Sharon stumbled forward, but Carver held her back.

"Let me go!" she cried, and twisted out of his hands. She knelt beside her brother and tried to untie the knotted rope.

Carver used a pocketknife to slice the ropes. He checked Argent's carotid artery, then carefully touched the man's head and moved it slightly. He shook his head.

Sharon sat on the bed staring at her brother.

"I'm sorry, Sharon," Carver said. "He's dead. A broken neck. Sometimes during a severe beating, it happens. There are men with the strength to do it."

She nodded listlessly. She continued to gaze at the dead man. Her brother. Tears glittered on her cheeks, and she buried her face in her hands. Her body shook with silent sobs as though electric shocks were jolting her. Finally she turned to Carver.

"What do we do?"

"Call the police."

"And then?"

"Things take its course."

"I see," she said, although she was just saying words.

Carver went to the phone and called Homicide, asking for Sergeant Ludlow. The sergeant was off-duty, but Carver insisted, and the police said they'd try to reach him at home.

He returned to the bedroom and leaned against the door-jamb and watched Sharon looking at her brother. What kind of thoughts were running through her mind? Or was she thinking of anything?

Whoever killed Frank Argent had worked him over first. That was obvious. They had wanted something, or they had wanted Argent to tell them something. Was this killing connected with Lou Piombo's murder? Carver felt the inside man—the hunter, the ferret—take hold of him, a long-familiar animal who lay craftily hidden most of the time. But, when needed, that hunter-beast would come out faithfully. Often unbidden. All right, he had called the cops . . . but now he was going to look around the apartment.

He went through the drawers in the bedside table and then the dresser. Nothing. And he didn't find anything in the front room, nothing that would get a man killed. Only some correspondence and some payroll deduction slips that told him Frank Argent worked for a freight-forwarding company.

Another drawer was full of loose maps and railroad schedules. Several were wrapped with rubber bands. Just the sort of things a freight dispatcher would have. Nothing there.

Carver returned to the bedroom; she was still sitting there. He took her arm and gently pulled her to her feet. He led her back through the apartment where they waited on the stairs. The air was thick and leaden, as though the streets smoldered under a branding iron.

Again he scanned the area, matching previous details. The dark sedan across the street had exhaust trickling from its tailpipe. The vehicle could be harmless, simply waiting for one of the tenants to come out. Carver would keep his eye on the car.

"Is that why you wanted to stick around, Ed?" Cholly asked in irritation. He stared at the two figures on the front stairs of Argent's apartment.

"Yes, and shut up, Cholly," Ed Zinn said. His voice was grating and whispery. "And keep your goddamn head down."

Cholly slunk farther down on the passenger seat. He could just see past Zinn's forehead to Argent's apartment across the street.

One big one, that was what was on Zinn's mind. Had been since he had done time. One good score. The old-timers were always talking about it like it was some kind of fairy tale, like something the pop-generation of hoods and thieves couldn't understand. Zinn could, oh, yes, indeed he could. When he had been tied with Lou Piombo in a cell for six months, he never dreamed of anything this big.

Dollars, that's what he and Piombo talked about. Ol' Lou, all he talked about was how goddamned clever he was, how he jiggered things, like making art copies and such. He was a fascinating little crook. And that's what made the world go around. Bucks.

Six months in jail here, nine months there, for Zinn, over and over again. But Zinn had never been to the Big Wall. Thank God for that. Just little stuff. But he was over forty years old and what did he have to show for it? Nothing worth a damn. Friends? Hanging around banana-brains like Cholly.

Some of the old ex-cons had talked about percentages, dividing how much they made by the years in prison, by the years outside. Somehow it never paid off. A goddamn street sweeper made more money in the long run. So what was the answer, unless you really wanted to sweep the street? The big score! And that's what Lou thought he had. Something safe, with little chance for the Wall. Now Piombo was dead. Who the hell killed him? That's what Ed Zinn wanted to know.

"We oughtta get out of here," Cholly Lehm said, his voice quavering. "A fuckin' half hour we been here. It's crazy. We never should've stuck around. This car is hot. But maybe they won't have it on their whatchacallit."

"Their hot sheet."

"Yeah, the hot sheet. They won't have it on that this fast. We're okay. Huh?"

"I'll do the thinking. Frank's phone ringing twice like that. There was a good chance someone might come around to see him. I wanted to see who it was."

"We want to know where the squeeze lives?"

"You got a brain, Cholly."

"This waitin'. Makes me hungry, Ed. Sorta thought we might stop for a bite. A sandwich or a pizza."

"Cholly," Zinn said in exasperation, "eat a hambooger."

"I don't like this waitin'."

"I know. You've told me. But it paid off. That's the guy who said he was a private detective."

"How can you tell, Ed?"

"Jesus, whatta you, some kinda racist? All smokes look alike? I got eyes and I'm telling you that's the same guy. Maybe I should've killed him, but . . ."

"Yeah, I know. Why make more trouble? Shit, Ed, we're in deep already."

"So let your greed be your guide."

"I'll shut up. But . . . Son of a bitch! Here come the cops."

A half hour later the police technicians had completed most of their work: the photographer had taken pictures of the victim, the bedroom, the front room; the fingerprint woman had completed dusting; and the M.E. had verified that Frank Argent had died of a broken neck, probably the result of the savage beating. Whether it might have been accidental or deliberately inflicted, he was unable to say.

As Argent was zipped into a body bag, Sergeant Ludlow sat on a sofa in the front room. He looked at the African mask on the wall and the crossed asagais beneath it. Why didn't they just stab the poor bastard? he asked himself. Maybe it was accidental.

Sharon Argent and Carver Bascombe sat nearby, next to the open window. Still no relief from the heat. Sharon had watched the arrival of the cops and technicians, but she was barely aware of them. Sergeant Ludlow had nodded grumpily. Carver was silent, with his own thoughts and questions.

Dr. Wolfram came out and told Ludlow his estimate of the time of death. Just a short time, within the last hour or so. Ludlow wrote this down, and then gestured to Carver and Sharon. They repeated their story a second time. Ludlow wrote notes.

"And that's it?" Ludlow asked.

They nodded.

"What? I didn't hear that, Jack."

"Yes, Sergeant," Carver said, "that is all."

"Umm," Ludlow said indifferently. "Okay. If that's what you say, that's what you say. And now, Miss—or you prefer Ms.?"

"Whatever you're comfortable with, Sergeant."

"I'm not comfortable with anything. Tell me about your brother. Where did he work?"

"He was a freight dispatcher for a company on Townsend. I don't remember the name of the company."

"Truck or train freight?"

"Both, I think," Sharon said.

"It's Bay Forwarding," Carver added.

"How do you know, Bascombe?" Ludlow asked.

"I saw the name on a payroll stub."

"Looked around, did you?"

"Yeah."

"You know I don't like this," he said, glaring at Carver, "and you know why."

"Tell me."

"One fuckin' day you're involved, and already two dead people are laid in my lap. I got nothin' better to do—"

"Stop it, Ludlow. You don't do the outraged public servant very well. Why give Miss Argent the wrong impression? She's liable to think you don't like your work."

"Don't wise off." Ludlow grunted. He removed his hat and wiped his brow. He lit a cigarette and crushed the match-flame with his fingers. He stared at Carver and Sharon. No blink. "Okay. . . . Get out of here. Drive careful. Go to bed." He gestured his big hand like a broom. "Go."

They went. Driving along Guerrero they said nothing. Sharon was deep within her thoughts. Carver kept his eye on the rearview mirror. He had done so since leaving Argent's apartment. He didn't want to frighten her, but he had seen a car pull out and follow them. The car from across the street. He wasn't mistaken; he knew that it wasn't a coincidence—the car had gone a half block before the driver had turned on his headlights.

Was there something Sharon had not told him? Was she lying about not knowing where Tom Ferrik was hiding? In his office, her concern for her brother had seemed artificial. Had she known that he was already dead? There was the possibility that Sharon had already visited the apartment, found the body, and then used Carver as an alibi of sorts. It wouldn't be the first time a woman had tried something like that.

He didn't like being underestimated.

Was the car tailing him—or her? Or both?

"What's the matter?" Sharon asked.

"Nothing. Just thinking." No sense in alarming her about the tail.

They were silent, letting the warm night air rush against their faces. Sharon began snuffling and tried to hide her tears in a handkerchief.

"He meant so much," she finally managed to blurt out. "To me. So much to me. Frank was—was so full of fun. He used to tell me bedtime stories that he'd make up. Fairy tales. Such a fantastic imagination."

"Don't talk if—"

"No, it's . . . I want to talk, Carver. Frank . . . he used to come up with wild and silly schemes when we were kids. The perfect crime, the perfect robbery, and even the . . . the perfect murder.'' Sharon sobbed openly. "Murder . . . Oh, God . . .''

Carver was without words. He parked and followed Sharon up the stairs. The lights in the landlady's apartment were on, and through the gauze drapes Carver could see the flickering bluish light from a television set. Sharon took out her key and opened the door.

"I'd invite you in for a cup of coffee,'' Sharon said, "but I'd really rather be alone. For a while. I'm still shook up about—about . . .''

"Yes, I understand,'' he said. He moved closer and put his hands on her shoulders.

This was the first time he had actually touched her, and she felt warm, trembling, and vulnerable. He looked into her eyes. Sharon looked away and he stepped closer, sliding one arm along her back. She looked at him, her eyes moist. Several tears moved slowly down her cheeks.

"No, Carver. Please.'' She gently removed the hand from her shoulder and moved from Carver's embrace. "I do appreciate everything. All that you've done . . . but I do want to be by myself.'' She looked at him with a slight smile that had little warmth in it. The smile was merely polite and nothing more. She had nothing to put into it.

Carver was embarrassed. Mentally, he chided himself for making such an obvious move. Too early, he told himself, too damned early. Obviously Sharon was struggling desperately to hold back the tears. Couldn't he wait? No, another voice inside said, he couldn't wait, he had to make a move. He pushed that voice away.

"All right, Sharon,'' he said huskily, "but please call me. Tomorrow? Early?''

"I'll see. I don't know how I'll feel when I wake up.''

"You're tired.''

"Yes, but I don't know if I can sleep. Good night.''

He felt uncomfortable, as though he had committed a foolish act. Tomorrow? Yeah, he'd settle for that. He waited for Sharon to enter the apartment and turn on the lights. He went back to the Jaguar and stood beside it, listening to the sound of the engine ticking as it cooled off.

"A warm night," he muttered to himself. A lot happening. The thing inside, that consciousness that filled his mind with the thrill of the hunt, seemed to grin. All right, so Sharon wasn't ready. Until this case was finished they'd be together often. Plenty of time. A negative feeling crept through his body, almost as though the hunter inside was saying no, no, there was too much to do. No time for a woman.

He looked down the street and picked out the car that had been following them. Whoever they were, they knew where Sharon lived. Were they cops? Had Ludlow put a tail on him? Carver didn't think so; it wasn't Ludlow's style. He shut off the burglar alarm and slid in behind the wheel, where he sat, slumped, as though he were going to stay for a while. Wasn't that part of a private detective's job? Just sitting around watching? Sure it was. Boring.

But Carver's mind raced. Who was in that car? He looked at Sharon's apartment and saw the lights go out. The lights in the landlady's apartment were still on. After twenty minutes, he carefully opened the car door and slid to the sidewalk. The street had few street lamps and one was out. He maneuvered behind his car and opened the trunk just a crack. He reached in, unlocked the custom-made compartment, and removed the Colt Python. He closed the trunk and then made his way down the hill, car by car. He was sure he hadn't been seen.

The last distance was going to be difficult. He had to take them by surprise. He wasn't too concerned about them being armed. If they were the killers, wouldn't they have shot Argent rather than break his neck?

On the other hand, it would be slightly amusing if they were cops tailing him.

Moving cautiously, crouching low, Carver was next to the car just in front of his target. With luck, they were watching Sharon's apartment or his own car. He made the last few feet on hands and toes, then reached for the door handle. He cocked the hammer of the Python and then jerked open the car door. He was looking forward to their expressions.

Surprise!

The car was empty.

SEVEN

The ceiling seemed cloudy, as though all through the day the heat had risen in Sharon's bedroom and collected there.

Or was it her eyes?

She brushed away the tears. She resisted the urge to turn on the light. She had to lie in the darkness. Had to. From time to time, bursts of soft sobbing racked her body.

Her only brother was gone. It seemed so unreal. They had played as children, and he had often been there to protect her. He had been the one to urge her to continue her art studies. Frank had understood her so well. She was different, and she knew she was different; Frank had known it, too.

Their father . . . "It was just a phase," he had said. "Besides, girl, blacks didn't get into this fine art stuff. No money in it. Bad enough for white artists." What did families know? She had battled so much for her own self, and to have had to battle parents—it was just too goddamn much. Sometimes. Sometimes, when it was dark, she could still feel the loneliness.

Her parents had worked so hard, and all they had known was day-to-day survival. The pay of a trolley operator had been good, but it had still been difficult.

How she hated these thoughts, reducing her own life to just a few pat phrases. Life was difficult. What the hell, just what the goddamn hell did that mean?

Frank had been the strong one. Even when the auto accident had killed their mother and father, he hadn't broken down.

Sharon twisted in bed, shuddering, trying to drive the thoughts and memories from her mind. None of it did any good. She knew what she wanted: to work, to cut steel, to bend metal, to throw herself into a nightmare fever of hard work.

And now she was really alone. Frank was gone. All she had left was Tom—and where was he? Why hadn't Tom called her? Didn't he think she could help him out of whatever trouble he was in? Didn't he trust her enough for that?

Asking questions was useless. She had no answers.

Sharon yawned, her mind going drowsy, her hands falling slowly to her side. Her eyes closed. There were so many questions . . . Frank could not have been involved . . . not with anything like . . . he was killed by . . . burglars. Yes, that was . . .

She finally fell into a tortured sleep.

Carver waited patiently in his car. Her lights had been out for a long time. One hour. Two hours. He could hardly keep himself from yawning. God, he was tired. Maybe he was mistaken. Maybe the men in the car that had tailed him and Sharon had nothing to do with her brother's death. So far nothing had happened.

Carver had left the empty car undisturbed, but had walked up and down the street, gun in hand, checking all the doorways. Then he returned to his car and sat behind the wheel. Waiting.

He was going to fall asleep. Which wouldn't do. He had to chance leaving—if only for a few minutes. He drove off and found a saloon that had a telephone booth in the rear.

The first two P.I.'s he phoned were not available, but he scored on the third call. Mike Tettsui was home and willing to do a watchdog job. Carver's next call was to the police. He drove back to Sharon's building and parked. Sharon's apartment seemed peaceful.

A couple of cops in a squad car drove up and talked with Carver. The sedan? Stolen, about four hours ago. They took Carver's report and had the sedan towed to the police garage. The owner was going to be both happy and pissed off; the towing fee and storage charge was stiff. Everybody made out except the victims. Someday the suckers would get smart and the entire society would consist of nothing but criminals. No innocent victims.

As the tow truck hauled away the car, Mike Tettsui drove up in a paneled pickup. The Japanese detective came to work complete with a thermos of coffee, sandwiches, and cups of ramen noodles. Carver described the job.

"No sweat, Carver," Mike said, settling into his pickup, his eyes on Sharon's apartment. "Go on home, my man. You look all in."

Carver asked him to call later that day. There might be more work. He thanked Mike and then drove off. In his apartment-cum-office, he fell onto the bed. He slept wretchedly, awaking many times.

Sweat-drenched sheets. Open windows and noises from the streets. Belching buses. Angry drivers honking. Carver slept fitfully. He woke and stared at the night-gray ceiling. He remembered—he had been dreaming of Sharon Argent. Erotic dreams. Pleasant dreams. Again he fell asleep.

The second time he awoke, he washed the sweat from his body in the kitchen sink. He drank a glass of water. Visions of a man on a morgue slab had haunted him. How about a bottle of beer, old perspiring detective? With the third awakening, he had a dialogue with himself. Dreaming about Sharon didn't mean a thing. Or did it? Filled with regrets? Desires? Ironic questions?

Had he done the best thing? Calling Mike Tettsui to watch Sharon's house? Was she really in danger? Possibly. The sedan had been empty. Where were the men who had been in it?

He was glad when daylight began to filter into the bedroom. He arose, naked, made coffee, and fixed a bowl of wheat flakes and a glass of orange juice. He dressed in slacks and another short-sleeve, loose-weave shirt. In an airline bag he put two changes of clothes.

Already the office was stifling.

The phone rang. Carver answered it and listened to Mike Tettsui's report.

"Listen, Carver, that woman is a real doll, but does she ever get up early. Sharon Argent left the house about an hour ago and took a taxi. Guess where?"

"Can't imagine, so tell me."

"The taxi dropped her off near your office. She went inside but paused in the lobby, like she was making up her mind. She left after a couple of minutes and then walked to a parked car. She got in and drove off. Her own car, I figured."

"Yeah, she drove over here last night."

"Anyway, she went to this place near Townsend where she has a studio. She's there now, so I took the time to report."

"What kind of car does she drive?" Carver asked, reaching for a note pad.

"A Japanese coupe, dark blue, about six years old, I guess."

He gave Carver the license number, and Carver thanked

him for the report and for coming to the rescue the night before.

"Glad to do it," Mike said. "You said there was more."

"Yes. Make yourself available at Rose Weinbaum's."

"When, Carver?"

"You need sleep, too. How about this evening, around six or seven?"

"You got it. Anything else?"

"No. Send me a bill."

Carver hung up and gazed out the windows. He found himself in the kind of thoughtful state he usually said was unproductive. He shrugged, picked up the airline bag. Before he left the office, he turned off the fan. Conserve energy.

"God, God," De Anza muttered. He rummaged in the kitchen cabinets, cursing under his breath. He held his head, slowly shaking it from side to side.

His wife, Laura, entered the kitchen. "Now sit, Raphael," she ordered with just a trace of condescension. "I'll make the coffee. Instant? Or the real thing?"

"Whichever stops this doomsday machine in my head." He sat at the butcher-block table and put quivering hands to his throbbing head. "What time is it?" he asked peevishly.

"It's seven-thirty," Laura replied quietly. A soft answer turneth away wrath, but hath no effect on drums and cymbals of ye hangover, she thought.

Laura De Anza was a lovely woman, somewhat younger than her husband. She moved about the kitchen with practiced ease, her long black hair swinging in rhythm with her body. She smiled tolerantly at her husband, her large, dark, almond-shaped eyes twinkling with amusement. In minutes, coffee was perking, filling the kitchen with its wonderful aroma.

She poured the coffee into two cups and placed one in front

of De Anza. He sipped it gratefully, letting the minutes drag on until he almost felt human once again.

Unfortunately, the front doorbell rang, sending shock waves through De Anza's long-suffering head. Laura started for the door, but Raphael said he'd get it. Muttering vile curses to himself, he flung open the door.

"Good morning, Raphael," said Carver Bascombe.

"Do you have any idea, any idea, what godforsaken time it is?"

"Of course," Carver said, and made an elaborate show of looking at his wristwatch. "It's seven-thirty." He looked up at the bright sky. "In the morning."

"Funny, very funny. Well, for God's sake, Amigo, don't stand in the doorway letting in all that hot air. Come in, come in."

De Anza led the way down the hall of the old frame house. In the large kitchen, he indicated a chair at the butcher-block table. Carver exchanged greetings with Laura.

"Coffee?" she asked.

"Fine, Laura," he replied, then turned to De Anza. "You said last night . . ." Carver began.

But De Anza held up his hand like a traffic cop. No. Unh-unh. *Nada. Nyet. Nein.* Whatever the language, there was to be no speaking. Yet. Carver sighed and settled back in his chair. The only noises in the room were the coffee bubbling, the rattling of cups and saucers, and the sound of Laura's slippers slithering over the bare wood floor. She poured out coffee for Carver.

"Okay," De Anza said after taking several big gulps of coffee, "what did I promise you last night? It better be good, or you made this trip for nothing."

"You don't remember?" Carver asked.

"Not much, but go ahead. Don't be embarrassed, Laura knows I came home pissed to the eyeballs."

"It is not something," Laura said, "that happens frequently. I forgive him."

"That's not what you said last night. I don't recall the exact words, but I do remember the mood, a nasty, vile mood. And to inflict such pain on a man in my condition . . . What insensitivity, such a lack of understanding . . ."

"You remember nothing. I was only angry for a minute, and then I realized what a waste of time it was. Who do you think helped you get your clothes off, helped you brush your teeth, helped you at the toilet—"

"All right, Laura, you don't have to embarrass me further."

"I got him into bed," she said to Carver, "and he was unconscious even before I had the sheets under his chin."

"I was asleep."

"Unconscious. Passed out."

"All right, woman," De Anza warned. He finished his coffee and held out the cup for more. When Laura went to the stove, he winked at Carver and then gazed admiringly at his wife. With admiration? No, more like adoration.

"We talked last night," Carver began, "about Piombo's rooms."

"Oh, yeah," De Anza said, and waited while Laura refilled his cup. "You wanted to get inside and look around. Okay, okay, but I don't think you'll find anything we didn't. But if you insist, I'll get the address and let them know you're coming. That okay?"

"Yes. And thanks."

De Anza called his office and gave Carver the address. In return, Carver gave him Barbara Stahl's Sharp Park address. They chatted, with Carver promising to keep De Anza up-to-date on the Ferrik case. Carver also promised not to step too hard on Ludlow. Of course, there was no such promise that Ludlow would treat Carver with kindness. Not expected, either.

Half an hour later, Carver had parked on Mason Street, more than a block from Piombo's address in the North Beach area. That was as close as he could get.

The neighborhood was Italian, loosely bordered by Columbus Avenue all the way down to Fisherman's Wharf and Battery. The hub was the crossroads of Columbus and Broadway. Old-time Italians sat in espresso cafés twirling their bandit mustaches. Sightseers looked into the windows of ravioli and spaghetti factories. The heavy morning air was filled with the aromas of roasting coffee and brewing chocolate.

Carver had not known North Beach in what was called the Good Old Days by the old-timers. Every neighborhood had its Good Old Days, and they were always better than the todays. So they said. So what did they expect the current generation to do, hang their heads in shame because they hadn't been born sixty years before? Carver thought of the tales he had heard of The Black Cat, of Izzy Gomez's Green Door, and of the Montgomery Block, a long-gone building that had housed and nurtured hordes of artists (and would-be-artists).

Then came the beat generation and their bookstores, art galleries, and the new Bohemian bars: City Lights, Vesuvio's, The Scene Gallery, Miss Smith's Tea Room, and others.

All generations had their tales. The stories were endless: police corruption, illegal boozing after-hours, houses of prostitution, artistic rivalries, mad poets berating one another.

Hooray for the Good Old Days. Whenever they were.

The old-timers in North Beach couldn't see the place the way the young people did. To the younger generation it was exciting and had a breath of romanticism and freedom. And it was their time, their generation. Someday these would be their Good Old Days.

Carver went up to the door and identified himself to the cop sitting in a black-and-white at the curb. The cop was a gabber and talked cheerfully about the weather: Wasn't it just too fucking hot? And like that. He lifted the yellow crime-scene banner and opened the door to Piombo's apartment. Number 4. Carver went in, and the talker went back to his squad car.

Piombo had not lived too well. To put it bluntly, the man lived like a bum. The front room was tiny, furnished with a card table and a chair. In the corner were a couple of mattresses with old ratty blankets. No sheets. Against one wall was a dresser made of some kind of cheap pressed-wood pulp with a plastic veneer. The closet was barely big enough to hold half a dozen shirts and pants. The kitchen had barely enough room for a two-burner stove and a midget-sized refrigerator. Carver looked in the fridge. There was a half quart of sour milk, a can of tuna, and some kind of cheese that was best left unidentified.

Tossing the place took less than an hour. It was as thorough a search as possible, unless Carver stripped the walls and wood molding. A big nothing. An overweight zero. But this was no place for Piombo to sculpt. So where did the dead man do his work?

Of course it was possible that Piombo shared a studio with another sculptor. Oh, yeah. Carver shook his head. He had to see Myron Moseby. If Myron didn't know where Piombo sculpted, then he might know someone who did.

But first there was Amber. She was his main client, and she might remember where her daddy took her camping. Given enough time and money, Carver believed he could find Ferrik, but he had a hunch that time was running out. Then there was that odd question: When? Somebody was in a hell of hurry to know when, whatever it was.

At first Carver thought the sound was the closed window shade scratching the window. But it wasn't. Someone was on the fire escape trying to break in. Carver stepped into the closet, cracking the door about an inch.

The window slid open and a woman climbed in, muttering curses under her breath. She carried an enormous rattan handbag and a black plastic sack. She put the sack down and wiped the sweat from her face with an old-fashioned red bandanna. She shook herself like a wet dog, her frowzy gray hair flying. A drowned muskrat had better-looking hair.

She looked cautiously, nervously, around the room. She reached into the handbag and pulled out a nickel-plated .25 automatic. In her big hand the gun looked more like a Crackerjack prize.

EIGHT

Through the slightly open door, Carver watched as the woman went immediately to the bed and dragged it to one side. She pulled her voluminous skirts aside, an unconscious parody of daintiness, and knelt on the floorboards. She pried up a loose board and began pulling things from the hiding place.

Carver stepped out quietly.

"Hello, Magda," he said.

"Jesus!" she yelped, and spun around, sprawling on the bed.

He stepped close and plucked the little automatic from her hand.

"Bascombe," the woman said, "what the hell are you doing here?"

She pushed quickly with her legs, catching Carver behind one ankle and sending him tumbling onto the mattress. She laughed uproariously, then caught herself and smothered her chuckles with the red bandanna.

"Bascombe, you gotta watch it," she said with a smile.

Her teeth were large and white. "Someday somebody is gonna take you way down."

"Magda, if it happens," he replied, laughing, "you'll probably be the cause of it."

Lying on his side on the mattress, he dropped the pistol's clip and jacked the slide back. Nothing came out. He looked at the clip. Loaded.

"You didn't have a bullet in the chamber, Magda," Carver said. He smiled tolerantly at her. "What good is that?"

"Hell, I don't wanna hurt anybody."

"You just plain forgot."

"That's what I said, I forgot. So what are you doing here?"

"More to the point, Magda, what are you doing here?"

"I'm looking for some money that Lou owed me."

"And you didn't want the cops to find it and impound it."

"Hey, smartie, you're as fast as ever."

She turned and continued tossing things out of the hiding place in the floor. Papers, receipts, bills, a roll of money that she stuffed into her handbag, some kind of rock, a gold watch, and a checkbook.

Carver reached for the jumble, but Magda playfully slapped his hand away.

"No you don't," she said. "Just a bunch of knickknacks and good-luck-charm stuff." She swept all the papers and objects back into the hole and popped the floorboard back into place.

"How much did Piombo owe you?" Carver asked.

"None a your beeswax."

"Why did he owe it to you?"

"What difference does it make? He owed it to me. What I found wasn't enough, that I'll tell you."

"Come on, Magda," Carver said, "you and he were on some kind of scam. As usual."

"Hey, I'm a law-abiding person."

"Never," Carver said. "You're a street hustler, a con artist."

"That's what I said, I'm a crook. Just an ol' bag lady."

"You're not so old, and you're not a bag lady."

"What is this?" Magda asked, pointing to her handbag. "A Gucci purse?"

"Tell me about Piombo."

"Nah, Bascombe, I couldn't do that. Code of the streets an' all that."

"I could call the cop downstairs and you'd be up before another judge in the morning. Breaking and entering."

"Nah, you'd never do that." She paused, looking at him. "Would you?"

"Try me."

"How can you be such a cold bastard in all this heat?"

"Because a little girl's life might be in danger. And Lou Piombo is dead. Whoever killed him is walking around free."

"I might talk better with a little breakfast in me."

"For you, Magda, anything you want."

"All right, I'll meet you at the Café Florentine. Coupla blocks from here."

"I know the place."

Magda Cantera punched Carver playfully in the shoulder. She took her plastic sack from the floor and looked out of the window, checking the police car below.

"Donkey cop," she said under her breath, then climbed out onto the fire escape.

Carver looked around the room and then left.

"Hey, waiter, make that two more cappuccinos."

"Tell me about Lou Piombo, Magda," Carver urged.

"One cappuccino just barely makes me awake. The other two are for the taste. I like cappuccino."

They sat by a window looking out on to Columbus Avenue. Carver drank iced coffee. Magda swallowed the last of the first cappuccino, then put the cup down on the marble tabletop. A waiter brought a ham-and-cheese omelette, country-fried potatoes, a half-dozen slices of bacon, four sausages, two English muffins, and a glass of orange juice.

"So I won't starve today," Magda said, tucking in, talking between mouthfuls. "Me and Lou? We had the usual stuff going, him making little trinkets, what they call objay dee arts." She shoveled some of the omelette and a sausage into her mouth. "He used to give me a bunch of them so I could sell 'em to the tourists. Well, about two months ago he had some kind of deal cookin' and he needed some dough. What he called seed capital."

"Did he say what it was for?"

"Nah." She thanked the waiter for the two cappuccinos as he put them on the table. "You knew Lou. Always a scam, but he was cagey. Said this was his big score. So like a goddamn fool I loaned him some money."

"How much?"

"Coupla hunnerd. He tells me he's in this with some guys, and after they pull it off he's gonna retire, he said." She ate more of the food. "Well, he sure as hell retired. Real permanently. And I never got my dough. Except what I found in the hidey-hole. Roll a dollar bills. Twenty-four bucks."

"Who were the guys that were in on this big score?"

"I don't know. I know most of the guys Lou knew. But once I saw Lou walking down Broadway with a couple a guys I never saw before."

"Would you know them again?"

"Nah, Bascombe. I don't think so."

"Was one of them black?"

"Yeah, now that you mention it. I forgot."

"Did one of them have a pony tail and wear a headband?"

"Nah, just a guy. I didn't know him, never saw him before. Never saw the black guy before either."

"There's a possibility that Lou Piombo was somehow tied in with another sculptor. Tom Ferrik. Did you know Tom?"

"Sure did," Magda said, wiping her chin with a napkin. "I know lotsa artists. An' I can tell you, it wasn't Tom I saw with Lou and the black guy."

Across the street from the Café Florentine, Ed Zinn and Cholly Lehm sat in a gray sedan. They had stolen the car two hours before.

"What're they doin', Ed?"

"Eatin', whatta you think."

"When we gonna get somethin' to eat, Ed? I'm real hungry."

"Shut up, rat fucker."

"Who's the old broad Bascombe is talkin' to?" Cholly asked.

"Who knows? Shut up, Cholly."

"Magda," Carver said, "tell me about you and Tom Ferrik."

"That was some time ago. Back in Tom's Bohemian days. Yeah, us and Tom and his old lady, we were sorta like the four musketeers. Lou being a small-time hustler didn't bother Tom. There were a lot of characters running around North Beach in those days. Too bad him and his old lady didn't work out."

"I met her yesterday," Carver said.

"I guess Barbara divorced him—or versey vicey—just too soon. He was still scuffling along then, doin' those window display things. Then he got lucky. Got a big commission. Twenty-five thousand, I unnerstan'. Too late though. The divorce was final."

"Did you ever see Tom after that?"

"Yeah, coupla times. He got a few more big commissions for some big corporations down the peninsula. Bought that fancy house in Berkeley, put the little girl—what's her name, Jewel?—in a good school."

"Amber," Carver said.

"That's what I said, Amber. Real smart that one." She drank the last cup of cappuccino and pushed away the empty plates.

"You're sure one of the men with Piombo, when you saw him on the street, wasn't Tom Ferrik?"

"Course I'm sure. I know Tom, even if I haven't seen him for a few months."

"And that's it?"

"Whatta you want, Bascombe? The name of the guy who shot Lou?"

"That sounds good for a start."

"I don't know who did it, but I sure hope you find the bastard. Not that it'll do any good. Lou might've been a real jerk in some ways, but he never did anything to get blasted for."

"Not till now, Magda," Carver said.

"Ed, I still think we shoulda grabbed Frank's sister."

"Ferrik knows a helluva lot more than that broad," Zinn said. He squirmed in his seat, looking past Cholly at the café across the street. "We follow Bascombe, we gotta chance to snatch Ferrik's kid."

"What if she don't know where her daddy is? Whatta we do?"

"We'll figure that after we— Hold it, Cholly. Start the engine. Bascombe is leaving the café."

From North Beach to Rose's house was about a fifteen-minute drive. Carver enjoyed the scenery as he drove along Bay Street, then turned toward the bay and tooled along the marina. On his right was the long green sward, then the yacht club and the harbor, with many sailboats barely bobbing on the water. Plenty of sailboats were out on the bay, moving slowly in the humid air.

Opposite Golden Gate Park, he parked on Fulton and then

rang the bell. Rose lived in a pleasant two-story house, cream-colored with forget-me-not blue trim. There was no answer, but they should be home. Carver stood on the sidewalk, looking at the upper windows. Breaking and entering in broad daylight was not a cool number. A next-door neighbor, an Asian woman, probably Japanese, clipped a hedge. Carver spoke to her. Yes, the neighbor knew Rose Weinbaum, a nice person. They were good friends, good neighbors.

"I'm her boss," Carver said, "and she should be home. She's taking care of a little girl."

"Yes, Rose has spoken of you, her partner, often," the woman said. She pointed across the street to Golden Gate Park. "I saw them only a few minutes ago. They went into the park. I spoke with them and they said they were going to see the fishes. I would guess that means the aquarium?"

Carver thanked the woman and hurried across Fulton Street. The aquarium. It could take hours for them to return. Sure, he could have breakfast somewhere and wait, but he didn't want to take the time. He could catch up with them. After all, how fast could an eleven-year-old walk?

He moved swiftly, his long legs eating up the distance. Sweat gleamed on his face, and dark circles formed under the sleeves of his shirt. Eucalyptus leaves crunched underfoot. Dense shrubbery blocked his view. The aromatic trees and dusty flora seemed to droop in the heat. Slow down, Carver ordered himself, or you'll have a heat stroke.

Along the paths and roads were dozens of roller skaters, turning, dodging, skating backward. The skating-mating dance of young men and women. Carver ducked around them, his eyes moving methodically over the scene. He turned onto the main drive. He didn't see Rose or Amber.

The wide main drive connected with other roads, and he could see the spire of de Young museum, the bandstand shell, and, far away, the complex of buildings that housed the aquarium. Which way? All of the roads were bordered with shrubbery and trees. The skaters were everywhere on the trails and footpaths. Dozens of cars and cyclists passed by, many turning onto the connecting roads. Visibility wasn't perfect.

Carver crossed the main drive and scanned the road to the museum—and caught a glimpse of a woman and a child off to the right. Yeah, near the playground, just the other side of the underpass. He lost sight of them for a moment as he crossed back over the road, but saw them again as they entered the long tunnel that went under the main drive.

He scrambled down a slope and entered the tunnel. The other end opened into the olive tree grove that fronted the shell bandstand. Yes, it was Rose and Amber. They had reached the other side and broke out into the suffocating sunlight. He called to them, his words echoing in the tunnel. And then it happened.

A man, thick with fat, his face covered with a nylon stocking, came in from the other side of the tunnel. Moving fast. He grabbed Amber with one hand and backhanded Rose with the other. Rose went down. Amber screamed, but her yell was cut off when the man clamped a meaty hand over her mouth.

Carver was already running, dripping sweat and cursing that he wasn't armed. Amber was dragged out of sight. Rose rolled onto her feet and gave chase, holding on to her purse.

She saw the fat man struggling up the grassy slope. He was heading for a sedan on the upper road, its engine revved up, the driver gesturing wildly. She could see the driver clearly; he wore a stocking over his face, too. Rose heard running footsteps behind her. Had to be Carver. She had heard his voice calling when the man grabbed Amber. Things were happening so fast that she hadn't time to think of how Carver came to be there.

The running man was only yards from the car, and Amber was struggling in his arms. Several roller skaters looked in surprise at the action. The driver swung the rear door open and then gunned the engine. In seconds the big man would hurl himself and Amber into the car.

Rose skidded to a stop and, with a smooth action, almost without thinking about it, pulled a .38 revolver from her purse, flicked back the hammer, and squeezed off a shot. Cholly stumbled as bits of flesh and blood tore from his shoulder. He dropped Amber and clutched his left shoulder. He looked wildly at Rose. Surprise and fear oozed from the stocking mask.

Amber yelled and rolled away. Two women roller-skating screamed, lost their balance, and fell. The driver yelled at Cholly to hurry up, forget the kid, and get in the car!

Rose was about to shoot again when Carver ran past. He took the last few yards, gasping, drops of sweat flying from his face, and landed on Cholly. A single shot went over their heads.

The windshield shattered in front of Ed Zinn.

Carver tried to drag the fat man to the ground. The stocking mask was gray with sweat around Cholly's face; his gasping, open mouth was dark and dank with spit. He pushed Carver's face, unrecognizable swear words sounding like hissing snakes.

Zinn thrust a shotgun out of the window and fired. The grass exploded between Rose and the struggling men. She ducked and rolled over onto Amber, shielding the girl with her body.

Cholly slammed a fist into Carver's stomach and Carver let go. Another fist slammed into Carver's chin and he fell to the grass.

"Go! Go!" Zinn yelled to Cholly.

Holding on to his bloody shoulder, Cholly stumbled the last feet to the car. Over the angry sounds of his own curses, he heard people screaming. Fuck 'em. Not enough sense to get the fuck out of the way! He threw himself onto the rear seat, and Zinn stomped on the gas.

Carver rolled into a kneeling position and watched as the car roared off. He breathed in great, ragged gasps. Good God, that fat bastard was fast on his feet. And had one hell of a punch. Carver felt as though he were going to throw up.

Rose gently led Amber by the hand, and they came over to Carver. He was still kneeling on the grass, trying to get his breath.

"You all right?" Rose asked. She put the revolver into her purse.

Carver nodded wordlessly.

"Is . . . Amber . . . okay?" he finally managed to ask.

"I think so," Rose answered. She knelt down beside the girl and held her close.

"I'm okay, Miss Rose," Amber said seriously. A faint grin crept over her face. "I know it's bad . . . but I thought that was very exciting."

"Amber, Amber," Rose said, shaking her head.

Carver Bascombe got to his feet, brushing twigs and grass from his pants. He let out a sigh, looking down the road where the sedan had disappeared.

"Who were they, Carver?" Rose asked.

"I think the driver was the same guy at Ferrik's house yesterday. I never saw the big guy before."

"Why did they want Amber?"

"I don't know for sure. Maybe for the same reason I wanted to talk to her. Find out where Tom Ferrik is hiding. We damn well missed a chance. My fault." He slowly shook his head. "I got in the way. Should've let you do the shooting. Their tires."

A small crowd began to form around them, and Carver told them to go away. The police would be called.

"Did that already," one skater said, holding up a cellular telephone. He put the phone back in a vinyl case on his belt.

Carver and Rose thanked the man and then sat on the grassy verge. Rose held on to Amber. They refused to answer questions, and the crowd moved away. Several die-hard gawkers stayed close by.

"Rose . . ."

"Yes?"

"Thanks."

"For what?"

"For having the brains to carry a gun."

"That's part of my job. Bernie always said that. And I know you don't like to carry yours."

"Don't rub it in."

"I'm not. Only when you have to. You've told me that many times. Forget it."

Carver was silent, brooding, plucking at the grass between his feet. Finally he stood and stretched. Then he knelt beside Amber and took her hand.

"You and your daddy, you went camping."

"Yes, Mr. Bascombe. I liked it a lot."

"Okay. Do you remember where you went?"

"It was a nice cabin in the woods, near a river. I think Daddy called it the—the . . . like that funny square thing you twist and turn with all the colors."

"Rubik's cube?" Carver asked.

"Something like that. There was a town with a funny name. Eruption City. I think."

"What about the cabin itself, Amber. Any idea where it was exactly?"

"I don't think so. A few miles from that town. Esecushun, I'm sure it was called that."

"There is an Execution City," Rose added, "beyond Placerville in the Sierras."

"I can't wait for the cops, Rose," Carver said. "I must see Moseby. You tell the cops exactly what happened, but not one word about Execution City or the river or the cabin.

Everything exactly as it happened, without the location of Ferrik's cabin.''

"I understand. Exactly as it happened. But nothing about the cabin.''

"Right," Carver said, tucking his shirt into his pants. "I don't think they'll question Amber. They might make trouble for you, though.''

"Trouble? For me? Why?''

"You shot a gun inside city limits. That's against the law.''

"You're serious?''

"Very," he said.

"Don't worry, Carver. We'll be fine.''

"I know it," he replied, looking at her purse.

Carver walked away, taking the same route back to his car.

NINE

"Ya gotta stop, Ed!" Cholly cried. "I'm bleeding to death."

"Shut up!" Ed Zinn ordered. "It's only a scratch."

He resisted the urge to speed, to vent his anger with fast driving. He held to a steady speed. In the next few miles he wanted to ditch this stolen car and get something else. But Cholly was the car thief. What did Zinn know about hot-wiring a car? Nothing.

"Goddamn! What a foul-up," Zinn spat out angrily. "Can't you do anything right, Cholly? Just snatch a kid! Fucking simple!"

Cholly wriggled around in the rear seat, clutching his wounded shoulder. He groaned constantly, crying for Ed to get him a doctor. Zinn ignored the fat man.

Zinn cursed their luck, cursed the fat man's clumsiness. Cursed the black detective they had followed to North Beach and all the way to Fulton Street and then into Golden Gate Park. Cursed the bitch with a gun in her purse. Who the hell would guess things could go so damned wrong?

"Ah, Ed, please, for God's sake. I'm hurt real bad. Damn that woman. Never woulda guessed that skinny broad would have a gun. These liberated women are gonna kill me yet."

"I'm telling you, Cholly, just shut up! I'm thinking."

"Yeah?" Cholly said between gritted teeth. "About what? We ain't gonna get a chance to grab that girl again. Fuckin' woman's gonna have a flamethrower next. Listen, Ed, let's give it up. We ain't gonna find out where Tom Ferrik is, and we sure ain't gonna find out when that shipment is movin'."

"I'm thinking'," Zinn said, and wheeled the car along the Great Highway. Oh, he had to think all right, and damned if he was going to listen to that tub of guts in the rear. No, there had to be another way. All he had to do was think. Oh, and find some bandages for Cholly the nose-picker.

Carver took the stairs down from the parking area on the roof of the Moseby Art Gallery. Before driving downtown, he had changed clothes again at his office/apartment. Fresh clothes can boost a man's morale, and he felt a hell of a lot better in grass- and dirt-free slacks, clean shirt, and a seersucker jacket. He took the stairs from the roof down to the gallery.

The gallery was a sanctum of plush, wine-red carpeting, and beige cloth-covered walls. Replicas of antique chairs and divans were placed for the art lovers to contemplate the muses. The ambience was designed to lift the patrons' money in as painless a manner as possible. The paintings, drawings, and sculptures were lit by soft concealed lights. The larger sculptures were on the floor; smaller, and very, very expensive pieces, were inset in nooks. The total mood was of gentility and taste.

Myron Moseby had never been to a business-marketing class. Imagine that. He had a native sense of good taste, combined with an ability to present a client with a six-figure price with élan.

For Carver Bascombe, the single most important aspect of

the gallery was the cool, refreshing air-conditioning. He breathed the air with a sigh of relief. Carver found a lithe, impeccably dressed Myron Moseby standing in front of a Theodore Roszak sculpture.

"Ah, dear boy," Moseby said with genuine affection. "How nice to see you again. How charmingly you grace my humble sanctum."

"Good thing there are no customers to hear that. They'd probably throw up."

"Ah, direct and crude. How unlike you, Carver."

"What do you think of it?" Moseby said, gesturing at the sculpture.

"Good. I've always liked Roszak. What's it worth?"

"No, no, Carver, you're slipping. Remember what I taught you. The intrinsic worth of art has nothing to do with crass money. Leave that sort of thing to the neo-appreciators, the self-appointed curators, the social climbers, the old and new money of this fair city. That is the only judgment they can make of artistic worth. How much is it! Bah."

"So how did you get it?"

"The previous owner wouldn't put it up for consignment sale. Rather, they wanted to auction it through Sotheby's. I offered immediate cash." Moseby pulled the corners of his mouth down and cocked his head; alas, all too sordid, he pantomimed. Money, money. "Naturally, they took it."

"Okay, so satisfy my curiosity. How much?"

"I do believe you have been needling me. However, it would be more than you will earn in the next two years."

Moseby took hold of Carver's elbow and guided him into his private suite of offices. His movements were graceful, economical, and artistic, like a ballet dancer. He selected his clothing with luxury in mind. Today he wore a pale blue silk suit, with a pale yellow silk shirt open at the throat. The whole ensemble couldn't have weighed more than a dozen butterflies.

Baguette rings on his little fingers glittered when he moved his strong hands. Moseby stroked the gray wings of carefully styled hair over his ears. He was in his late forties, but appeared a good ten years younger. He cultivated a pallor, preferring, as he put it, to create an aura of Moonlight Madness rather than the suntanned cancer look of the Côte d'Azur. He stood at the side of a large, well-polished oak desk and started to open a silver box.

"I almost forgot," Moseby said, "you don't smoke."

"No," Carver replied.

"Many of my clients do." Moseby indicated three identical silver boxes. "Dunhill's, Sherman's, Sobrante's. An offering for any taste."

"Snobbery," Carver said softly.

"But, of course, dear boy." Moseby draped one leg carefully over the corner of the desk. "Now, you have been naughty. I have read of your latest escapade in the morning newspaper. The Piombo matter, of course. And the death of Sharon Argent's brother. Would you say they were connected?"

"I don't know."

"Well . . . two sculptors, one dead, the brother of another also dead. A connection might be implied."

"I can't say," Carver answered with a smile.

"Do I dare hope that I can be of some small service?"

"Yes, you can be of some small service."

"Wonderful. Into the thick of crime, I daresay. Even if it's the only way I can see you these days."

"Hard to believe," Carver said with a grin, "but I have been busy."

"Of course!" Moseby said, flicking the air with a forefinger, a gesture implying a faulty memory. "Your bar exams. Well, soon you will be hanging out a shingle. And there goes your private detective business. You have given that some thought, I presume?"

"Yeah, I've been thinking about it."

"No matter. I shall miss being embroiled in our criminalistic exploits. Even though they are often fraught with danger." Moseby fingered his ribs, where a female killer had once shot him. Carver had saved his life then, and Myron Moseby would never forget it. "You know I demand to be the first legal client. I shall transfer all my legal activities to your office." He paused, a finger on his lips. "On one condition."

"Only one?"

"One, Carver. You must indulge in a new suite of offices. After all, I can hardly do business with you on Fillmore Street. My Rolls would be stripped in a trice."

"What in hell is a trice, anyway?"

"But a moment, a blink of God's eye. At any rate, you'll need something more in keeping with a wealthy clientele. A proper front, shall we say."

"Maybe I don't want that kind of clientele."

"Yes, Carver, I know. A storefront lawyer—helping the poor, the disenfranchised, all that. But there is nothing that says your office has to look destitute to do that. Besides, you would be depriving me of a singular pleasure."

"Oh? And what would that be?"

'Why, the chance to see some of our city's better citizens, in all their finery, in your waiting room, rubbing elbows with, shall we say, a bunch of ragged poor."

"I can't guarantee I'll accommodate your sense of fun."

"Ah, well." Moseby shrugged. "Now, as to your reason for coming here . . . Lou Piombo. Isn't that right?"

"He had a studio and I hoped you might know where it is."

"Yes, I do. It's south of Market, near Townsend Street." He went around the desk and opened the center drawer. "I believe I have the address somewhere. Yes . . . here it is." He copied out the address and handed it to Carver. "As precious as life is, I don't mourn for Piombo. A charlatan as a sculptor, even though he had a modicum of talent."

Carver looked at the address. It was across the street from Sharon's studio. He folded the paper into his breast pocket and then looked at Moseby.

"Tell me about Piombo."

"A man who faked pre-Columbian work—and faked replicas of anything he could get his hands on."

"Faked replicas?"

"Yes. A lucrative business. You know, a sculptor creates a piece and has it cast in bronze. Depending on the original method, he—or she—might have many copies cast. There are many of Rodin's *The Thinker*, for example. Or a museum might take a popular item, say, a small ivory statue from Roman times, make copies in plastic or porcelain or some other material similar to the original, and then sell them as replicas of the original. You understand?"

Carver nodded.

"So," Moseby continued, "Piombo would buy one of these replicas, make another mold, and cast his own replicas of the replica. And he was good enough so that few could tell the difference. I know a few museum curators who have been fooled. A moderately lucrative racket, but not exactly heavy on appreciation from the art world. Which is what Piombo wanted more than anything."

"How did he cast these replicas?"

"As I said, in a similar material—plastic, glass, metal, whatever gave him the look and feel he needed."

"Metal casting," Carver mused, recalling the foundry next door to Sharon Argent's studio. Hutte and Son. He looked at Moseby. "Have you ever heard of any connection between Piombo and the Hutte foundry?"

"No—and I'm not familiar with the name."

"It's a casting foundry, and from the address you just gave me, it's not far from Piombo's studio."

"Do you think there is a connection?"

"Maybe. I have an offer of a tour of the foundry from the

son. After I take a look at Piombo's studio, I'll visit the foundry.''

''Would you like me to come along? I'd rather fancy a break in the routine of the gallery business. Besides, Leroy is perfectly capable of carrying on in my absence.''

''Not this time,'' Carver replied. ''What can you tell me about Tom Ferrik?''

''Is he involved in this affair?''

''He's my main target. I'm looking for him. I'm not interested in who killed Piombo—''

''Not yet,'' Moseby interjected. ''But I know you, Carver, and I know that obsession of yours. You'll get into the thick of it yet. If you aren't already.''

''About Ferrik?''

''You know, the gallery has several of his pieces. I'll show them to you before you depart. Well, I think he's a good sculptor. Not a great one, but he is young enough for further development. Most of his pieces are for showing in galleries. Modern, of course, but comprehensible. Not your giant steel block on a point in front of a corporate glass tower.''

''I've seen some of his sketches in his home.''

''Then you know what I mean. Not controversial at all.''

''What kind of man is he?''

''Ah. That's what you really want to know.'' Moseby tented his fingers and stared above Carver's head. ''I believe Tom Ferrik to be sensitive but temperamental, egotistic but not overly ambitious. He has had several opportunities to make his mark on the local scene, buttering up to corporations and to critics, and he ignored them. He believes himself to be a better artist than he actually is—but that may be my prejudice.''

''Have you ever heard of any place where he might hide out?''

Moseby laughed.

''Dear boy, what a question. California is a big state and anyone can disappear anywhere. Tom Ferrik wouldn't even have to leave the city or county. It would take weeks to find anyone. Why don't you enlist the aid of the police?''

"The cops are looking for him. They figure him to be a possible material witness in the killing of Lou Piombo.''

"What do you think?''

"They have a point. But I hope I'll find him before they do.''

Ernie Ludlow was angry. He stood next to Raphael De Anza's desk in the Homicide Division office. As he talked, he punctuated his words by pounding the desk with the palms of his big hands.

"What I don't like,'' Ludlow said, forcibly keeping his voice low since there was no reason for the other detectives to overhear everything, "is the fact that Bascombe went over my head. And you didn't tell me. You told him Piombo's address. Goddammit, Raf, the guy is a civilian!''

"Lots of people knew where Piombo lived, Ernie. Carver would have found out the address sooner or later.''

"So what? Let him find out his way. You're letting your friendship for that black bastard get in the way of my investigation. And now—now he doesn't even wait around after a shooting and an apparent kidnapping attempt! Imagine! He's a fucking witness! What does he do? He lets that secretary tell the story to the cops. And where is Mr. Bascombe? Running around chasing clues. Just what the hell . . . Do you want to throw away that promotion?''

"Easy, Ernie.'' De Anza kept his own anger in check. No reason to add fuel to Ludlow's inferno. He locked his hands on his desk and looked steadily at the black homicide detective. "I grant you, from your viewpoint, I bent the rules a little—''

Ludlow snorted, squinting his eyes.

"—but the information I gave Carver was harmless.''

"Yeah, but you also paved the way for him to enter a murder scene."

"Piombo wasn't killed there, so it wasn't a murder scene. And I didn't give him Piombo's studio address."

"It wasn't right, and you damn well know it. You're rationalizing and it doesn't change one damn thing. Okay, we know from forensic evidence—or the lack of it—that Piombo wasn't killed at either his rooms or his studio. The fact remains, Bascombe is butting in again."

"He is a licensed detective," De Anza said.

"So let the jerk look for philandering husbands and wives. Murder is our business. Not his."

"He's looking for a missing man. That sculptor, Tom Ferrik."

"So the fuck are we," Ludlow said, emphasizing each word harshly. "So are we. And we damn better find him before Bascombe does."

De Anza grinned and then immediately settled his face soberly.

"We'll find Ferrik," Ludlow continued, "and we'll find out everything else, too." He paused, then finally sat in the chair facing De Anza's desk. He lit a cigarette and moved an ashtray close to hand. "Why would those guys try to snatch the girl? My guess is they also want to know where her father is."

"It seems a fair assumption," De Anza answered. "What are you doing about it?"

"I've put a couple of men watching Rose Weinbaum's house and the local squad car comes by more frequently, about every twenty minutes or so."

"Think another snatch attempt might be made?"

"Could be," Ludlow answered. Privately, he didn't think anyone would be so stupid as to try again—at least not out of a guarded house. He almost wished they would, just so they could be nabbed. A lot of questions would get answered. Or

117

they might try to shoot the kid. Somebody had tried once; why not again?

"What did the autopsy show?" De Anza asked.

"Just that Piombo was shot in the back at close range—with a seven-point-sixty-five-caliber weapon. Possibly a foreign make weapon. Maybe a Luger, Walther, or Berretta. The slug matches the one we dug out of the statue in Ferrik's studio."

"No idea where the murder was committed?"

"No—and don't tell your pal any of this."

"Afraid he might find out before you do?"

"No. Like you said, he's looking for Ferrik. We've got Sergeant Stein and some other guys checking all known friends and enemies of Lou Piombo's."

"And?"

"Nothing, Raf. Damned discouraging. Every hour past the first twenty-four hours of a murder makes it tougher. All of Ferrik's acquaintances are being checked. Although Sergeant Stein has a name, a sculptor named Herd. I've already talked to Ferrik's ex-wife. And guess what?"

"I can't imagine, Ernie," De Anza answered.

"Bascombe didn't even ask her where she was that morning, the time when the girl was shot."

"See? He isn't interested in the murder. Did she have an alibi?"

"Yeah, for what it's worth. She says she was at home, waiting for a phone call for a modeling job. Her friend, read that 'lover', a guy named Hermano Grabar, says he kept her company. And she's his alibi. At least Bascombe didn't get any of that."

"He's doing his job, Ernie. And you do yours."

"Balls!" Ludlow snorted. "I know that guy. He's going to get involved. And that's bad. For him." Ludlow stubbed out his cigarette and looked at De Anza. "Just remember, Raf,

Bascombe gets in my way. I'll have his black ass decorating my desk."

Ludlow stared at De Anza, and then stood and walked away.

De Anza also had his own thoughts. What was going on? So far, the only linking factors seem to be the sculptors. Was someone tying to steal a valuable statue? He didn't think so, but just in case, he telephoned the Art Crime division to check the de Young museum, the Museum of Modern Art, and the California Palace of the Legion of Honor to see if there was a particularly valuable statue or objet d'art that might be a target for thieves.

Piombo's studio was small and messy. The heat was stifling. Dirty clerestory windows in the high ceiling let in some sunlight. Carver left the front door open and then pushed open a nearby window. Any kind of circulating air was better than frying in here.

Where to begin? He rubbed his chin, feeling the scarred indentation, the result of a teenage fight. There was so much junk. . . . Clockwise was as good a way as any. Carver moved among the benches and drawing tables. He skimmed through the sketches and the litter of bills, invoices, and memos. Just a mess, indicating the state of Lou Piombo's daily life.

The studio walls were littered with crayon scribbles and pinned-up drawings. One of the tables had molds, bits of rubber and plastic, and smearings of clay and wax.

Along one wall was a rack of storage bins, containing a variety of sheet-metal stock and iron bars and rods. Another area had a raised asbestos platform for welding. Carver recognized a basin as a washing and patina area for statuary. Another table, under an exhaust system hood, had materials for brazing bronze and brass. The hood would carry off poisonous fumes from the molten metals.

Against the far wall was a kiln, and he popped open the door and looked inside. Nothing. He poked his fingers in a casting pit; the sand was cold.

Carver shook his head. What a waste of time. The place was a jumble of papers, scribbled drawings, and the remains of molds and castings. He sat in a rickety chair and brooded. There had to be something. But what? He gazed at the door and the dusty windows.

Idly, his eyes went from the windows to the benches lining the walls. Just junk. Broken molds. Of what? He went over to the bench and began piecing small chunks of torn rubber together. He turned the rubber inside out. Looks as though Piombo was trying to make a mold of a small, irregular shape, he thought. Some kind of modern art? Didn't look like anything of commercial value. Some kind of experiment?

If so, then where were the results?

Carver moved around the room, looking into wastebaskets, cardboard boxes, and makeshift cabinets. In a cabinet near the kiln, he found a half-dozen black objects; pitted and scored, they looked like rocks. Spray-painted black. He'd seen one like them in Piombo's hiding place in the floor.

What had Magda Cantera said? Some kind of good-luck charm?

Next to the table, he found several cans of heat-resistant automobile engine spray paint. The wall next to the table was clouded by black paint. Obviously, Lou Piombo had been painting the rocks, but for what purpose? Carver held one of the rocks in his hand. Seemed heavy for a rock.

Carver heard a sound behind him and turned.

Two men stood in the doorway, then walked into the studio.

For a moment Carver was afraid that they were the two men in Golden Gate Park, but neither of them was big and fat.

''Who are you?'' Carver asked.

"Who wants to know?" one of them asked.

His words had an arrogance that Carver recognized, a prelude to trouble.

"Yeah," the other man said.

Both were in their middle or late twenties, Carver figured. And neither of them wore stocking masks. Grateful for small favors. As they circled the studio, Carver studied them. He had a bad feeling he might have to identify them in a lineup. One was of medium height, say five seven, with narrowed, sullen eyes; he nervously brushed lank hair from his eyes. He breathed through an open mouth, his lips tight against his teeth. Some smile that was.

His buddy was taller, about five ten, and had a habit of rubbing one hand over the knuckles of the other. A telegraph signal Carver didn't like. He didn't like the man's eyes either, big, ugly, and dark—like drowned beetles in cream.

The two men flanked Carver. His hand closed over one of the black rocks.

A fist lashed out at Carver's stomach, but he twisted to one side and shoved the other man aside with all his strength. He kept on moving fast, but a foot struck him between his ankles. He fell and rolled, lashing out with his legs. He caught one of them in the knee. Carver had a moment of satisfaction, seeing the man's face grow red like an instantly heated iron.

Carver went into a crouch, ducking and weaving. Out of the side of his eye he saw it coming. The blow rocked him. He tried to dodge. No use. He was hit with a storm of fists. Blood spattered over his shirtfront.

Carver threw several of his own—flailing the air. One landed. His knuckles felt broken. The beetle-eyed one slammed a beefy fist into his gut. Carver bent double, then felt a steely arm grab him around the neck in a stranglehold. Carver gritted his teeth and threw a backward punch at the stranger's face. The man grunted, the sound a garbled chuckle.

The other man, beetle eyes, slammed several more vicious punches into Carver's stomach, and then the strangler let go. Carver fell to the floor. He retched, gasping in vain for air, for breath. He was kicked in the ribs. After that he didn't know who kicked or punched. He felt several kicks, and one punch in the neck. Mostly he was aware of the cold cement floor, gritty and damp under his face.

His nose felt as though it had been split with a hatchet.

He was barely aware that the two men were moving around the studio, muttering obscenities, throwing papers and tools around, opening cabinets with a clatter and a bang. That impression of the two men searching for something lasted less than ten seconds. Carver passed out.

TEN

"Hey, mister, you okay?"

The voice was muzzy, unclear, the syllables all running together. Heymisteryouokay. Sounded Swedish.

Carver felt himself being lifted into a sitting position, then cold water trickling into his mouth. He sputtered, swiped at his lips, and tried to open his eyes.

"Leave him where he is," another voice said. "Looks better on the floor."

Carver wondered if it was going to be worth all the trouble. Opening his eyes could be very dangerous to his health. That second voice sounded familiar.

"Come on, mister," the first voice pleaded, "please snap out of it."

Something wet was put against Carver's forehead. Well, now, that felt good. He might live out the day after all.

"Jesus, Bascombe," the second voice said, "you take forever to wake up. Whoever worked you over did a good job. You look like shit, Jack."

Ah, Carver knew that voice. He tentatively opened his lids a slit. "Mr. Bascombe regrets," Carver said, "that he will not be dining today." His eyes opened fully and he looked at the man standing over him. "Hello, Ludlow."

He struggled to his feet, helped by the stranger. Sergeant Ludlow stood apart, no help at all, flipping through Piombo's scattered papers.

Carver stood, swaying, slowly regaining control.

"Are you all right?" the man asked. "Want me to get a doctor or anything?"

Carver shook his head. He took deep breaths, feeling his ribs grating. Probably fractured one, he figured. He looked at the man who had helped him. Looked familiar. Knew that face. Dark. Curly black hair, Clark Gable mustache, stocky build.

"You're Hermano Grabar," Carver said as he stumbled to a sink. He washed his face and soaked his badly bruised hands. No broken bones.

"Yes, but how did you know? We have never met, you and I."

"Oh, Bascombe is a real detective," Ludlow said sarcastically over his shoulder, still sifting through Piombo's papers.

"What happened to you?" Grabar asked.

"Couple of guys beat me up," Carver replied.

"Couple of clients you overcharged?" Ludlow asked.

Carver ignored Ludlow's remarks. He had a couple of snappy rejoinders, but what the hell, what good would it serve? Just make Ludlow more unpleasant. Besides, talking made his lungs move and that made his ribs hurt like hell.

He moved to the table and searched among the papers, then bent to look under the table. He felt momentarily dizzy and took two painful breaths. He looked at Ludlow.

"See any rocks?" he asked. "Black rocks?"

Ludlow shook his head.

Carver turned to Hermano Grabar. "Why are you here, Mr. Grabar?"

"I was curious about those two men leaving here. You see, I was visiting Sharon, paying my respects to her on her brother's death. I offered my help in arranging the funeral. There are many details that often a grieving relative forgets."

"I understand," Carver said, and mentally kicked himself for not offering his own help under those circumstances. "How is she?"

"She is well, but she is trying so very hard to bury her own grief in her work. She is driving herself very hard. To forget, you understand." Grabar paused and looked around the studio. "I do not understand—there is so little here. What could those men have wanted here?"

"I think they wanted those rocks," Carver said.

"Je-sus," Ludlow said, "there you go again with those rocks."

"They were arguing as they left here," Grabar said. "I was just departing from Sharon's studio when I saw them leaving. I wondered what they were doing here since they did not look like police. Does that answer your question as to why I was here? I was curious as to what those two men were doing here."

"Yeah," Ludlow said, "he was looking into the open door when I drove up. Piombo seldom locked the place during the day. He often slept here, and when he did leave, he put a padlock on the door. So how did you get in here, Jack?"

"Picked my way in," Carver answered. He sucked in his breath as his ribs began to ache.

"That's illegal," Ludlow said.

"Prove it. The door was open, the lock was only hanging there."

"Don't be a smartass, Jack."

"Mr. Grabar," Carver began to say, "I don't suppose—"

"Please, call me Hermano."

"You didn't get the license number of their car?"

"They had no car. They walked to the end of the street and turned the corner . . . out of sight."

"About those rocks," Ludlow asked Carver, "what kind of rocks were they?"

"Just rocks, as far as I could tell." He gestured at the wall with the painted black cloud. "I figure he put the rocks on that table and spray-painted them black for some reason. The wall behind caught the overflow. The spray cans are on the floor under the table."

Ludlow rubbed the side of his face, then checked several sheets he pulled from his inside pocket. He scanned the pages carefully.

"Yeah, the inventory mentions six rocks. In a cabinet. Is that where you found them?"

Carver said it was, then described the two men and the beating he had taken. Ludlow shook his head; why would two thugs want to take a bunch of rocks? None of it made much sense. Carver agreed, but could add nothing to Ludlow's speculation. He was grateful they didn't kill him. He thanked Grabar for his help, and the three men left the studio.

They headed for Sharon's studio. Ludlow wore a scowl and wiped the sweat from his hat. Carver put on his sunglasses.

"Tell me," Carver asked the olive-skinned sculptor, "did you know Lou Piombo?"

"No, I did not. He was not the sort of man, and certainly not the kind of sculptor, I would associate with."

"Why not?" Carver asked.

"Surely you know. Piombo had a very bad reputation. He was not an honest man."

"You didn't think much of him as a sculptor?"

"If you want to see good work, come to my studio. I am proud of my abilities."

"Where is your studio?" Carver asked.

"Not around here," Grabar answered. "I've recently moved to a small garage in Sharp Park."

"To be closer to Barbara Stahl."

"Of course," Grabar said with a grin.

"You knew about Piombo's so-called artistic enterprises?"

Grabar spat contemptuously into the street and went into a long discourse about Piombo's dubious ancestry, his lack of integrity, his greed, which destroyed any talent he might have had, and a series of curses on such men who had the nerve to call themselves artists. Carver listened patiently. The three men stopped outside the door of Sharon's studio.

"Couple of items, Hermano," Carver said. "Alex Marteau, one of the art commissioners—you had a beef with him. Knocked out some teeth and broke his arm."

"Yes, I did. He deserved it."

"Why?"

"Hey, just a sec, Jack," Ludlow said to Carver, "how'd you know this stuff?"

"Confidential sources, Sergeant." Carver turned to Grabar. "About that fight . . ."

"I would suggest you see him about that. Then come to my studio and talk."

"Sounds fair. Now, the last item. Tom Ferrik—did you know him?"

"No, Carver, I did not. I know only what Barbara tells me of her ex-husband—and you know what that means. She is biased. I do know Ferrik's work, of course. I have seen it often in galleries and museums. It is good, but it comes mostly from the mind, not from the heart. It is more David Smith and not Auguste Rodin. You understand the difference I am trying to make in my poor way?"

Carver nodded and said he'd visit Grabar's studio. The two men shook hands, and Hermano Grabar walked away. Carver and Ludlow stood by the studio door.

"You're going in?" Carver asked.

"Yeah, with you," Ludlow answered. "Any objections?"

"Are you going to follow me around all day?"

"Any objections?"

"No."

"Good."

"After you," Carver said, opening the door.

"Thanks, Jack. I'm interested, really interested, in how you do your job." Ludlow's words carried with them a tone of sarcasm and superiority. "Yeah, you got a way with questions, you do."

Carver grinned.

Bob Hutte, the foundry owner's son, and Sharon were drinking cold beers. Sharon was in her overalls again, and Hutte was dressed in slacks and a short-sleeved shirt.

"My God, Carver," Sharon exclaimed, "what happened to you?"

"Bascombe here got himself beat up," Ludlow said, "just across the street. Sort of on your doorstep, you might say."

Carver introduced Ludlow to Bob Hutte, who offered them beer. They accepted, and the beer tasted good.

Under Sharon's urging, Carver explained what had happened, leaving out the part about the rocks. He also did not mention the stakeout in front of her apartment or the abandoned sedan.

He noticed the dark rings under Sharon's eyes, the sweat on her forehead, and her quiet attitude. Based on Mike Tettsui's report of Sharon working early at her studio, he guessed that she had worked out much of her sorrow and shock.

Ludlow strolled around the large studio, gazing at the huge piece of metalwork.

Bob Hutte looked at Carver and winked.

"What do you think, Sergeant?" Hutte asked. "Do you like it?"

"What the hell is it?" Ludlow replied. "Looks like a big

piece of scrap. What are these things supposed to be?'' he asked, pointing to large forms that grew from within the piece. "Some kind of leaf or a tail?"

Sharon did her best to explain that it might be a symbol of nature gone rampant. Perhaps an outcry against pollution, she wasn't sure. Carver could see that it wasn't easy for her to explain, since words are a difficult form of communication for visual artists. And she was not finished with the piece, her mind still open, considering avenues of attack, letting the creative juices flow.

Her words fell flat, as though the more she tried to explain, the more her art seemed contrived or, worse, a sham. Obviously Ludlow wasn't buying any of it. Carver wondered if he was using a psychological ploy to get Sharon talking, to think about something other than the death of her brother.

"Why the hell don't you sculptors make statues the way they used to," Ludlow demanded, "something people can understand. A famous guy on a horse or some politician sitting in a chair. I've seen the Lincoln statue in Washington, D.C., and it looks great, real majestic. I don't think it would be so great if it looked like something dredged up from the bottom of a swamp."

"There are artists who still work in that manner, Sergeant," Sharon said, "but most of us, we're part of the twentieth century. Aren't you?"

"So what? Guys two hundred years ago, a thousand years, all had two eyes. Just like me. I know what I can see."

"The traditional way," Sharon said patiently, forcing back an exasperated sigh, "was for a sculptor to find his image in a block of marble or wood, and then carve it *out* of that material. We're not bound by that concept. Are you bound to use a horse and buggy just because it looks fine outside a palace or trotting in a park? Would you give up your automobile just because someone thinks a horse and carriage is more aesthetic?"

"It's not the same," Ludlow said.

"The hell it isn't," Sharon said bluntly. "There are materials we use that weren't even around a hundred years ago. Aluminum, for instance, or steel in great quantities. Would you actually suggest that housewives go back to using clay pots, maybe even making the things themselves?"

"Don't get pissed, lady, because we don't understand it," Ludlow said, swigging his beer. "Whose fault is that? And you actually sell stuff like this?"

Sharon sighed. She was so tired of this sort of conversation. She put up with it only because she didn't know how far she could push this homicide detective.

"Okay, forget all that crap," Ludlow said to her. He gestured at Carver. "Did hotshot over there tell you about this morning?"

"What about this morning?" Sharon asked, looking at Carver.

With an almost sadistic pleasure, Ludlow related the police report on the incident in Golden Gate Park. Sharon looked aghast, and Bob Hutte narrowed his eyes and shook his head.

"That settles it," Sharon said, looking with concern at Carver. "You want to find Tom—and so do I. Where you go, I go."

Carver shook his head, indicating with a jerk of his hand that he didn't want to discuss it with Sergeant Ludlow around. Sharon caught on and nodded her understanding.

Ludlow accepted another bottle of beer from Hutte.

"I've never seen a casting foundry before," Ludlow said. "You got time to show me around—and Bascombe, too?" He tipped the bottle to his lips and stared at Carver over the neck of the bottle.

"I've seen it," Carver said. He wanted to stay with Sharon— and he didn't want to play Ludlow's game, whatever it was.

"Come on, Jack," Ludlow said, his words harsh, almost

an order, "it'll be educational. You're the one who's artistic and well educated and all. Besides, maybe you can talk Mr. Hutte here into becoming one of your legal clients."

"Glad to show you around," Hutte said. "I gave Mr. Bascombe a standing offer to look at the operations, but if he doesn't want to—"

"No, that's okay," Carver said, relenting. He had to keep Ludlow from talking with Sharon; she might tell him about the Sierra cabin, and Carver's job was to find Amber's father. Ludlow's job was to find Piombo's killers.

"Fine," Bob Hutte said, gesturing toward the foundry door. "Come along."

In the foundry, several workers huddled over two halves of an object made of some kind of gelatine. Another worker stirred a vat of hot wax.

"A casting foundry is an extension of the sculptor's studio," Hutte explained to them. "We've been lucky most of the time with casting orders. Occasionally, we have to close the shop for a day—put the workers on half pay." He gestured broadly. "And this is where the work begins. An artist comes in with his sculpture, and we make a gel mold. Once it's dry, we open it up and coat the inside with layers of wax—"

"Yeah," Ludlow said, "I've heard of that. The lost wax process."

Carver looked at the homicide detective. Didn't the guy ever forget anything he read or heard or saw?

"Yes," Hutte said, "*cire-perdue*. The traditional method of casting. The wax is a microcrystalline petroleum product, much finer, able to hold the most subtle marks an artist can create."

For the next few minutes, Hutte explained the molding and casting process.

"My dad used to have several other foundries, one over in the East Bay, one in Los Angeles, and a small one for custom jewelry in Atherton. Economics prevailed, so we sold two. We still have the one in Atherton. Come on."

Hutte gestured for Ludlow and Carver to follow him deeper into the foundry, where several muscular workmen were handling a large crucible. An anxious-looking, middle-aged man stood nearby. Using the overhead hoist and handling shanks, the workers maneuvered the bubbling crucible to a large pit in the floor, where a mold had been placed and packed around with sand.

"Stand back," Bob Hutte said to Carver and Ludlow. "The heat is terrific—and we don't want you splashed accidentally with hot metal. The artist—that's him, the nervous one—has created a piece which is to be cast. Now the workers are ready to pour the bronze or brass. Or whatever metal the artist prefers. Now!"

The workmen tipped the crucible over the main funnel.

A cloud of steam and gas billowed out, hissing and whooshing from the casting pit.

"In about six or eight hours," Hutte said, "the metal will be cool enough. In really large pieces, cooling might take days. We break apart the investment mold and check the condition. With luck—and a lot of experience—there'll be no cracks or defects."

Ludlow shook his head, regretting having asked to be shown the workings of the foundry. Christ, should've done this in winter, when the heat would be welcome. He looked at his clothes: his jacket hung over his arm like a wet rag, his pants bagged around his ankles, and his shirt . . . Hell, the less said about that the better. Use it to wipe off the car.

Hutte showed them the cleaning area, the acid baths, and the various kilns. They were just returning to the main foundry area when Karl Hutte came down from the mezzanine.

"I told you, Robert," he began angrily, "that I did not welcome these—these sort to my foundry."

"Who's this asshole?" Ludlow asked.

"My father," Bob Hutte said. He tried to introduce Ludlow to Karl Hutte, but the big man merely waved his hands in front of him, as though fending off an attack.

"No, no," the older man yelled. "They have no business here. They do not do business with me. Never!"

Ludlow flashed his detective's shield at Karl Hutte. The old man ignored it.

"What is that to me? Get out. I do not want *schwarzers* here."

"Oh, yeah," Ludlow said, bristling. "Don't step on me, Pop, or you'll find yourself in a lot of trouble."

Carver Bascombe stepped back a pace into a shadowy area. He grinned to himself, and Bob Hutte joined him.

"This is a white country," Karl Hutte said patronizingly, "and should stay a white country. But, no, you and your kind are interlopers, trying to fit in. Trying to mix with whites. No! It is an impossibility."

"You're right there, Pop," Ludlow said.

"What!"

"Yeah, Pop, you said the truth. We didn't want to be brought here as slaves. But white guys like you did it, with a little help from Ay-rabs and enemy African black tribes. But here we are—so let us alone. Or give us the means to start our own country. I think California would make a terrific country for us to live in. So why the hell don't you guys get a bill passed in Congress and give us this state."

"You are crazy," Karl Hutte muttered. "Crazy."

"Sure. Just like you, Pop. You don't like blacks. Hey, I don't like whites."

"Ja, but think—you even had to ask me to get your country for you. You do not make it yourself. Bah. You are all alike. Lazy and stupid."

"Anyway, think about it," Ludlow said. "I kind of like

this business. Looks mighty interesting. Tell you what, you have it appraised and I'll give you ten cents on the dollar for it on the day you leave California to us niggers.''

Hutte's face grew beet-red, his lips moving in and out. Not a word came out.

"Think it over, Pop," Ludlow said.

"I do not have to think. You are the crazy one. This is a valuable business. What kind of a man would even consider such an offer? This is my business, where skill and strength are required, and experience and the appreciation of art. Things which you would not understand. Blacks are only good for making water jugs, and ugly masks, and ugly jazz music.''

"Like I said—think about it, Pop."

Karl Hutte stared at the black man and then angrily returned to his office on the mezzanine.

Ludlow watched the older man. Yeah, now there was an interesting case. A real fascist. He wondered if Karl Hutte had any kind of record. He'd check on it.

Leaving Carver Bascombe behind, Ludlow walked outside. The heat of the day seemed cool by comparison. He wiped the sweat from his brow and then put his hat back on. A cold shower would feel great, but it wasn't in the cards. He had a report to write. One more item: Two white men had beat up a private detective. Did anyone care? Was it even important? Oh, yeah, don't forget the rocks. Guys don't get mugged over worthless rocks. They had to mean something, had to have some importance.

Carver shook Bob Hutte's hand and returned to Sharon's studio.

"Now what about this idea of yours . . ." he began.

"What idea was that?" Sharon asked innocently.

"Following me around."

"I did not mean following you. I'm going to be with you. Where you go, I'll be at your elbow."

Carver knew she meant driving with him to the Sierras. How wonderful it would be to take an all-day drive with her. But it might be dangerous. Piombo's killer might follow them. His thoughts were jumbled, conflicting; his emotions battling.

"You don't go," Carver said, his brain winning over his heart. "If Tom Ferrik is hiding out in the Sierras, then I want to find him. Alone."

"Do you think I'll get in your way?"

"Yeah. I work better alone. I've tried the other way—and it usually doesn't work out."

"What are your plans for now?"

"Patching myself up," he said with a rueful grin. Yeah, Band-Aids and a cold beer. First he'd tape up his ribs and douse himself with rubbing alcohol. Then a visit to Alex Marteau. The day was still young.

Sharon smiled enigmatically as Carver left the studio. He just didn't know her. She had her plan and, dammit, she was going to follow it through. She waited for a minute, then threw off her coveralls and dressed rapidly. She knew where Carver's office was located. Patching himself up, was he? She'd see for sure. She was going to be right there if he went anywhere. Every step of the way.

When she locked the studio door, Carver Bascombe was nowhere in sight. Her six-year-old coupe was parked on the next street over, on Townsend. She got in and tried to start the motor. Nothing happened. The starter merely clicked and clicked. Sharon raised the hood . . . and saw a white paper and a ten-dollar bill stuck on the opened distributor. The rotor was missing. She took the money and read the handwritten note. She shook with anger.

The paper read:

Sorry, Sharon. I'll return the rotor to you tomorrow. Here's cab fare.

                                    Carver

ELEVEN

"All right, Ernie," Lt. De Anza asked as he entered his office, "is Grabar a prime suspect or not?"

Sergeant Ludlow leaned an elbow on De Anza's desk.

"Not. Because I couldn't dredge up anything about him. Nothing I can recall—except for the fight with that art commissioner, Alex Marteau. I recall that real good."

"Then you figure he's off the hook?"

"Until I get some hard evidence."

De Anza filed papers in cabinets, then leaned back in his chair. He lit a cigarette and offered one to Ludlow. The black detective took it.

"How did the commission grilling go?" Ludlow asked.

"Easy, Ernie, very easy," De Anza answered. His face flickered with a self-satisfied grin. "Nobody's in the running. A couple of days and I'll be Captain De Anza." He looked around the office. "I'll kind of miss this. But having a private office compensates. So . . . to business."

De Anza read Ludlow's typed report, fingered his mustache, and smoked his cigarette.

"What else is happening with Piombo's case?" he asked.

"Nothing. We're hitting zeros. No motive. You know me, if Piombo had been a bigger crook, or if I'd ever arrested him, I'd have it all up here." Ludlow tapped his temple. "Detective Applegate is checking Piombo's probation officer for a list of guys Piombo knew in the county jail. Should have it in a couple hours. Also me and Stein, we're going to check on that sculptor who knew Piombo. I mentioned him earlier. Elliot Herd."

"I remember—and it's in your report. Any luck on finding Tom Ferrik?"

"Not yet. This Herd guy, maybe he knew Ferrik, too."

"What do you think about the timetable on Piombo and the little girl?"

"I don't like it." Ludlow narrowed his eyes and dragged on his cigarette. "First off, the killer would've had to shoot Piombo, prop his body in the Vaillancourt Fountain, then get on the trail of Amber Ferrik and take a shot at her. Raf, he'd have to do all that in a hell of a hurry."

"It wasn't planned? One of those precision timetables?"

"More like spur of the moment stuff. I think . . . Look, he kills Piombo, maybe planned, maybe not, but the girl . . . He follows her, waiting for an opportunity. He runs out of time when he realizes she's close to her destination and then shoots her. Okay, he misses, and, for some reason, he doesn't take another shot."

"Probably panicked. Or too many people got off the bus. Do you suppose he knew Amber was going to Bascombe's office?"

"Raf, I'll know that when I collar him."

"Is Bascombe getting in your way, Ernie?"

"Nah. He just rubs me wrong. Right now he's all bruised

up. Mostly his ego though. Grabar told him about the fight with Marteau.''

"Carver seems to put some significance on those rocks in Piombo's studio."

"Right. The only stuff missing from the studio. Those two hoods grabbed them. We've got their descriptions circulating, but you know what that's going to bring?"

"El Zippo, El Nada," De Anza said dryly.

Ludlow blew smoke at the ceiling and watched the designs made by the thin smoke.

"I haven't seen anything of the autopsy on Frank Argent."

"Just what you figured last night," De Anza said. "Broken neck caused by severe blows to the face and neck."

"So far I ain't seen no one that's built strong enough to do that. Except for this guy at the foundry, Bob Hutte."

"According to your report, most of the men who work there look like army tanks. I suppose any of them could've done it."

"I suppose. This Marteau guy sounds like a scrapper. I'm going to see him before Bascombe does."

"Then you'd better move your ass, Ernie."

Ugh! A terrible pain racked Carver's body. He continued to roll the cloth bandage around his chest. His flesh trembled. When he finished, his torso shined with sweat. He pulled on a clean shirt, then turned on the stereo and selected a record. He took a bottle of Anchor Steam beer from the office refrigerator.

A dirty trick, stealing Sharon's rotor. Had to be done. There were too many people running around with guns, and she might get in the way of a bullet. And besides . . . Once before a woman had used him, thinking him outclassed. She had accompanied him on a case with every intention of finding out what he knew when he knew it. And then betrayal. (He still could not say her name—just thought of her as *she.*) She was also an artist. An opera singer. A lovely voice. Never more to be heard.

Carver stood at the open window and listened to Hector Berlioz's *Benvenuto Cellini,* with Colin Davis conducting the Covent Garden Chorus and the BBC Symphony. Was he in love with Sharon? No, he didn't think so. He'd only just met her, and he didn't much believe in love at first sight. And yet Sharon meant more to him than just a sexual conquest.

He knew he would see her again. To return the distributor rotor. He wanted to see her again.

Had to get his mind off that.

He telephoned the art commission office. Marteau wasn't in. Carver asked for his address, but his secretary would definitely not give out Marteau's home address.

Marteau wasn't listed in the phone book. Carver took out the city directory from his desk and in ten seconds he had Marteau's address. Fifteen minutes later, he parked on Jackson Street, two blocks from Marteau's home. That was the closest he could get.

Heading west, he crossed Octavia Street. The area abounded with expensive homes, mansions actually, complete with spiked fences, Samoan gardeners, chauffeurs, limousines, and maids. Marteau's home was typical: a scaled-down version of Jefferson's Monticello, with cypress trees at the corners of the house and Doric columns flanking the entrance.

He rang the bell and waited.

A maid answered. "Yes, mister?"

"I'm an investigator working on a case. I'd like to ask Mr. Marteau some questions."

"Again? The others have left Mr. Marteau very disturbed."

Carver figured she meant the police. He shrugged in a manner that said, What can you do? She let him into the rose-white-tiled hallway. She asked him to wait and, in a few minutes, returned and asked him to follow her.

They passed through a vast living room, with white and

brown velour furniture. A Betsy Lombard pastel of a 1949 Ford woodie went well with the decor. They passed through an atrium where ferns brushed against Carver's arms. They finally entered a room containing a number of small sculptured pieces and several paintings. Carver recognized a Lee Bontecou and a sagging man-sized clothespin by Oldenburg.

French windows opened on to a patio, where Carver could see a lush lawn beyond. Sprinklers tossed umbrellas of water onto the grass and several miniature rainbows hovered over them.

Alex Marteau was a small man, under five three. He stood near an easy chair with a drink in his hand.

"I've already answered the other detective," he said without preamble. He did not offer to shake hands; he kept his hand tight on the glass. "What now?"

"I'm not with the police department," Carver said. He pulled out his ID and showed it to Marteau.

The little man grew red. The color seemed to harmonize with his plump-tomato nose, melon-round head, pursed, thick beet lips, chunky arms, and pale fingers. Alex Marteau looked as though he had stepped full-grown from a vegetable patch.

"Get the fuck out!" Marteau said angrily. He drained the last of the clear liquid in the glass.

Carver smelled gin. In the brief time he had been in the room, he had seen the little man toss down at least four ounces of gin.

"Just a question or two, Mr. Marteau."

"If you don't get out, I'll call the cops." He went to a wet bar and poured himself another full glass.

"I only want to know a couple of things. Do you know Tom Ferrik? And I'd like to hear your version of the fight with Hermano Grabar."

"You're a private dick. I don't have to talk. I don't want to talk. I've had it up to here." He gestured with a slash across his stubby mouth. "I certainly don't have to talk to a private cop. So get the nell out of my house. I'm going to fire that maid. Goddamn her for not checking! Can't stand incompetents."

"You're being harsh, Mr. Marteau," Carver said.

Marteau slugged down half the gin. He balled one hand into a fist. An eggplant. He stepped closer to Carver.

"Okay, so I'm harsh. It's my house. What the fuck, I'm talking, and you're still here. What is this?" He turned to the wet bar and picked up a telephone. "I'm calling the cops. You've got ten seconds to get out."

"What happens if I don't?" Carver asked. "Maybe I'll just wait for the cops to arrive. Might take them ten minutes, or it might be half an hour. I can ask a lot of questions in that time."

Marteau put down the phone. "Then," he said slowly, and put down his glass, "we settle it my way." He balled both fists. Two eggplants.

Moving lightly on his feet, Marteau moved to Carver's left. He had a boxer's stance. He grinned, his lips pulled tight against his teeth. Carver wondered what the hell this little guy was going to do. Reach up eleven inches to put one on his chin? Hell with that. Besides, he'd already had his ribs caved in a couple hours ago. Enough was enough.

Carver moved fast, slid one leg behind Marteau's foot, and shoved him in the face with the flat of his hand. Marteau windmilled, tripped over Carver's foot, and fell heavily into the easy chair. Carver stood back.

The fist that slammed into Carver's stomach caught him by surprise. Marteau had leaped out of the chair and thrown a punch with startling swiftness. Carver doubled over and backpedaled. Ah, Christ! His ribs felt as if an oxyacetylene torch was scouring them.

Instinctively, he went into a martial arts stance, twisting, striking out with his hands. Nothing but thin air. The pain from Marteau's punch racked his ribs. Damn! He shouldn't have moved into action so damned fast! Carver sucked in air through clenched teeth, fighting back the agony.

Alex Marteau stood back—and laughed.

"Hot damn! You look stupid. All that fancy Jap stuff. What a lot of nothing. I think I could take you. But I won't."

He went to the bar and picked up his glass.

"Want one?" Marteau asked. "Ice cold."

Carver breathed deep, his ribs aching, aching.

"Come on," Marteau urged. "It's over. You did me. I did you. We're even. I'll even talk to you. Too fuckin' hot to fight."

Yeah, why not, Carver thought.

"A beer," Carver said.

"Okay. What kind? I got everything."

Carver asked for Anchor Steam, and Marteau brought several bottles out from the cold storage behind the bar.

"I guess you think I'm a nut," Marteau said.

Carver said nothing and sipped his beer.

"Okay, I lash out. Why keep stuff bottled up? It's bad for the digestion. What was your name? On your identification license? Bascombe? So you want to know about Ferrik? And my fight with Grabar? Okay. I told the police. It's no secret. What do you know about the art commission?"

"Only what I read in the papers."

"We do a lot of stuff. Neighborhood art programs. Running the annual art festival. All kinds of things. But the beef with Grabar was about the building art percentage. See, every public building that goes up in this city, the commission levies two percent for art. Say a new city auditorium is built. Costs twenty million. Four hundred thousand goes for artwork. You can imagine the competition! You get the idea. It's good for artists. More cities should have such a plan."

"And Grabar wanted a piece of the action?"

"You got it, Bascombe. See, a good percentage of that art

143

money often goes to sculptors. Oh, an occasional mural gets done, but mostly it's big sculptural pieces. Grabar wanted special consideration. For himself and a couple of other guys.''

"You wouldn't give it to him?"

"Hell, no. I got integrity. I know what it takes to sculpt. I'm an amateur myself. Got a small studio just off the patio. Want to see it?''

Carver agreed, his curiosity whetted; he'd seen plenty of sculptors' studios in the past forty-eight hours. Marteau poured himself another drink and then led the way across the patio. The studio was neat and carefully laid out: drawing tables and clay throwing tables, a kiln, and a small casting pit.

The studio was also air-conditioned. Carver was grateful.

"This is just for fun,'' Marteau said. "Anyway, I've had my arguments with plenty of artists. Hermano was just one.''

"And Tom Ferrik?"

"Hey, I can read newspapers. I know Tom is missing. Cops are looking for him. You, too, I suppose.'' He paused. "Yeah . . . I remember reading about it. The private detective—that's you, huh?''

"Yes. Did you know Tom very well?"

"Better than some. Less than others. He's a swell guy. I like him. But he's headstrong. Likes to do things his own way. Maybe that's why I like him. But he didn't feel he'd been cheated if he didn't get any of the public building commission money. Maybe that's why he got one job.''

"A big one?"

"He would've grossed over a quarter million.''

"Did Grabar know Ferrik?"

"Sure. They'd met. But Grabar tried to influence me. Offered me a kickback if I was to throw my influence at the other commissioners.''

"Did you?" Carver asked.

"How'd you like to get your black ass whipped into chocolate pudding?''

"No, thanks.''

TWELVE

"How often do they come by, Rose?" Mike Tettsui asked.

They sat near the front bay window in the house on Fulton Street. The late-afternoon light was fading; the shadows under the trees in the park across the street were deeply colored. Rich purples. Inky blues. The greenery was almost black.

"About every half hour," Rose replied.

Before Mike Tettsui had arrived, Rose and Amber had watched the police prowl cars. Amber made a game of it, setting an alarm clock every twenty-five minutes and running to the window to watch. Rose let her use an old clock that had belonged to her late husband.

Rose brought Tettsui up-to-date on all the incidents and dangers. She wanted to know if Mike was armed. Mike Tettsui stifled a yawn. He drank more of the tea that Rose Weinbaum had brewed for him. Five hours' sleep. Didn't exactly put him in the best conversational mode.

He carried a 9mm Heckler and Koch 15-shot automatic pistol in a shoulder holster under his jacket. Additionally, in an ankle-length lizard-skin boot was a small five-shot .32 revolver.

Rose was satisfied. She and Amber had played games or watched television most of the afternoon. Tettsui wondered where he would sleep. They decided that Amber would sleep with Rose, and he could have the spare bedroom.

Amber came running in from the front room.

"Mike, another one went by. That's five minutes late. Thirty-five minutes since the last one."

"Okay, what do you want us to do?" Tettsui asked. "Should I call the local station and upbraid them?"

"Upbraid . . . ?" Amber repeated. "What does that mean?"

"Take them to task. Tell them off. Give 'em hell."

"You're funny," Amber said.

Bodyguard duty was never fun, Tettsui thought. Sometimes it was necessary. He thought of his own two children, Cynthia and Evan. Six and four. Because of them he always kept his weapons locked in a gun safe. Maybe it was better not to carry guns. Maybe Carver Bascombe had the right idea. Maybe. What was Bascombe up to now?

Thirty minutes of driving took him to Sharp Park. He found the Palmetto address Hermano Grabar had given to him earlier. Grabar's studio was a disused auto garage; no attempt had been made to change its appearance. Someone might still drive up and ask about fixing a radiator or carburetor. Carver noted two cars parked on the sloping cement entrance ramp. He jotted down the numbers of both license plates in his notebook.

"Ah, Carver," Grabar said pleasantly when Carver entered. Barbara Stahl was with him, drinking a glass of lemonade. "You know Barbara, of course."

"How are you?" Barbara asked. Her question sounded forced, her words strained. "Have you found Tom?"

"Not yet," Carver said.

"Are you all right? Hermano told me about the beating this morning. I think . . . it's so terrible."

She sounded as though she meant it, but Carver noted more interest in her question about her ex-husband. When he first entered the garage studio, he thought he had interrupted lovers' talk—but maybe it was a lovers' quarrel. About what?

"So," Grabar said, "this is where I work." He swept a hand in a semicircle.

The garage no longer looked like a garage. Unlike Piombo's messy studio, and similar to Alex Marteau's, Grabar's studio was neat and clean, with a place for all the tools and everything in place.

On several worktables were small models of sculptured pieces that Grabar was working on. A large—almost finished—sculpture stood in the middle of the room. The piece was made of thin bronze rods welded in an open-weave pattern, with angular boxes intersecting, playing with space, an eye-tricking effect of mathematics and spontaneity.

"I like it," Carver said. It certainly reflected Grabar's penchant for neatness.

Grabar thanked him. Barbara had said little since Carver had arrived. Grabar showed Carver sketches of designs he was creating, which would be sculptures of monumental size.

"I gather," Carver said, "that these drawings are proposals for commissions?"

"Yes, that is so. It is a fact of life. One has to try to interest these faceless corporations. Many do not see the benefit of public art."

"Hermano is always competing," Barbara Stahl offered. "Maybe that's why I love him."

"Is he that different from Tom?"

"I think I've said all I'm going to on that subject."

Carver turned to Grabar. "I've seen Marteau. He tells me you offered him a bribe."

147

"Ah . . ." Grabar said, and then chuckled. "Yes, he would say such a thing. But this is not true, Carver. In truth, it was the other way around. Many sculptors have never been considered for the two-percent public-building commission. I wanted the commission members to look at works by neglected artists. I included myself, naturally."

"Naturally," Carver said.

"He said he would see what he could do. For a price. It was quite apparent what Marteau meant. Although he did not speak directly. The offer was roundabout. But I knew what he was saying. We would have to pay him off."

"Is that—" Carver began.

"That is when I hit him. We fought with fists and feet for a minute, perhaps less. Alex Marteau, he is a very strong man. The maid called the police and I was arrested. I spent overnight in jail. The next day Marteau dropped the charges and I was let out. There were many newspaper reporters there. Even through his wired jaw he laughed over the incident, said it was all a misunderstanding. Said my English was not that good."

"I think your English is fine," Carver said. Did any of this have anything to do with Ferrik's disappearance? His thoughts were interrupted by Barbara Stahl speaking to him.

"Mr. Bascombe, how is Amber?"

"She's fine."

"I don't think so," she said, her words tight and shuddery. "I can read the papers. She was almost killed this morning."

"I don't think they wanted to kill her."

"Who were they?"

"I don't know."

"I think—I think they wanted to get Amber so they could get her to talk, to tell where Tom is hiding."

"You could be right," Carver said.

"And if they had, then they would have killed her."

"Amber doesn't know where her father is."

"Doesn't that make it all the worse? They would still have killed her!"

Carver did not reply. Barbara Stahl could be correct. She had a reason to be worried.

"Please, Mr. Bascombe," she pleaded, "let me take her. I can hide her. I know I can."

"Amber is well protected," Carver said bluntly, thinking of Mike Tettsui and of the district cops on patrol.

He thanked them for their time and left. Thirty minutes later, Carver entered his office, turned on the stereo, and checked his mail. Four letters had been dropped in the mail slot. Nothing from Sacramento. Double damn. He sat in his chair and brooded.

Forget about the bar exam letter. Think about the case.

Did he have anything that was going to bring him closer to Tom Ferrik? Were the killings of Lou Piombo and Frank Argent linked? He looked at the photos on the corkboard and then typed his notes. He arranged them in time sequence; there was no other order as yet.

Okay, Carver mused, concentrate on Tom Ferrik. What was he like? Impulsive, hard-working, arrogant. Figured he could handle anything. So Tom had a particular reason to disappear without Amber. Had a reason to send her to him. Because she needed protection? Why not send her to the police? Because . . . because he didn't want them to interfere?

Carver sat up straight and stared at Ferrik's photo. The afternoon light was fading. He turned on the desk lamp.

Yeah, it made sense. Tom Ferrik didn't want interference. Whatever was happening, he knew about it! And he didn't want the police—who would interfere—because Tom wanted the event to happen. Or . . . or he has to let it happen.

Couldn't he let this happen and still keep Amber with him? Apparently not. Tom had been threatened. But so had Amber.

Could Tom think Amber was better off separated from him? And protected. So he sends her to a private detective.

But why to him? Carver wondered. He telephoned Rose. As he had predicted, Rose did have a problem with the cops about her shooting the revolver in Golden Gate Park. Fortunately she had her permit. Amber thought the whole thing was fun.

Rose had helped Carver by getting Amber to look at a state map. Execution City was not far from Placerville, and it was only a short distance from a river named Rubicon; that was Amber's mismatch, the word that sounded like Rubik.

"Good work, Rose," Carver said, writing down the essentials. East on Highway 50 to Placerville. Execution City. In the hills. He gave her a brief rundown on his activities.

"Now what, boss?"

"I've exhausted everything else, so I think I'll try to pick up the trail in the mountains. I'm driving up tomorrow."

"Want me to do any more?"

"Find out who else knew Lou Piombo. Moseby was a blank there, and I haven't picked up anything further. Is Mike there?"

"He's been here for the past hour, boss. Is there anything else I can do?"

Carver told her no, and Rose hung up.

Carver went back to his musings. Forced himself back. What was Ludlow doing? The routine cop stuff, checking all of Piombo's acquaintances. Checking any leads to Ferrik. But neither Ludlow nor De Anza knew about Ferrik's camp in the mountains.

So . . . tomorrow, on the road. He looked forward to the drive. Into the hills and mountains. It reminded him of his hitchhiking days as a young teenager. Coming west to California. With a crazy desire to see the Pacific Ocean.

Memories crowded his thoughts. Detroit when he was a

boy. Later hitchhiking west. His time as a young military policeman. Then opening his investigation office.

Deliberately, he pushed the memories aside. Okay, think about tomorrow, on the road, east to the Sierras. Yeah, he had been on the road before. Detroit to the Pacific Ocean. Many thousands of days ago . . .

THIRTEEN

Salt air—he had never smelled salt air before. Seventeen-year-old Carver Bascombe stared out of the window of the bus. He strained his eyes but saw only brown hills and the highway snaking toward Los Angeles. He moved from his seat and sat closer to the driver.

"Whatcha lookin' for, sonny?" the bus driver asked.

"I want to see the ocean," Carver said.

"Well, that's gonna be kinda tough, see. It's over there, on your right, over behind those hills. 'Bout a mile."

"I can smell the salt."

"Yep, you sure can," the driver said. "What you're gonna have to do, see, is when you get into town, ask for a city bus out to Santa Monica. Might take a couple hours, but that's the best way to see the Pacific Ocean."

Carver thanked the driver, and when the bus dropped him off in the middle of downtown L.A., he followed the man's advice.

At sunset he stood on the beach at Santa Monica. The great

ocean pushed breakers up onto the sand, crashing with a wild roar, shaking and beating the earth. Carver was wide-eyed. This was land's end. The ocean stretched farther than the eye could see and that appealed to his young soul. He sensed the mystery of time, the limitless possibilities of life.

The air was cool, tangy with the smells of iodine and salt tickling his nostrils. He walked the beaches barefoot, feeling the warm sand and tide foam between his toes. On the board-walk he watched spiky palm fronds toss in the sea breezes.

For several days he hop-skipped from cheap hotel to cheap hotel. He looked for any kind of a job and worked for a week as a bellboy in a middle-class hotel. The older and bigger bellboys tried to bully him. But they were stupid, not survi-vors, not used to dealing with a streetwise kid who had grown up in a Detroit ghetto.

"See, pard, it's like a business," a tough-looking twenty-three-year-old said. "You split your tips with me." The guy flicked a thumb at the upright collar on his bellboy uniform.

They were in the hotel's kitchen, at night. The twenty-three-year-old was named Max. He was big, with a beer gut already stretching the uniform at the brass buttons. Several others, a young black janitor and a middle-aged, weasel-faced bellboy, stood nearby. They grinned, as if they had practiced this routine many times.

"What happens if I don't split my tips?" Carver asked.

"Ah, shit, pard," Max said. He leaned negligently against a stainless steel counter, rattling the pots and pans hanging on racks. "That would be a terrible thing. For you."

Carver reached quickly for a frying pan and hit Max be-tween the eyes. The man went down onto his knees, his eyes rolling up, blood streaming from his forehead. Carver hit him again, on the back of the head, and Max bounced on the tile floor. He faced the other two, the pan in his hands. The two men backed away. Carver tossed the frying pan onto the counter and pulled off his uniform jacket. He threw it onto the unconscious Max.

"Extortion is illegal," Carver said—and walked out.

He moved on to different jobs. Pumping gas at a cutrate service station. Working at a down-at-the-heels gymnasium, washing towels and occasionally getting into the ring as a sparring partner. Shortly after his eighteenth birthday, he had saved enough money to enroll in college. He passed the entrance examinations.

"So, Mr. Bascombe," the college counselor had asked—and no one had ever called him mister before—"what sort of major interests you?"

They sat in a cramped office, with books overflowing from shelves and cardboard boxes.

"I'm not sure, sir," Carver said.

Of course Carver knew what his own interest was, but he felt strange that he was placing his career in the hands of a white man. A stranger at that.

"Call me Stan," the man said, a friendly attitude flowing through his words. "Well, then, may I suggest a liberal arts curriculum? We have your grades transcript from your high school in Detroit and, to tell you the truth, I don't think your grades are good enough yet."

"No, sir."

"Stan, please. Not that your grades are bad, Mr. Bascombe, but you need some brushing up. What we call bonehead courses. Actually, they're fairly tough, but get through them and you'll be equal to any freshman in this college. Anything else?"

"I guess not . . . Stan," Carver said. He hesitated. "Actually, there is . . . a major I'm interested in."

"You bet. Fire away."

"I'd like to study law."

"A legal career? Want to be an l, capital L, lawyer, hey?"

"I'd like to use the law to help people."

"Well, far be it for me to discourage you, but it's a long haul to get a law degree. And then you have to pass the bar exam. And in this state, that test is a killer."

"Oh."

"But, like I said, don't let me discourage you. We have some law courses here. Get you acquainted with the stuff, anyway. Finish a couple of years here and use that time to look for a good law college. Who knows, you might get into the university law school system."

"All right, that sounds all right."

"Now, your other problem, a job. We have a pretty good job placement service here, but there are no guarantees. We usually have to wait for someone to ask us if any students want jobs."

"I'll keep looking on my own."

"You bet. Good luck, Mr. Bascombe."

Cheap rooms near the college were hard to find, but using the student grapevine, Carver found a room with a tiny kitchen. Cooking his own meals would save money, and the green stuff was running out.

On campus, Carver often felt girls' eyes on him. He liked the company of women; he didn't turn them away. He made friends easily. He didn't think of himself as particularly good-looking; he saw himself as too skinny. He wasn't aware of his own grace, his smooth, lithe movements, his economy of motion. He seemed to glide on ice as he walked, in contrast to the jaunty, cock-of-the-walk style of a few of the other black students.

Carver was a good listener. The problems and life plans of his student friends seemed more interesting than his own. Several of the female students found their way to his rooms.

"Is it so different in Detroit?" a lovely young black woman asked as she squirmed into a more comfortable position on Carver's bed.

Joy was twenty, with two years of college. She was a

physical education major, and her glowing medium-brown color was enhanced by sunbathing under the Southern California sun. That was Joy all over. Good-looking and proud of being black.

"Yeah, it is," Carver said in answer to her question. "If you haven't been there, then there's simply no way of telling you. The black experience—in Detroit it really is a black experience. Like a pit."

"You said your folks died there?"

"Yeah. My dad was killed in an auto accident. After that, my mom sort of died of a broken heart. I loved them. I really miss both of them."

"I don't know . . . you seem very self-reliant. Now, with me, it was different. . . ."

Joy told him about growing up in Encino, about her goals. She had tried gymnastics, with an eye to getting on an Olympic team. She just wasn't good enough as a gymnast. She shrugged. Joy looked at him, her head cocked to one side, as she rolled a joint.

"What about you, what do you want?" she asked, taking a drag. She handed the cigarette to Carver.

"Just getting more of an education." He took a long drag, holding his breath, the smoke deep in his lungs. After a few moments, he let it out and passed the joint back to Joy. "I'm hoping to get a better job than pumping gas."

"Yes, me too. Through the college placement office?"

"Yes," Carver said.

"All that's well and good, but what about now?" She looked at him, her eyes on his face. She smiled, then moved her gaze down his chest. "Right now?"

He did not decline the offer.

Several months later, at the semester break, Stan the counselor sought out Carver. He had a possible job for him. They sat on a wooden bench under a cypress tree.

"I don't know if this job would appeal to you," Stan said,

"but the pay would be good. It's certainly different, and it's something you can do at night. Won't interfere with your classes. If they accept you."

"What is it, Stan?" Carver asked.

"A process server."

"Oh. What law firm would I work for?"

"Not a law firm," Stan said with a grin. "Like I said, it's different. It's a private investigation agency. The Carrier Detective Agency."

Carver's mind danced with the possibilities. He'd heard that serving subpoenas and summonses was good money.

"Interested, Mr. Bascombe?" Stan asked.

Carver nodded. He was too excited to talk.

"I bet on it," Stan said, and handed Carver an envelope. "This is the address and an introduction from the college personnel office. You see a man named Rost—Felix Rost—at eight tonight. Which sounds like he has a job already lined up."

"I'll be there. And, please, call me Carver."

"You bet," Stan said.

"You come highly recommended," Felix Rost said.

Carver said nothing but nodded once.

Felix Rost stared at the young man sitting opposite. Carver's color meant little to him. He liked what he saw—and what he didn't hear. He distrusted people who talked too much at an interview; it indicated they were nervous. And this job needed a cool head and a man fast on his feet. A quick thinker.

Physically, Rost was as narrow as a four-in-hand tie. His favorite outfit was a baggy, two-toned sport coat, pleated slacks, and a casual wide-collar open shirt. He also liked brown-and-white golf shoes.

Carver flicked his eyes over the office. Only a few desk lights were on, but he could see a large bank of file cabinets against a far wall and four desks, each with at least two telephones. The floor had wall-to-wall carpeting, and old-fashioned English hunting prints were displayed on the paneled walls. The office had a feeling of get-the-job-done solidity.

"So okay," Rost said, "we'll give you a try. In this envelope is a summons—here's the address—and deliver it to a man named Gale Silber. Any questions?"

"No."

He knew better than to ask dumb questions like: Should he take a taxi or use city transportation? Should he call in after he delivered the papers to the man or come back to the office? Should he type a report or tell Mr. Rost personally? None of that.

Carver took the envelope, thanked Mr. Rost, and left.

The address was downtown. He called Joy and borrowed her car, an old Volkswagen with eighty thousand miles on it. Ten minutes later, he parked on Coronado, not far from the Hollywood Freeway.

The neighborhood was mostly old homes, slowly being taken over by developers putting up modern (and more expensive) apartments and high-rise office buildings. Carver found the address, a new condominium. The doorman on duty was no help.

"Look," Carver said, "I just have to deliver this to Mr. Silber."

"What is it?" the doorman asked.

"Gee, I don't know," Carver replied, putting on a real-nice-teenager voice. "It's from overseas, some kind of message from his office." He hoped that Mr. Silber really did work in an office or, if not, that the doorman didn't know otherwise. It was taking a chance, and he felt excited taking that chance. "See, I work there, and his boss said for me to deliver it."

"Kinda late, ain't it?" the doorman asked suspiciously.

"Oh, gee, you know how it is. I shoulda been here a

couple hours ago, but my girl wanted me to pick her up downtown, and she kept me waiting and waiting.''

"Yeah, yeah, kid, I know how it is, but I can't help you. Mr. Silber ain't back yet.''

"Gee, I'm going to be in a lot of trouble. My boss said Mr. Silber has to send out some kind of report before morning.'' Carver looked downcast, then brightened. "He must be out to dinner? Maybe you can tell me where he eats?''

"Look, kid, I shouldn't tell you this . . .'' The doorman looked around, as though he were about to sell a military secret to the Russians. "He goes for a walk. Not too far from here. You know MacArthur Park?''

Carver said sure, it wasn't far away, and the doorman told him that Gale Silber often walked there in the evening before dinner.

"Sorta looking for a dinner guest,'' the doorman said, "if you're old enough to get my meaning.''

"He's cruising,'' Carver said.

"Yeah, and I never said a thing.''

"Never heard a word, mister—and thanks.''

Carver rejected the idea of driving to the park; he might miss Mr. Silber walking back. He set off at a trot, with one question nagging him: How would he recognize his quarry? Asking the doorman for a description would have given the game away.

MacArthur Park featured a sprawling lagoon surrounded by palm trees. The scent of mimosa was in the air, and a splashing fountain in the lagoon added a lighthearted touch.

Carver wandered about the footpaths, the manila envelope tucked into his lightweight windbreaker. He noted the men walking the paths: some single, others paired up, and several laughing trios. Many in tight jeans, rough-cut biker denims, or superswish gaudy casuals, pink and lavenders and tropical-parrot-colored shirts.

Use the brain, Carver thought. Silber lived in an expensive

condo. So he probably dressed in a business suit or expensive sport clothes. It was a reasonable assumption and eliminated a lot of possible types.

He decided on a ploy. He passed dozens of men and tried his tactic on one man, but it wasn't Silber. He saw another man, well-dressed, talking with a guy in tight-ass pants, a shirt open to his belt, and a waterfall of gold chains around his neck. Carver walked alongside.

"Hi, Gale," he said, trying to sound casual, as though he knew the man. If it didn't work, he'd plead mistaken identity.

The well-dressed man turned, a smile on his face.

"Oh, hello," he said in a friendly voice, trying to remember where he had met this very handsome young black stud.

"This is for you," Carver said cheerfully, and handed him the summons. He turned and walked away, pleased with himself. Not a bad job, and kind of fun. Like an adventure, doing something out-of-the-ordinary . . .

He heard a shout and turned. Gale Silber was running toward him, his face purple and twisted in anger. His friend was faster and grabbed Carver, and Silber threw a punch into Carver's chest. His breath was knocked out of him and he retched violently, collapsing to his knees. Silber slapped him several times across the face, hurling curses at him with each taloned strike. The other guy—or was it Silber?—kicked him.

Then somehow the two men were not hitting him. On his hands and knees, Carver was aware of shouts and yells and a vicious scuffle nearby. He opened his eyes, his throat gagging. He tried to use one hand to wipe his mouth but fell over onto one side. Oh, he was in swell shape. Then he felt a pair of hands helping him to his feet.

"I don't believe those chaps will bother you," the stranger said. His voice was smooth and mellow. He looked at the young black man, steadying him with a strong grip. "Dear boy, are you all right?"

Carver looked into the stranger's eyes and saw concern mixed with a twinkle.

"Yeah, I think so," Carver said, hand-sweeping dirt from his knees. He took deep breaths. He ached like hell.

"I detest an unfair fight," the man said. "I really don't like bullies."

"Thanks," Carver said, his breathing almost normal. "Thanks a lot."

For the first time, Carver took a good look at his benefactor: a man in his middle or late thirties, with a faint silvering of the hair at the temples, and a well-cut long hairstyle. He was slender, with an erect stance as though he were a military officer on parade review. His superbly cut dark blue velvet three-piece suit blended with the night. A ring on each little finger twinkled in the moonlight.

Carver looked at the two men several yards away, one on his knees, the other sprawled flat on the path.

"What did you do to those guys?" Carver asked. "You really laid them out."

"A bit of this and a bit of that. Karate, you know. A very useful method of self-defense. Additionally, it helps keep my body in shape. May I inquire what caused the fight?"

"I gave the guy a legal summons."

"I see," the stranger said. "At first I thought perhaps . . . you're not gay?"

"No."

"I thought not," the man said, slightly rueful. He smoothed the wings of hair over his ears. "You are aware of what goes on in MacArthur Park?"

"Yes, but I figure that's their business, not mine."

"And serving summonses, that is your business?"

"I hope so. It was my first. I just started this job."

"How interesting. You're young, and if you are going to stay in the process-serving business, may I recommend that you learn karate or one of the other martial arts of self-defense."

"You've got a point there."

"Allow me to introduce myself. Myron Moseby."

Carver gave his own name, and they shook hands.

Moseby offered to drive Carver to his car. As they walked out of the park, they talked, and Carver studied Moseby. He was a handsome man, with a straight nose and twinkling eyes. Slightly under six feet, very slim and trim, with muscles like rocks. Carver had felt them as Moseby helped him to his feet. Undoubtedly Moseby was a fruit, but Carver didn't think he was on the make.

They had arrived at Moseby's car, a Rolls-Royce.

"God" was all that Carver was able to say for a moment. "Is this yours?"

"Yes . . . my other car is a 'forty-eight Willys."

Carver laughed and climbed in. He relished luxury, the incredible smoothness of the automobile. Myron Moseby asked Carver about himself, and Carver gave a brief history of his leaving Detroit and coming to Los Angeles to attend college. His ambitions? Still unsettled, unfocused. His spare time? Carver spent a lot of time studying and going to concerts and museums.

"Really, dear boy?" Moseby asked. He parked behind Carver's borrowed car. He laid a strong hand on Carver's arm. "If you will allow me . . . I'm staying at the Biltmore, and I'd like to invite you to a party next week."

Carver gave him a dubious look.

"Oh, not to worry," Moseby said, chuckling. "I find you interesting, and I am a capricious sort. It'll be a good party, and you'll meet some interesting men—and women. Perhaps even a movie star or two. If you decide not to come, then I would appreciate your telephoning me."

Carver agreed, then shook hands. He left the Rolls-Royce, with an envious backward glance, and drove off in Joy's VW.

A week later he attended the party and enjoyed himself hugely. He felt somewhat out of place but Moseby assured him that slacks and sport coat were just fine. For a brief exciting moment, Carver ogled the bountiful buffet, the thick carpets, and was dazzled by the designer dresses and gowns. He forced himself into a casual attitude, as though he were not impressed by all this wealth and status.

But it was difficult to maintain a false front. Carver was introduced to Tony Musante and his wife, Jane, along with several other motion picture and TV actors. Across the glittering room, he saw Sidney Poitier talking with Ossie Davis and Ruby Dee. Vincent Price shook his hand and then strolled through the crowd. That was when Carver found out Myron Moseby's profession.

On the far side of the suite were four original paintings on easels. Carver recognized a riverboat painting by George Caleb Bingham and a disturbing subway painting of George Tooker's. Two other artists' works he didn't recognize. Myron Moseby was an art dealer, and this party was a way to introduce his latest acquisitions. Vincent Price held several guests in thrall with his analysis of the paintings.

Moseby explained to Carver, dear boy, that they were not for sale. Not yet. It was part of his usual strategy to whet the interest of potential buyers. Although he believed neither the Tooker nor the Hyman Bloom would sell easily.

Carver wanted to know why, and Moseby told him some of the prejudices against unknown or unpopular art and artists. Carver was fascinated, and Moseby sensed a kindred art-loving spirit.

Moseby's gallery was not in Los Angeles. He was driving up the coast on the weekend—would Carver be interested in joining him? Moseby laughed at Carver's discomfort and assured him that he had no desire to seduce him—only an interest in continuing Carver's art education. And the closest museums of any worth were four hundred fifty miles north of Los Angeles.

Carver didn't accept the first time, but he drove up with

Moseby months later. Once there, he accompanied Moseby to Puccini's *La Bohème*. It was Carver's first opera and it left him speechless. In the days to follow he savored the grandeur of the California Palace of the Legion of Honor and the de Young museum. Moseby enjoyed his new role as artistic mentor.

In Los Angeles, Carver continued to work successfully as a process server for Felix Rost at the Carrier Detective Agency. He knew that his life had changed for the better.

"Listen, kid," Felix Rost said after Carver had been working for a year, "you have a natural knack for this work. I like the way you figure things out, using your head. You should think about being a private investigator. You're good at it."

The jangling of the telephone jarred Carver Bascombe to the here and now. A drop of sweat fell off his nose, as he came back to the present. Yeah, stop the dreaming. Back to work. He reached for the phone.

"Carver, is that you?"

He recognized the voice.

"Yes, Magda," he said. "What do you want?"

"Have you heard anything . . . you know, about Lou?"

"Nothing I can tell you."

"Do you think I'll ever get my money back?"

"I doubt it, Magda," Carver said. "You never had an IOU or anything like that, a piece of paper or a receipt. Did you?"

"Nah, nothin' like that. Okay, smartass, I'll be talking to you." She hung up.

Now what the hell was that all about? Carver thought about it. Yeah, there was that black rock in the Piombo's hiding place. Yes, Magda Cantera sure pushed it back into the hole fast enough. A lucky charm, she'd said. And then six more in Piombo's studio. They meant something. Carver was positive of that.

He sat behind his desk and slid his feet out of his shoes. He wriggled his toes and rubbed his feet over each other. Ah, that felt good!

So there was a connection between Ferrik and Piombo, or why would someone try to hide Piombo's identity by putting Ferrik's coat over him at the Vaillancourt Fountain? The killer must've known Piombo's identity couldn't be kept hidden for very long.

And there was Frank Argent. He was probably the black man Magda had mentioned seeing with Piombo. So Argent and Piombo were in on something illegal together. And who else? The killer? What was this? Thieves fall out?

He looked up when the telephone rang. Carver wondered who it might be—and chuckled. Probably Sharon Argent. Better brace himself for a chewing out. He picked up the phone on the third ring.

"Carver Bascombe?" a man asked.

Carver didn't recognize the voice, but a sudden chill ran down his spine; he knew who it was before the man identified himself.

"This is Tom Ferrik," the man said.

FOURTEEN

The voice was a baritone, intermingled with static from the telephone. The man sounded anxious.

"You're a hard man to contact. I've phoned, but you haven't been in your office much."

"How do I know you're Ferrik?" Carver asked.

"Oh, yes," the man said, "I was told you might be cautious. You've seen Amber?"

"Yes." Carver waited.

"She has faint scars on her back."

"Not good enough. Somebody else might have seen them."

"I see. Then we are in a predicament."

"You made it when you ducked out on Amber."

"Then you believe I am Tom Ferrik?"

Carver moved a hand over his face; it was wet with perspiration. From the heat of the day?

"Maybe. Why did you run out on your daughter?"

"I had to. My life was in danger. Hers was not." He paused. "At least I didn't think so. Not at that time. Mr.

166

Bascombe, after that shot came through the window, I ran out so fast I didn't stop for anything. I knew Amber could take care of herself, and I phoned and told her to go to you. For protection. She's a very good survivor for a girl her age.''

"Yeah. Go on.''

"That's all. I want you to make sure she is safe. I'll be able to handle any fee. You have no fear on that.''

"Wait a minute,'' Carver said harshly. "I want to know why you didn't take her with you.''

"I guess there's no harm . . . Because she would slow me down. She would be too conspicuous. I've been running from cheap hotels to flop houses. No, taking Amber would've been terrible. . . .''

"Okay, Tom. Why did you send her to me?''

"I'm a friend of Gwen Norris. You remember her?''

Carver sucked in a breath of air. Oh, sure, he remembered Gwen. From time past. A lot of it seemed to have been washing over him in the past hour.

"Gwen is an old friend,'' Ferrik continued, "and she told me you were a man to be trusted. She was a godmother to Amber after she was born.''

Carver barely heard the words. He squeezed his eyes closed, then slowly opened them. A mild exorcism.

"What's going on, Tom?'' Carver asked. "You can't leave us in the dark.''

"I have to,'' Ferrik said, sounding sorrowful. "I can assure you that it will be over in—'' Ferrik caught himself. "It'll be over soon.''

"How are you involved? Maybe we can help.''

"I'm not really involved, and you can't help me.''

"If you're not involved, then what harm—''

"Because!'' Ferrik said angrily. "Because I know what is going on.''

Carver was silent, and then he spoke one word loudly. "When?''

"When is the—" Ferrik paused. "Forget it, Mr. Bascombe. Nice try. It'll be over soon. Please make sure that my daughter is safe."

"You've read the papers?" Carver asked, keeping the conversation going, hoping to catch Ferrik in a slip. "About the attack in Golden Gate Park?"

"Yes, of course. It's been on TV. And I thank you from my soul. God bless you and your secretary. But, please, don't take Amber outside again. Not until this is all over. Then I'll meet with you."

"Look, Tom, there's more to this—"

The telephone sounded a click and then the line went dead.

Slowly, thoughtfully, Carver hung up. His fingers twitched on the desk. He forced them still, then wiped the sweat from his brow. A tiny, rueful grin flickered over his face.

The day was rapidly fading; the streets were shadowed in warm gray colors. The heat still shimmered, and belching city buses added oily smells to the humidity.

He could very well just leave the Ferrik case alone. He could camp out at Rose's house, play patty-cake with Amber. That's what Tom Ferrik wanted him to do. Let the police turn the case upside down. Ludlow would probably solve it. At any rate, whatever was happening would be over. Ferrik had said so. Yeah, just let the cops fix everything.

The secret creature deep inside him just laughed. Oh, no, none of that! The trail was hot! The case was sizzling! There would be no rest. Carver would go on until he dropped from the heat of the hunt, the chase. And he'd love every second. Dwelling on the past paid few dividends; it interfered with the aim of the bow, the sight along the barrel, the lighting of the fuse. The amused voice of the huntsman spread throughout his body and mind.

First, a simple dinner here in the office, and then a good night's sleep. Tomorrow would find him on the highway to the Sierra mountains.

FIFTEEN

Twisting heat waves warped the highway, as though some evil one had melted the road, then stirred it with a black-magic wand. Sergeant Ludlow squinted against the bright shimmer, concentrating on his driving. Sergeant Stein kept one beefy arm out the passenger window. Trails of sweat trickled down their faces, silvery in the harsh morning daylight, like paths of snails.

"How far?" Sergeant Stein asked.

Ludlow grunted.

"That far, huh?"

"Another couple miles," Ludlow finally said.

"Hey, don't let me spoil your concentration."

Again Ludlow grunted and didn't say another word until they came to the turnoff. The sedan bumped over rutted roads until it stopped.

"Dead end," Ludlow said.

"No shit," Stein commented as they climbed out of the car. "Why, I thought you could just drive into the ocean."

"You're not funny, Stein," Ludlow said.

They hooked their badges onto their belts and left their coats on the front seat. Ludlow locked the car, knowing the car would be an oven when they returned. They started off down a path that led to a run-down house. Ludlow took off his hat and wiped his brow.

"Whatta ya think, maybe there'll be a beer in this guy's pad?" Stein asked.

Ludlow winced. Pad? Did they still use words like that? Or was Stein left over from some older, artsy-fartsy, Bohemian generation?

A violent explosion rammed into the air!

Ludlow dived for the sand, while Stein flopped into a clump of dune grass. They watched as a dark, oily cloud climbed into the sky. Stein moved first, clumsily, but going forward. He came to the crest and squatted.

"What the hell?" he muttered.

In front of them, on the beach fifty yards away, a stocky man stood near a still-smouldering hole in the sand. A table-sized sheet of metal was in the hole, bent and creased in odd shapes. The man used gloves to pick up the metal and look at it. He smiled, running his hand over the indentations and creases in the metal.

"I say again," Stein said, "what the hell?"

"Come on," Ludlow said, stepping off the crest toward the beach, "we're not going to find out just standing here."

As they trudged on the hot sand, the man on the beach noticed them. He waited for them.

"Well, gentlemen," the man said when the two men were close, "what do you think?"

He held up the bent and creased metal.

The man was in his late twenties, early thirties, Ludlow guessed.

"A little polishing," the man said, admiring the metal, "and it'll be just what I wanted." He looked at Ludlow, then at Stein. "You men are police." He didn't say it as a question but as a statement.

"Just what the fuck are you doing?" Stein asked.

"Are you Elliot Herd?" Ludlow asked.

"That's me," Herd replied, "and I'm working on a sculpture."

"It's against the law to set off explosives," Stein said.

"You're in San Mateo County, officers," Herd said with a smile, "and I can set off all the explosives I want. This is my property—"

"Private property don't mean shit—" Stein started to say.

"—and I have a permit," Herd finished. "Now what?" He looked at each man, a challenge in the question.

"Let's see the permit, Jack," Ludlow ordered. He held out one hand, the other on the butt of his holstered revolver.

"Oooh, you don't have to reach for that," Herd said playfully. "As a matter of fact, I don't have it on me. It's in the house."

"Jesus, Ludlow, the guy's got a lot of nerve. Gotta hand him that."

"It's true," Herd stated. He paused. "About the nerve."

Ludlow grunted and pointed the way to the house. Inside, Herd offered them beer. Stein grabbed his bottle and gulped down several big swallows. Ludlow thanked the sculptor and took a swig. Herd pointed to a row of framed permits on the wall.

"That's them," he said, "duly authorized by the State of California and the County of San Mateo. Blasting powder permits and a permit to blast on my property."

"Why, Jack?" Ludlow asked, sipping at his beer.

"That's my artistic process for making sculptures. An act of creativity unique in the annals of art. See, I'm after shapes you can't make by hand. Look around," he said, his arms sweeping the large room.

Weirdly bent and shaped pieces of metal of all sizes were

on pedestals. Several of them were turning on motorized bases. The dazzling sunlight came down through skylights and glared off the artworks. The sculptures suggested the shapes of the wreckage of war or the gigantic blossoming of some mutant flowers. Others seemed to be just abstract shapes, ugly, grotesquely bent, and defying description. They existed for their own sakes alone, a statement about controlled destruction.

Most of the pieces were unpainted, highly polished, with designs made by tool marks. Several pieces had been left to rust. A few pieces had been painted in bright colors, some glossy lacquered, another flat black. One was the color of arterial blood.

"What are they supposed to be?" Stein asked.

"Symbols," Ludlow offered, almost grunting the word.

"Close enough," Herd said. "Let me tell you how I do it. When I get the idea for a piece, I sketch it out roughly on paper, and then—and then I take an appropriate sheet of steel or aluminum down to the beach. I don't bring the sketch with me, having it in my head, but mostly because I don't want to be tied down to a preconceived idea. It's sort of a blueprint in my mind.

"Then I dig that design in the sand, cavities, snaky ridges, all kinds of shapes, depressions, and whatnot. Then I put the sheet of metal on top. Placing it just right is a real skill. Then comes the fun! I put plastic explosive on the metal, figuring out just how much goes where. Now that's a real art."

"I get it!" Stein exclaimed. "When it's just the way you like, you set the whole thing off. The blast forces the steel down into the holes, and the design is done. Right?"

"That's the way," Herd said. "It's a hell of a damn sight faster than cutting with a torch and welding—or beating the hell out of it with hammers. Oh, sometimes I've planned a piece that took more than one sheet, and then I weld the whole faloofa together. But I really like seeing how complicated I make things just in the sand. Different textures, too. Sometimes I put seashells and driftwood or rocks and seaweed in the hole. Very interesting results. Even the sand itself gives different textures, depending on whether it's wet or dry.''

"Okay, Jack," Ludlow said, "enough of the art lesson."

"Of course. I didn't think you came down to buy one of my sculptures. What's up?"

"You were a friend of Lou Piombo's?" Ludlow asked.

"That I was. Sorry to hear he was killed. Any idea who did it?"

"Sonny," Stein said, "we were hoping you could tell us."

"Why would I know that?"

"You were a friend of his," Ludlow said, "and maybe you knew his other friends?"

"Some of them. Hell, fellas, let's not banter about. I want to get back to work. Lou's friends were not good for him. Lou was in the jug, you know. . . ."

"We know," Ludlow replied.

"Okay, so he met guys in jail—and they came around to Lou's studio when I was there. One guy in particular. Zinn was the guy's name, Ed Zinn. Do you know him?"

"Yeah, Jack, I know him," Ludlow said. He closed his eyes and let his memory flip through mental file cards. The facts came rapidly to mind. "Not a very nice guy."

"I agree, Lieutenant—"

"Sergeant," Ludlow said, "just sergeant."

"And then I also met another guy named Cholly Lehm."

"We know him, too."

Herd gave them several other names, and Stein scribbled them into his notebook.

"We'll check them out," Ludlow said. "Any others?"

"None that I can remember."

"Swell. Now what about you? Didn't you help Piombo in some of his scams?"

173

"Never! If I had, my blasting license would be in jeopardy. The state could revoke it for almost anything. Hell, I don't even drive if I've had more than two beers. I need that license to create."

"How'd you meet him?" Ludlow asked.

"He heard about me, about the way I worked, and he was interested. He came out here, oh, I guess it was about three years ago. He was frank about his past, and I sure didn't hold it against him. His little art schemes didn't interest me, and I didn't see any big money in them."

"Yeah, Jack?" Ludlow said dubiously. "What do you call big money?"

"My sculptures sell for . . . How much money do you make, Sergeant?"

Ludlow told him and Elliot Herd chuckled. He earned over twice Ludlow's annual salary for one piece.

"And that's when I'm hardly trying. Why, once, I contracted for a one-man show in Dallas, twenty pieces, and I blew them up in one weekend. I even invited the police department and the district attorney's office to come out and watch. You should have seen it! On a Saturday I had the whole beach covered with designs, and I blew up sheets of steel one after the other. Bang! Bang! Bang! Just like that. On Sunday I spent the day polishing and painting. I had an assistant who helped. That night I air-expressed the whole show to Dallas. Opened the next day."

"The show did well?" Stein asked.

"Sold every piece in two weeks. I took the rest of the year off and went to Europe."

Ludlow grunted. There wasn't anything more they were going to learn here. But they had one name that interested him: Ed Zinn. A real psycho, a killer, but never caught out. Zinn was lucky—and careful.

"Anything else, Officers?" Herd asked.

"Yes, indeed," Stein said. "Your explosives."

"What about them?"

"We want to see where you keep them," Ludlow said.

"I sure don't keep them in the house. Come on, out in back, I'll show you."

Herd led them outside to a dilapidated shack. He unlocked the padlocked door.

"See," Herd said, "caution to the point of paranoia. You'd need a tank to move this shack. And no one gets in without the keys and the combination."

The sculptor eased open the door. The shack was camouflage for a steel shed inside. Herd gasped and dropped his keys in the sand. The steel doors had been torched open, the molten metal like a gaping wound around the combination lock.

"Oh, my God," Herd stammered, "someone burned through my locks. . . ."

He pulled the thick steel door open. Inside were wooden crates.

"What's missing?" Ludlow demanded.

Herd grabbed a clipboard hanging by the door. Nervously he flipped through in-triplicate sheets. He went from box to box, checking the inventory of plastique and dynamite. He opened one large box—and stared.

"It's missing . . . gone!" Herd said in disbelief. He stared at Ludlow and Stein. He flipped through the inventory pages once again. He licked his lips. "Dynamite and timed fuses. Detonators."

"How much?" Ludlow demanded.

"Enough! More than enough to blow up a mountain!"

SIXTEEN

"It was a dirty trick, Carver," Sharon Argent said, "so you owe me one." She held up a hand, anticipating Carver's objections. Her eyes narrowed. "I'm going with you. I have to find Tom, and I think I can do that by sticking with you."

In the early morning heat, they stood by the Jaguar parked next to the gasoline pumps at the Hi-Valu service station. Sharon had a suitcase by her feet. Her eyes sparkled angrily like dark stones that had been polished in a mountain stream; they were shaded by a large floppy straw hat. She ran one hand nervously over her other arm. Her pale golden dress was radiant, the white bonnet a saintly halo.

"Listen to me," Sharon said, her words hard, almost spitting from her lips. "Someone killed my brother. Tom is missing. Maybe the two incidents are connected. Maybe not. Do you know for sure?"

Carver was deliberately silent; he wasn't about to explain his belief about her brother and Piombo scheming to do something crooked.

"Then I have to find Tom," she repeated. "Maybe he knows, maybe he doesn't. We know his daughter is in danger. And you're the only one who seems to be doing anything."

"The police—" Carver began.

"Screw the cops! They don't tell me anything. Obviously, I can't tag along with them. Not that I'd want to. Not with that racist—that Ludlow. I have to do something!"

Carver shook his head in disbelief; she was certainly persistent. And she looked fantastic, quite cool in the blazing morning light. Hammering away at her sculpture the day before hadn't diminished her anger or her grief.

"Sharon, you're still not coming."

"Don't fuck with me, Bascombe."

"No, you're not coming. Not a chance."

"Where the hell're they goin', Ed?" Cholly Lehm asked.

"East," Ed Zinn snapped back.

"Yeah, yeah, I can see that," Cholly said nervously. He squirmed in the seat of the stolen van as though he had to go to the toilet. "But how long do you think—"

"Christalmighty, I can't read their minds. I don't know where they're going! So far, over the Bay Bridge—and the Carquinez Bridge."

"Okay, Ed, okay. My bandage is makin' my shoulder itchy. And them two ain't stoppin' or nothin'. And Sacramento is the next big city."

"We'll tail 'em as long as we need to."

"Okay, yeah," Cholly said. He thought for a few minutes. He used part of the time to dig around in his nose. "I guess we didn't grab the dame 'cause you wanted to see where she was going?"

"Yeah. It's easier than trying to beat out of her. Especially if she doesn't know where he is, but that private dick might. Anyway, we'll just keep moving along behind Bascombe and Frank's sister."

"They might catch on we're tailing them."

"So we snatch another car or somethin'." He glanced at Cholly and slapped his hand away from his nostrils. "And stop that!"

Behind the Jaguar, the Sacramento valley shimmered and danced in the heat. The air was still, musty, and fevered. Ahead, Highway 50 rolled gently upward into the mountains. They were at the two-thousand-foot level. Carver kept the accelerator at a comfortable sixty MPH. The twelve cylinders purred easily. He had watched for any car tailing him but had spotted nothing; he'd relaxed since leaving Sacramento.

Sharon held on to her bonnet with one hand, a map on her lap, and chatted about her work. Carver listened with half an ear; her conversation sounded artificial. She had avoided mentioning her brother or what funeral arrangements she had made.

Before Sharon had showed up, he had called De Anza to ask him to put in a good word with the sheriff's department in Execution City. Sheriff Marvin Clay had called, stating that he had never heard of Tom Ferrik. Carver had told Sheriff Clay that he would be in Execution City sometime in the late morning.

"Placerville," Sharon said as they passed the old mining town. "Where do we turn off?"

"Ice House Road, just this side of Riverton."

"Oh, yes," Sharon said, looking at the map.

He didn't know what to make of his emotions. He felt ambivalent; on the one hand, Sharon would be sitting next to him for hours. On the other, she was engaged to Tom Ferrik. The more he saw of Sharon, the more intensely he felt about her. Did he really want to find Tom?

All around, the hills were brown, dried out, almost an inferno of tans, browns, and reds. The green trees seemed to droop in the hot air. The brush was parched, dead-gray; the sparse grass listless; the gullies and erosion scars, crumbly and dry. Even at three thousand feet the air was hot, as though the sun beamed more easily through a thinner atmosphere.

Steadily, the highway climbed. And then the turnoff. Carver slowed, holding his speed to about forty-five along Ice House Road. The trees and rocks closed in around them; the temperature was like a baking oven. The chrome on the Jaguar was untouchable.

In another twenty miles, they climbed another two thousand feet. They had passed a lake on their left but resisted the temptation to cool off with some wading; Sharon was determined to get to Execution City.

They pulled up at the sheriff's office. The main street was a dusty road, with old frame buildings along one side. The sidewalks were made of planks, and needed five hundred pounds of nails to cure their ramshackle condition. Sweat began to form on Carver's and Sharon's faces as soon as the car stopped.

"Come on, Sharon," Carver said, taking her hand.

"Why, it looks like something out of an old Bob Steele western. And look at the people."

"I saw them."

They walked hand in hand to the wooden walk. Her hand was moist in his, and he gave it a gentle squeeze.

The walkway was shaded by a wooden roof, with shafts of sunlight beaming through numerous cracks. Several older men stood in front of the general store, and others leaned against rickety posts. With slight variations, the men were dressed in khaki pants, gray work shirts, and dusty, heavy boots. Two very old men sat in chairs next to the sheriff's office. No women were to be seen, and no young men. The bystanders stared with undisguised interest at Carver and Sharon.

"I don't think I ever saw so many suspenders," she whispered. She held on to Carver's hand.

He smiled. He liked the feel of her hand in his, and he wanted to prolong the contact.

They entered the sheriff's office.

"Welcome, folks," a tall man said heartily. "I'm the sheriff. Marvin Clay's the name."

Sheriff Clay loped around the ancient scarred desk and shook Sharon's and then Carver's hand. He whipped off his battered hat and slapped at the dust on two chairs. He aimed a clattering fan in the direction of the chairs.

The desk, the chair, the man, were all of a kind: weather-beaten, lined, scarred, and no-nonsense sturdy and service-able. A tree burl might have been hacked off and whittled to create his face. Around his narrow hips rested an ancient leather army holster, showing the butt of a .45 automatic. His semimilitary-style shirt and jeans were colorless but might have been tan once. The jeans were jammed into dusty, scuffed boots.

"Make yourselves at home," he said, jackknifing himself back into his own swivel chair. He smiled and lit a cigarette. "You're the private detective. Carver Bascombe. Talked to you earlier on the phone."

Carver showed him his ID and introduced Sharon Argent.

"Yep, nice to know you, Miss Argent. Say, I'm going to call you Sharon and you Carver. Last names sound sorta formal, like we gotta ask permission to speak to people. You call me . . . Sheriff!" He laughed at his own humor. "Well, there's nothing I like better than meeting new friends. Sorta cuts down the monotony."

Sheriff Clay leaped to his feet, like a grizzled praying mantis.

"Goddamn—pardon my French, miss," he said, "almost forgot my manners. Hot out there, and I got some iced tea in the back. Won't be a moment."

As they waited for the sheriff to return, Carver moved

around the office and looked out of the dust-covered windows. The air seemed to clog in his throat.

Sheriff Clay returned with a pitcher of iced tea and three filled glasses. Carver and Sharon thanked him, and they clinked glasses.

"Why is this town called Execution City?" Sharon asked.

"Well, now . . . coming up Highway Fifty, you passed Placerville?"

She nodded, sipping the tea.

"In the Gold Rush days," the sheriff said, "Placerville was named Hangtown. You can imagine why."

"I presume they had a lot of hangings," Sharon said.

"Well, this little town here never had a name in those days. The old-time miners had to take care of claim jumpers their own way. Not too legal, I suppose. Used to be a lot of claim stealing then, what with all the gold mines and such around here." Sheriff Clay hitched one lanky leg over the other. "The miners figured they were too far from Hangtown to bring in the law. They had a sorta trial and then shot the claim jumpers. Rough justice all right. The town was soon called Execution City. Hangtown got respectable, called itself Placerville . . . but we didn't, I guess. Get respectable, I mean."

Carver let a few moments go by, sipping his tea. "About Tom Ferrik, Sheriff?"

"Like I said on the phone, never heard of the man. Not around here . . . although that doesn't mean much. There's a lot of territory out there. Now, out in front of the town is the south fork of the Rubicon River. And the Rubicon itself is one long river. He could be anywhere."

"My information is that he had a cabin near Execution City, close to the river. Which probably means the south fork."

"Like I said, can't help you, but that don't mean someone else can't. Like I said earlier, I'll introduce you around. One old mountain goat of a prospector in particular. A few others. Some might not want to talk to you. You two are a bit out of place. We don't see many Nee-groes hereabouts. As a matter of fact, you two are about two hundred percent more than we've seen in six or eight months.''

''Tom Ferrik had a black man for a cabin guest.''

''That so? I don't recall any white man with a Nee-gro friend.''

Sheriff Clay stood and finished off his tea with a lip-smacking sound. He stubbed out his cigarette, then gestured, as if gathering a crowd around him, for Carver and Sharon to follow him. Outside he looked at Carver's Jaguar and shook his head.

''Yep, that's one pretty blue car. But it won't do for climbing the roads we're going. Dabney, down at the gas station, can rent you a four-wheel rig. I'll come along and vouch for you. Just park that Jaguar in the shade and come along.''

Carver agreed, and in half an hour he and Sharon were in an off-the-road FWD truck following the sheriff's jeep. They drove for fifteen minutes along a rutted, twisting, boulder-strewn road. At a dead-end ridge they stopped.

''Can't go any farther here,'' Sheriff Clay said. ''From here, we walk. Sharon, you can stay—''

''No, Sheriff,'' she interrupted, ''I brought along some practical shoes in my bag. I'll have them on in a minute.''

''What're they doin' now?''

''Shut the shit up, Cholly,'' Zinn ordered.

He lowered the binoculars and leaned on the large boulder. Zinn wiped his forehead. He looked with naked eyes at Carver, Sharon, and Sheriff Clay. He let out a heavy breath.

''What, what are they doin'?'' Cholly asked.

''She's putting on a pair of shoes.''

''Huh?''

"Goddammit, just be quiet!"

Cholly Lehm shrugged philosophically. He looked at the white-blue sky overhead and scratched at his armpit. Gee, feel that, he said to himself. All oily an' sweaty. Yuck. Smells bad. Drivin' and walkin' around these mountains— what else could be expected? Sure works up a hunger.

"Come on," Zinn said, clambering around the large boulder he had used as an observation post. "I want to get closer."

"God, Ed, I can't take all this walkin' like this. My shoulder really hurts. Why don't you go on, and I'll—"

"Cholly!"

"Okay, okay."

As they clambered up the ridge, Carver could see the south fork of the Rubicon curving below them. Overhead the sky boiled, and he wished he had brought along some kind of cap. After twenty minutes of hiking and heavy breathing, they arrived at a cabin. A trail of smoke drifted from the rock chimney.

"Hey, Tilly!" Sheriff Clay called out.

The front door opened and a stocky, older woman stepped out. Sheriff Clay introduced Carver and Sharon to Tilly Lot, explaining their reason for coming to the cabin. Lot merely listened and stood erect, her large head thrown back, studying the visitors. Her hands were thrust into old corduroy pants; her shirt was freshly laundered and short-sleeved. She looked Carver over, blinking her eyes, then wagged her head toward the interior of the cabin, inviting them inside. She followed them in.

The main feature of the cabin was bookshelves: except for the fireplace, all the walls were floor to ceiling with books.

Tilly Lot gestured for them to sit at a homemade timbered table. She nodded slowly, her long gray hair waving gently around her. She blinked her eyes several times.

"Contact lenses," she explained. "In severe temperatures such as we have experienced in the past week, my contacts feel dry more often. Very important to see, for the eyes are sentinels high in the tower of man." She looked at Sharon and Carver. "When fortune smiles, it smiles wide, for it has brought you and the lady to my door. What can I do for you?"

Carver explained quickly, with Sharon voicing her own concern. Sheriff Clay added only what little he knew and then lit another cigarette. He threw the match into the fireplace.

"Tom Ferrik, hey?" Tilly Lot said. "A name that is not brought to mind."

"He's a sculptor," Sharon explained, "and often brought his daughter up here, a little blond girl. And recently he brought my brother here several times."

As Sharon talked, Carver walked about the cabin. In the far corner near the popping, crinkling fire was a pile of prospecting equipment: rucksack, pick, shovel, and several empty leather sacks.

He looked at the books on the shelves. Some books on minerals and engineering, but mostly books on philosophy. The works of Jack London, Katherine Mansfield, and Hart Crane were also prominent.

"They said," Sheriff Clay began, when Sharon had finished speaking, "that this Ferrik fellow and this Frank Argent, that's her brother, stayed in Ferrik's cabin near the river, probably near the south fork."

Tilly Lot nodded, her eyes opening, a grin growing on her weather-tanned and windburned face. Finally she cracked a big smile.

"Sure, I know him. So do you, Sheriff. Tom Irons."

"Irons?" the sheriff said. "That's him, Tom Ferrik?"

"Certainly. I guess you just never saw the black friend with him. I did, and spent quite a few hours at the cabin. The act of discussion is often a voyage of mutual discovery, and sometimes a journey harmful to prior conceptions. We discussed many things of interest to both of us." She turned to Sharon. "The cabin is only a mile or so from here, a hundred feet from the river."

"I didn't know Tom used a different name when he stayed here."

Tilly Lot laughed out loud. "Oh, yes, and it was obviously his little joke. Tom Irons, indeed! Humor is often best when limited to one's own appreciation."

"I don't see," Sharon started to say, then checked herself. "Of course. Ferrik. Iron. Pertaining to iron." She joined in Lot's laughter.

Her laughter was a good sign, Carver thought. He was pleased to hear it. Sharon expected to see Tom soon, and he hoped she wouldn't be disappointed. He wasn't sure about his own feelings.

"Come along, Mr. Bascombe and Miss Argent," Lot said, "and I'll show you the way to the cabin. I haven't seen Tom for a while, and certainly not in the past few days, but that means little since I haven't been hiking about the mountain much."

Tilly Lot led them out. She walked beside Sharon down a well-worn path, while Carver and Sheriff Clay strolled behind. The path took them through pine trees and scrub oak and manzanita brush. Scrub jays squawked at the four hikers. Lot kept up a running discourse on the mountains, their place in prehistory, and the legends, truths, and half-truths of the Gold Rush days.

"There it is," Tilly Lot said after twenty minutes of hiking.

The cabin stood on a sloping plot, with trees surrounding it. Leafy shadows fingered over a steep roof that covered the thick-planked exterior. In front was a half-porch. Sunlight seemed to add another dimension to the large cabin. Except for the gurgling of the river one hundred feet in front, the place was quiet.

All the windows and doors were shuttered, clamped with iron and padlocked. Electrical lines snaked across the trees to the rustic structure, but no telephone lines were seen.

In the back of the cabin, Carver could make out another smaller structure. Probably a studio, he decided. He'd seen enough sculptors' studios in the past few days.

Carver stopped and admired a tree stump that had been carved into an intricate abstract leaf, complete with veins and insect-eaten holes. Yes, this was Tom Ferrik's cabin.

The group went up on the wide porch, and Carver fingered the padlock.

"Boarded up and locked," Sheriff Clay muttered.

A sobbing sound made Carver turn.

Sharon Argent was leaning against a porch railing, her shoulders heaving. Coughing, gasping sounds burst from her throat.

"He's not . . . he's not . . . here!"

She sat on the steps and let the tears flow. Carver went to her and put an arm around her shoulders. He felt confused, at once glad that he could comfort her, hold her, and ashamed that he was glad that Tom Ferrik wasn't here.

Sharon shook his arm off, then walked blindly off of the porch. She went to the edge of the riverbank. She knelt and splashed her face with cold water. After a moment she sat on a boulder by the side of the stream and put her head in her arms.

SEVENTEEN

"How do we get in?" Tilly Lot asked.

"With these," Carver answered, taking out a leather folder of picks. "And," he added, "with the sheriff's permission."

Sheriff Clay nodded, and Carver picked the lock. Heated air whooshed out as the door opened. They stepped inside, but it had been obvious from the first look that the cabin was empty.

From the dark interior Carver watched Sharon sitting on the boulder next to the river. He moved around the cabin, throwing open drapes and opening windows. He used the lock picks to open the shutters and let in the light. Tilly Lot sat in a leather chair next to a small statue, a smooth bird in flight carved from granite; she rubbed her hand over the surface. Sheriff Clay poked about and found Ferrik's collection of videotapes; he looked at several and looked around for the television set and the VCR.

* * *

The river rippled, made gurgling noises as it swept languidly around rocks. The water whispered and chuckled over worn pebbles. Sharon looked, her eyes taking in the kaleidoscopic reflections of moss and dry scrub, of stones and sandbanks. All the sounds and sights seemed far away, incongruous and unreal.

Where was Tom? she wondered. Why hadn't he called her? Maybe she could help and maybe not; at least he could have asked. Was this a presentiment of how their life together might be? Didn't he trust her?

Or did Tom know something about Frank, about Frank's death? Was Tom trying to shield her? From what?

A flock of towhees chirped at her and beat a fluttering path to a patch of trees a quarter mile distant. A shadow moved gracefully over the parched land; high overhead, a hawk glided to and fro.

She plucked absently at dry twigs near her feet, snapping them in half, then in half again. She dropped the bits into the swirling water and watched them meander downstream. A nice pattern. How interesting, the overhead sun cast patterns on to the river bottom. Nature was the best sculptor, always with harmony, always asymmetrical, yet in balance.

Shudders passed through her body, and Sharon bit back throat-catching cries.

In the cabin, Carver looked through the bedrooms and the closets, and made a mental note to do a more thorough search later. Maybe Frank Argent left something of interest behind. He walked out of the cabin and down to the riverbank.

"I'm sorry," Sharon said, wiping a hand over her eyes. "I didn't expect to—to fall apart like that. I was so sure Tom would . . . that he'd be here. I was holding my breath so much, I wanted him to be here, to see him, to hold him in my arms."

Carver Bascombe shuddered. A dagger had slid between his ribs and nicked his heart. What could he say? Certainly nothing that would not reek of hypocrisy. He'd never felt like this before. He nodded and turned away from her.

Was he really trying to protect her? Wasn't that a patronizing attitude? He was almost glad that he hadn't found Tom Ferrik. But there was a tangle inside himself; the hunter deep down floundered in a morass of perplexing emotions.

Did he want to find Ferrik or not?

The answer did not come easily.

He had to get his mind on something else. He returned to the cabin and saw that Sheriff Clay sat in the front room, a beer in one hand, watching television. The VCR was on.

"There's beer in the fridge," Clay said, waving a hand in the direction of the kitchen. "Don't think Tom would mind if we took a couple. He was a friendly guy." He nodded at the TV. "Watching tapes of the old Ellery Queen show, that one with Jim Hutton. Good show, don't you think?"

"I wouldn't know, Sheriff," Carver said, "I don't watch many mystery shows. Might make me feel inferior." He turned to Tilly Lot. "She really wanted Tom to be here. Did you ever meet any of his friends?"

"I met his little girl, a perpetual feast of sweet nectar. And I met his black friend, Frank. A fountain of questions, a seeker of ease without endeavor."

"Yeah," Carver said.

Yeah, Carver ordered himself, keep talking, keep all those other disturbing thoughts away. At his age he should know himself a hell of a lot better. He looked around the cabin. Then he tapped the sheriff on the shoulder.

"Mind if I look around?"

"No, don't mind," Sheriff Clay answered abstractedly. He was absorbed in the TV show.

Carver prowled methodically about the cabin. He was particularly interested in the guest bedroom where Frank would have slept. In less than thirty minutes, he had completely searched the room's contents. In a wastebasket he had found a railroad timetable. A schedule was circled: 10:00. A train from the Townsend Street station to all stops along the San Mateo peninsula. Atherton was circled.

He was sure it meant something, and it tickled the back of his mind. Hadn't he seen something like this before? Was this the *when* that the man with the shotgun wanted to know? If so, why? The train was an ordinary passenger train.

He continued to search. In the main bedroom there were still clothes in cedar chests, several old shirts and pants in the closet, along with several dresses in brown and tan. And women's jeans. Otherwise the cabin yielded nothing.

Carver walked outside. More scrub jays chattered at him. Around the back he picked his way into the small studio that Tom apparently had built. It was about the same size as Alex Marteau's studio. Everything was neat, and the tools put away. Anything out of place was easy to see, and Carver found a small, black, painted rock on the floor. The same as the painted rocks he had found in Piombo's studio. What did it mean? He put the rock in his pocket and returned to the porch where Tilly Lot stood leaning against a post.

"Did you and Frank talk much?" Carver asked, and glanced at Sharon, still brooding by the riverbank.

"Oh, certainly. He had never been in the mountains. I'd say Frank was a typical city man, proud of man's skill in building cities, but divine nature gives us the earth and the elements. But he wasn't afraid of the outdoors. He was really fascinated."

"In what way?"

"We talked about nature, the ecosystem, trees . . ." She paused. "Mostly he wanted me to tell him about my specialty."

"What's that?" Carver asked, still watching Sharon.

"Gold."

Carver turned and stared at Tilly Lot.

"Gold interested Frank," the old woman continued. "For that matter, the yellow element was the main reason I came to these parts. Gold—bright and yellow, hard and cold. I was a prospector, eager to study gold, to know its history, what happened all around here, and the philosophical ramifications of gold fever."

"Go on," Carver urged, his interest aroused.

"You, too?" Lot chuckled. "Well, it's an interesting element, a metal that has no intrinsic value, the last corruption of degenerate man. For thousands of years, something that mankind has lusted for."

"I'm only interested in Ferrik," Carver said.

"Are you? Possibly. Frank Argent, he was very interested in modern gold mining." She pointed to the river. "See that river . . . well, a lot of gold hunting goes on in rivers hereabouts. And it's not as dirty as grubbing about in a mine, swinging a pick."

"There might be a connection," Carver said thoughtfully, "between Tom and Frank and gold hunting. It's slim, but it's a possible connection or motive. Tilly, please tell me what you told Frank Argent."

"I sort of gave him a history of the area—this was over a period of several days, you understand—and the difficulty the old miners had digging shafts in the mountain or placer mining—that's sluicing gold out of the hills with water." She nodded at the nearby river. "That's why the mines in the hills up yonder were located here. Miners found gold flakes and nuggets in the riverbed and realized the rains had washed it down from above. So they dug for the source. A lust that overpowers conquest's rage."

"That's all?" Carver asked.

"No, I told him that the old mines petered out."

"I'd like to take a look at one of those old mines."

"Of course," Lot said, "anytime you want. There's one

just back of this cabin, up the mountain. But there's nothing there. Damn few people mine the mountains anymore. Although nowadays some fellows still mine the rivers.''

"How?"

"They use suction hoses and snorkel equipment. A modern river miner rests on top of a rubber raft, with a motor driving the suction hose and sluice filters to catch the gold. They wear wet suits and float next to the raft and guide the suction hose where they think gold might be caught.''

"Where would that be?''

"In rocky bays, where the river curves in on itself. The gold is very heavy and sinks to the bottom in these natural catchalls. The river miners use long metal rods to probe the crevices.''

"Is it really worth the effort?''

"Does it bring honor, friends, integrity, or success? Or do you mean can they find enough gold to make a decent hourly wage?''

"Yeah. Enough money.''

"Some do, most don't,'' Lot said. "I've known a few college men who made enough out of the Rubicon in one summer to put themselves through college, with enough left over to buy a new car.''

"Anything else that you told Frank?''

"That's about it, but of course, you understand, we went into great detail. He was not convinced that gold is no friend of man, that it corrupts and has no friend it does not betray.''

Carver nodded, thinking, wondering if any of this was going to help him find Tom Ferrik. He wasn't sure whether what Lot had told him was even a hint of a motive.

"Suppose, today,'' Carver said to Lot, "a person found gold in the river or even in the mines. What happens?''

"They'd sell it at the prevailing prices. An ounce goes for over three hundred dollars. Not too long ago it was more than double that.''

"They'd have to pay taxes, of course."

"Yes, but if they found enough, they'd be very wealthy."

Carver's mind churned. What if Argent had found gold? Where would he have found it? And if he did, where was it? Carver turned again to Tilly Lot.

"Would you know if Argent hunted for gold in the mines or the river?"

"Not that I know of. Probably not. Remember, you just don't wade into that river and poke around the bottom. You have to have equipment, a wet suit, snorkeling mask and tube, and a raft with a suction motor and hose. I never saw anything like that in Tom's cabin. He certainly didn't rent it in Execution City. No one around here has such equipment. And if there were, the town gossips would know about it real fast. A black man looking for that kind of equipment would surely stand out. And we never heard word one."

"What if he went somewhere else?"

"Closest place would be Placerville, and I'm not even sure he could rent it there."

Carver fingered the stone in his pocket. A hunch was building in his mind.

"How about digging for it in a mine? Wouldn't that just take a pick and shovel?"

"Yes, and probably some explosives. But I think I'd have heard something about it, from Tom if nowhere else."

"What about Tom?" Carver asked. "Was he ever interested in hunting for gold?"

"No, definitely not," Tilly Lot answered. "Tom's had his cabin for over ten years, and all he does here is read, walk around the hills, draw, and do what he calls meditating. And we almost never talked about gold. Why, I told Frank a hundred times more than I ever told Tom."

Carver mulled that over. He considered the time element: If Frank went digging in a gold mine or mining the river, when would he have found the time? He had only been here twice, and he had spent much of that time talking with Tilly Lot. Could he have returned to the cabin without Tom's knowledge? Or Sharon's?

If Tom knew Frank was gold hunting, and there was something somehow illegal about it, would that be enough to make Tom hide? And leave his daughter behind? Carver didn't think so. Would Sharon have any knowledge of what Frank was doing? If he was doing anything? But—dammit! Argent had to be doing something!

And, Carver now believed, Argent had to have planned it with Piombo.

"Miss Lot," Carver said, "have you ever met or heard of a man named Lou Piombo?"

"No, can't say that I have."

Carver nodded, rubbing his chin. He brought out the black rock. "Ever seen anything like this?"

Tilly Lot took the irregularly shaped stone and weighed it in her hand. "Pretty heavy," she said, "for its size."

"I noticed that. I've seen others like it. Did Frank—or Tom—ever show you anything like it? Or did you ever catch either trying *not* to let you see it?"

"Can't say that I ever saw it. Why is it painted black?"

"I've wondered that myself," Carver said slowly.

They looked at each other for long seconds—and then at the small black rock. Tilly Lot brought out her pocketknife, opened it, and scraped the paint.

Unconsciously holding his breath, Carver leaned forward, watching the curls of paint peel away. Dull metal gleamed beneath the paint. Tilly Lot dug at the metal. She fingered a small bit of it on the tip of her blade. She looked at Carver.

EIGHTEEN

"Lead," Lot said.

Carver repeated the word, then slowly shook his head.

"You see what talking about gold can do?" Lot said. "The lure of fortune's metal is often seen through hope's deluding glass." He continued to pick at the painted object. She scraped off more of the paint. "For some reason," she said slowly, "somebody mixed dirt and other stuff in it."

"I don't get it," Carver said, taking the lead stone and looking at it.

"I think you will, Carver," Tilly Lot said, her eyes narrowing. "You have the savage eye of the hunter, while I the serene patience of the noble spectator."

Carver's thoughts whirled furiously, trying to find some means to connect this painted object to Frank Argent. He had first seen one at Piombo's apartment. Six similar objects had been in Piombo's studio. Then one turned up in Tom Ferrik's cabin. Where Frank Argent had been a guest. That made some kind of thread running between Piombo, Argent, and Ferrik. Did Sharon Argent know anything about it?

He looked at Sharon, still sitting on the rock, thought about going to her but decided against that. He went inside.

"What're they doin' now?" Cholly Lehm said eagerly. "Lemme see."

"Knock it off, Cholly," Ed Zinn said, keeping the binoculars to his eyes. "They ain't doin' nuttin'. They're just going into the cabin. The dame is sitting by the river."

"Any sign of Ferrik?"

"Nah. He ain't here."

"What a waste of time," Cholly said under his breath. "Comin' all the way up here . . . for what? A waste of time."

"Shut up! What if Ferrik had been here? It was better than fifty-fifty he'd be here."

"Yeah, Ed, but he ain't."

"Shut up, Cholly."

A movement at the far corner of the scene caught Zinn's eye. He moved the binoculars. His fingers were slippery with sweat.

"Hey, hey," he said softly.

"What?" Cholly asked, eager again.

"There's somebody way behind the cabin, in a car, some kinda jeep, maybe one a those four-wheel jobs."

"Ferrik?"

"Maybe. Can't tell from this far. Car's parked among some trees. Could be a man or a woman."

"What's he doing?"

"Hidin' an' watchin'. Same as us."

Seeing Sheriff Clay drinking his second beer made Carver thirsty. He got beers for himself and Tilly Lot.

"How about one for me?" Sharon asked. She stood in the doorway, looking assured, her eyes dry, the redness gone.

Carver handed her his and got another for himself.

She assured Carver that she felt better. At least she knew Tom was still alive, somewhere, and that was enough for now. She was attracted to the VCR showing and sat watching, sipping her beer. Carver mentally went over each of the events of the past several days.

He shrugged. Another thread that tied things together was that many of the people he had met were sculptors. But then if he had been looking for a doctor, he would probably have met a number of physicians. Wouldn't he? Carver rubbed his chin, fingering the scar cleft.

Hadn't he read somewhere about some kind of scam about gold? He took his mind back. Yeah, salting a mine. What was that all about? Maybe Tilly Lot would know.

"Miss Lot—"

"Please, Tilly."

"Okay, Tilly . . . isn't there something called salting a mine?"

"Yes, there was. And I suppose there still is, but not just in gold or other precious metals. It's been done with variations with petroleum, vegetable oil, even crops."

"How does it work?"

"Simple. In a worked-out gold mine, new owners come along and try to prove to potential investors that there are still rich deposits in the mine. They plant a small amount of gold as proof and claim other diggers missed gold-bearing veins. Then the investors buy stock in the mine."

"Yeah," Carver said, drawing out the word. A hazy idea was forming in a pocket of his mind.

"Today, of course," Tilly said, "the con artists con the banks and stock and bond houses with faked documents that show an inflated value of goods in storage. That's modern-day salting. Years ago, the Billy Sol Estes case was like that.

Millions of dollars borrowed, or taken from investors, in non-existent vegetable oil in storage tanks.''

"I want to look at the mine shaft."

"All right, Carver. When?"

"Right now, while there's plenty of daylight."

Sharon turned from the television set.

"I've been listening—"

"I'm sorry, Sharon," Carver said. "I hope your brother—"

"He wasn't doing anything crooked!" she exclaimed. "Frank wasn't like that. But if you're going to look into an old mine, then I'm going with you."

Carver sighed; he'd lost several arguments with Sharon Argent and he knew he would lose this one. He agreed.

"Go ahead," Sheriff Clay said. "I'm going to stay and watch Ellery catch the killer."

"He always does," Carver said.

"Hey, Ed," Cholly said. He had the binoculars.

"What?" Zinn asked, munching one of the sandwiches they had brought along.

"They're moving outta the cabin. Three of 'em. The black dick, the dame, and the old gray-haired lady."

Zinn squirmed alongside Cholly and peered over the top of the rocky outcrop.

"Where the hell are they goin'?"

"How the fuck do I know? Where's the other guy?"

"The one keepin' outta sight?"

"No, asshole, I mean the guy who's gonna give us a million dollars for winnin' a lottery. Of course I mean the guy who's hiding."

Cholly looked through the binoculars.

"He's following them, too. Keepin' to the trees, outta sight. You wanna follow 'em, too, Ed?"

Zinn nodded, stuffed the sandwich into his pocket, and scrambled off the ledge. Cholly Lehm took a moment to grab the canvas pack with the water and sandwiches. He followed Zinn.

Trickling water echoed off the walls. Cool air pushed past their faces. Flashlights illuminated the rough floor and rusted narrow rails for long-gone ore carts. Splintery ancient timbers looked too weak to hold up the roof beams. Dust trickled down with each footfall.

The mine tunnel was rough-hewn from rock, with four-by-four uprights and angled beams every five or six feet. The timbers upheld crude supports overhead. Rotted timbers groaned holding back ancient earth. Dust still sifted down. All around was the blackness, the dust, the dank smell of rotting wood, the foul odor of slimy water seeping through myriad cracks in the walls.

"At least it's cool," Sharon said. She shuddered and stayed close to Carver Bascombe. Tilly Lot was in front of them.

"As you can see," she said, "there isn't much to see."

"Would you recognize signs of salting?" Carver asked.

"Oh, possibly," the older woman said. "But they would never put it so close to the entrance. Fortunately, this mine has only one tunnel. Many of them have three or four branches. Might take a week to look at all that."

They went farther, walking slowly, sweeping their flashlights over the walls, onto the floor. Would he know what he was looking for if he saw it? Carver wondered. Would Tilly Lot?

They came to a wide area, the walls lined with stacks of old timbers. Several dusty storage boxes were along one wall. Old leather harnesses and canvas bags were draped over the boxes.

"This is a storage area," Lot explained, "so the miners wouldn't have to go all the way back to the mine entrance. They put a lot of shoring timbers and tools here." She pointed her flashlight to the ceiling, the oval light pattern showing a foot-wide crack. A cool draft could be felt. "There's a natural narrow crevice that goes to the outside, so the miners got air. This was a logical place for the storage area. If you crane your head just right, you can see a small patch of blue sky."

"But no gold," Carver said. "Nothing that looks like it might have been tampered with. Sharon, I guess this has just been a waste of time."

"Carver, this place scares me," Sharon said. She shivered and hugged herself, the movement causing her flashlight beam to swing wildly, casting distorted shadows of Carver and Lot onto the walls and beams.

Suddenly there was an explosion! A wall of noise enveloped the trio. Their eardrums were assaulted by the sound. Support timbers split, shattered; earth and rock tumbled down, shrieking and crackling.

"Run!" Tilly Lot shouted, swinging her light farther into the mine.

Boulders fell from overhead, roof beams cracked and fell into their path, choking dust covered them, their flashlight beams slicing through the cloud like searchlights in a gray storm.

Carver grabbed Sharon's hand, and they followed Tilly Lot. They stumbled, tripping over rocks rolling in their path, and dodged falling beams. Sharon screamed. In seconds their clothes were in tatters, and they were cut and bleeding on their faces and hands.

The walls shivered, and a blast of superheated air blew down the length of the tunnel.

The floor rumbled, sagged, then fell apart under their feet. Carver tried desperately to hold on to Sharon. He grabbed at a railway beam, trying to lock his arm around it. He swung frantically, unbelievingly, into empty space—there was no floor beneath his feet.

Carver dropped his flashlight. In a nightmare of slow motion, the falling flashlight's beam slicing through the dust, he saw Tilly Lot disappear through the floor. Beams and debris fell all around him. Carver lost his grip and Sharon shrieked. They fell into blackness.

NINETEEN

"Jesus, Ed!" Cholly yelled. He dropped the sandwich he had been eating. "What happened?"

"That guy we saw—he followed them into the mine—he just blew up the mine shaft!"

Zinn clamped the binoculars tightly to his eyes. He ignored the trickles of sweat that dripped off his face. He licked his lips, tasting salt. What a blast! Nobody could survive something like that.

He swept the glasses over the face of the hill, catching a glimpse of the figure carrying a satchel. Probably a detonator, Zinn figured, maybe more dynamite. The figure clambered down the hill. Zinn shook his head in admiration. The guy must've had a hell of a load of dynamite to make a blast like that! Zinn dipped the lenses to the cabin and focused on the sheriff running out of the door. In seconds the sheriff was running toward the tunnel entrance a half mile distant.

Zinn refocused on the other figure, loping down the hillside. Out of sight of the sheriff. Zinn grinned, then caught himself. With Carver and Sharon blown to bits, he had no one else to follow. Unless—unless he followed the dynamiter. Sure, that was it.

"Come on, Cholly, back to our car."

"Hey, what's the hurry?" Cholly complained but moved his bulk after Ed Zinn.

"That blast must've killed Bascombe and Frank's sister. Come on."

"Okay, okay," Cholly said, huffing and puffing. "They're dead, so what's the rush?"

"We'll follow the one who set off the dynamite."

"Hey, that's not bad. Or is it?"

"Yeah, it's good. I think I know who it is."

"Hey, yeah? You do?"

"Yeah. Pretty sure."

"Okay!" Cholly said.

They reached their stolen car and Cholly started the engine. Zinn slid in beside him.

"Okay," Cholly repeated. "I get it. This guy, you think maybe he killed Piombo?"

"Yeah, I'd bet on it. And—"

"Yeah, I get it, this guy knows when!"

"You got it, Cholly. He knows when."

TWENTY

One beam shone through the blackness.

Coughing and retching, Sharon Argent crawled painfully toward the light. The other flashlights were out. Probably broken. She choked back a rising horror. She picked up the one working light and shined it around. The beam fell on Tilly Lot, hesitated, then deliberately moved away, searching. The light swirled on to Carver Bascombe. He was quite still.

Sharon moaned and her teeth chattered. How could she be so cold? Sharon fought the terror that lay waiting. She was going to die. She knew that. Carver and Tilly Lot didn't move. They were already dead. She knew that, too. She sobbed fitfully for a few seconds. The light bobbed up and down, throwing grotesque shadows on the damp walls.

Where was she?

She crawled over fallen timbers, puddles of greasy water, and loose, bone-stabbing rocks. She reached Tilly Lot. A heavy timber lay across her chest. Sharon bit her knuckles and tried to move the beam. It was too heavy. There was just enough room to press her ear to the woman's chest. Oh, God . . . Nothing. Sharon put her ear to Lot's nostrils, hoping to catch a faint breathing sound. Again, nothing. She turned back Lot's eyelids and shined the light into them.

Tilly Lot was dead.

Was Carver breathing? She wasn't sure. Her own breath was painful, with a horrible stab around her chest. Fear. Had to be fear.

She crawled toward him, keeping the bobbing flashlight beam on his face. Oh, God! He was alive. Still breathing. Her free hand splashed into an icy puddle. Sharon kneeled, put the flashlight on the ground, aimed it at Carver, and felt for her purse. She couldn't see it. Probably buried somewhere. She ripped the front of her blouse into pieces and dipped two of them in the water.

At Carver's side, she patted his brow with one of the wet cloths. She laid it there and wiped his face with the other cloth. Carver moaned and the sound echoed, a phantom sound that seemed to come from many different directions at once.

Sharon moved to his other side. Carver tried to sit upright. She placed the light on a large stone between them.

"How do you feel?" she asked.

"Lousy," he answered.

Carver looked into the blackness. He picked up the flashlight and moved the light around. The effort made him gasp. Carver shined the light on himself. A splinter had sliced open his arm for several inches. Sharon handed him a dry piece of cloth. He pulled the splinter out and staunched the blood with the cloth. His forehead was badly cut, with blood streaming down both sides of his face. His body was banged and bruised. His chest felt terrible, as though hot swords twisted in his chest. Probably broken ribs.

He shined the light on Sharon; her dress and blouse were

torn to shreds, her skin cut, bloody, and bruised. Her hair hung about her face in a dusty mop.

He found another puddle and splashed water on his face. At least they wouldn't die of thirst. He helped Sharon clean some of the blood from her face and hands. He felt her body trembling. and there was nothing he could do for her. Carver shined the flashlight up and down. Where were they?

"That explosion," he said finally, "I guess it busted open some kind of seam under the floor and it collapsed. We went with it."

"Where are we?" she asked again.

"I don't know, Sharon. Where's Tilly Lot?"

"Over there. She's dead—and we're going to die," Sharon said, choking on her words. Tears glistened in the light beam.

Carver felt cheated, unable to help her—or himself. He clamped down his teeth and lips and forced himself to think, to figure a way out. Which led to the most important question: Could they get out?

"I'm all right," Sharon said finally.

Carver didn't like the way she sounded. But what did he expect? A touch of hysteria? Panic?

He stood and swung the light around; they were in a sort of pit, about ten feet across, the walls arching overhead. Twelve feet over their heads, Carver guessed. If the pit had been another ten or fifteen feet deeper, he and Sharon would surely have been killed.

Carver felt along the walls, stumbling over fallen debris, timbers, planks, and rocks. There were no openings, no other shafts. The only way out was high overhead.

"We're in the bottom of a pit," he told Sharon when he returned to her side. He sat on a large rock and looked at her. "I've got to save the batteries in this flashlight. Do you understand, Sharon?"

She nodded, saying nothing.

"I'm going to shut this light off," Carver said.

She nodded again.

The pit was plunged into total blackness. A soft sobbing came from Sharon. Carver reached out and put an arm around her. She spoke in disconnected syllables.

"We're going to die here," she said.

Sheriff Clay ran toward the mine entrance. Smoke and dust still billowed. He cursed loudly. He jerked his eyes around the hill. Damn! Whoever had done this had run by now. No time to speculate about the motive for the dynamiting.

He pulled a bandanna over his nose and mouth and went charging into the tunnel. Fifty feet into it, he stopped. Enormous boulders blocked the tunnel. He stared at the rubble. No way was he going to get past that. All around there were the still sounds of timbers creaking, groaning under the weight of the mountain above. More of the roof could still collapse.

He had to get help! But first he took out his .45 pistol and made sure the safety catch was on. He used the butt to strike the rocks and waited for an answering signal. He waited and listened. Struck again and again. Waited and listened. He heard nothing.

"Don't lose him, Cholly," Ed said urgently.

"I won't," Cholly said.

Zinn kept his eyes on the rugged road and the car about a half mile ahead. He figured the other driver would feel safe in about ten or fifteen minutes. Then they'd close the gap, get a look at the driver. Then—then by God he'd know who had killed Lou Piombo and had tried to kill the little girl. And blown that nigger detective and the black chick and that old bitch prospector to bits.

He chuckled.

"Whatta ya laughin' about, Ed?"

"Nothin', Cholly. Shut up. Let me think."

Anybody not looking into Ed Zinn's mind would think he

sympathized with all those dead people. That wasn't the case. He didn't give a damn one way or the other.

What a detective he made, Zinn thought. In just a few minutes he'd know who the man was. When he knew that, he would have the biggest score of his life. He'd know when— know when the gold was going to be shipped.

"Did you hear something?" Carver asked.

"What?" Sharon replied slowly. taking several seconds to answer.

"Sounded like someone . . . I'm not sure. Sounds of tapping."

Sharon said nothing, but after a time she began to cry softly. Carver ordered her to shut up, then silently cursed himself for letting the darkness get to him.

Then a thought struck him. They didn't have to worry about the batteries—even if the other two flashlights were broken, their batteries might be intact. He looked around and saw faintly the two flashlights lying on the floor. He started for them—and stopped.

He could see them! Damned faintly, sure, but he could see them!

Carver flicked his flashlight on, then off. He could still barely make out images: the timbers, Tilly Lot's corpse.

There was light! From somewhere!

Carver glanced around, then looked up. Yes, there it was, a faint speck of blue. Far overhead was a patch of sky. He flicked on the light and aimed it up.

Twelve feet overhead, the floor had broken through under their feet. The patch of blue was higher . . . above the tunnel floor. The air crack that Tilly Lot had shown them. The explosion must have widened it. A crack to the surface!

"Look, Sharon!" Carver said sharply. He pointed the flashlight to the ceiling.

Sharon slowly turned her face upward. Her eyes looked

lost, as a child's eyes might look by a parent's graveside. Carver jerked the light toward the speck of sky. Could she see it? She nodded, then crawled painfully toward him. He helped her to her feet, and they looked at the blue spot.

"But, Carver . . . But how do we get out?"

She looked around, the faint daylight illumination showing the walls, wider than either of them could touch, higher than they could reach.

"I think we can," Carver said.

He picked up one end of a timber, raising it to his shoulders. Pain seared through his chest; he grunted with the effort. Not long enough to reach the top, the tunnel floor, and not long enough to span the pit walls.

He explained what he had in mind, and Sharon understood quickly. Her face brightened.

TWENTY-ONE

The car that Ed Zinn and Cholly Lehm pursued turned onto the highway; Ed and Cholly followed at a discreet distance. Then slowly Cholly closed the distance.

"Okay, take a look, Ed," Cholly said, "a good look when we pass."

Ed Zinn rolled down his side window.

When the road was clear in both directions, they passed the killer's car. Zinn got a very good look at the driver.

"I'll be damned," Zinn said as Cholly gunned the engine and passed the other car.

"So. okay, Ed," Cholly said excitedly, "who was it?"

"You ain't gonna believe it. Cholly."

"I will if you tell me."

Zinn told him. Cholly smacked his lips. He believed it. And for Ed Zinn a lot of stuff fell into place. He wondered why he hadn't figured it out sooner. But now he had the big slice, the whole score. It was all his.

And Cholly's, too. Of course.

Zinn shrugged.

In Execution City, Sheriff Clay had gathered a dozen men and several vehicles. With great haste they set off for the mine. They took a back road that would get them in close to Tom Ferrik's cabin, the same road that Ferrik had always taken to get to his cabin.

At the mine entrance they clambered out, carrying ropes, picks, shovels, sticks of dynamite, and fuses. Sheriff Clay led four of them inside, men who were knowledgeable about mines and cave-ins.

One of the men, a tough middle-aged man named Gus Bietel, looked at the rubble. He shook his head.

"Not a chance, Sheriff," he said. "It'd take weeks to clear this stuff out. Might go faster if we could get a digging machine in here, but it's pretty tight."

"Where can we get one?"

"Probably we could get one freighted in from Colorado or Utah, with men who know how to handle it." Bietel rubbed his chin. "Maybe we could have one here tomorrow. Twenty-four hours, maybe."

"Okay, I'll go back to town and order one."

"Right, Sheriff. We'll just go ahead and do what we can. We might get lucky."

"Do you think . . . ?"

"That anyone in there is . . . ?"

"Yeah, that's what I mean," Sheriff Clay said.

Gus Bietel shook his head. Not a chance.

Sheriff Clay grunted, rubbing a hand over his mouth. He left in his jeep, while the remaining men went to work manhandling boulders and stones and timbers out of the tunnel. He had only gone a few hundred feet when there was a shout from the mine entrance. He stopped and saw Bietel waving to him. He turned the jeep around and drove back.

The four men were by the entrance, doubled over, coughing and choking. A cloud of dust hung at the mine. Pebbles bounced down the hillside.

"What happened?" the sheriff demanded.

"Another cave-in," Bietel gasped. "We all had to run like hell. The damned thing is rotten. I don't think even getting a digging machine is going to be of any use."

"Could we use dynamite, blast a lot of that rubble into smaller pieces?"

"No, Sheriff, that'd just bring more of that damned mountain down on top of us. And on top of anyone inside—if they're still alive."

"But you really don't think they are?"

"I'm sorry, Sheriff," Gus Bietel said, "I just don't see how anyone could live through that. No, those outsiders are dead."

"One of them is Tilly Lot," Sheriff Clay reminded Bietel.

"Yes, I know that. She's dead, too."

"You're probably right . . . but I'm still going to get some kind of help. Some real mine experts."

"It'll take time."

"I'll move as fast as I can."

"Do you want us to keep digging . . . that is, if any of the men will go in after this cave-in?"

"That's up to them."

Sheriff Clay returned to his jeep and drove back to Execution City. He didn't really know those two Negroes all that well, but that didn't mean he was the sort of man who would abandon them. And Tilly Lot was a good friend, one of the best in these parts. His throat choked on him. Well, goddammit, he'd have to see all three of them dead before he'd give up.

Grunting with the effort, Carver tilted the longest timber against the wall. He looked around the floor, gauging the length of the other fallen timbers. Were they long enough? Were there enough?

"Will it really work?" Sharon asked.

"Yes," Carver said.

One of them had to be positive.

He lifted the end of another timber, satisfied that it was long enough. Many minutes went by and Carver soon had a number of timbers stacked against the pit wall. They were of various lengths and they were heavy. He hoped Sharon could handle them when he needed them.

Despite his pants and shirt being torn to ribbons, Carver made sure he still had the black-painted piece of lead. He had knotted it into the lining of his pants pocket.

The air in the pit was plentiful, but Carver could smell his own sweat and the odor of blood. His mouth was dry. He smiled thinly at Sharon, then took the longest beam and wrestled one end against the wall, as high as he could. About seven feet. He took the lower end and raised it a few feet, still jamming the high end against the wall of the pit.

"Come on, Sharon," he said bluntly. "Get some of the other timbers under it. Come on, move it!"

Sharon pushed two pieces of timber under the high end. She used other shorter pieces for more bracing.

"Okay, Sharon," he said, "when I raise the other end, get some more pieces ready."

Using all of his strength, Carver lifted the end to his chest. Sharon shoved a timber underneath, and then the two of them slowly raised that beam as high as they could. When they had pushed the upright as far as they could, Carver jammed it against the wall. Sharon repeated the process of bracing it. The timbers held in place.

"It worked," Sharon said, disbelief clouding her voice. "You did it."

Trembling from the effort, Carver took deep breaths.

"Let's take a rest," Carver said. "We have a long way to go."

He sat down on the floor, his back to the wall. Sharon sat next to him and leaned her shoulder against his. The flashlight still put out light, but Carver removed the batteries and replaced them. He had removed the batteries from the other flashlights and put them in his pockets. Cold batteries die faster. Carver and Sharon rested for about ten minutes, then he said that was plenty. Back to work.

For the next half hour they worked patiently, resting often. Their sweating body smells filled the pit, mingling with the dank smell of water trickling down the walls.

Sharon tried not to think about their trap. Oh, God, she said to herself, this just has to work. She didn't want to die; not like this. Slowly dying of thirst or starvation. Tilly Lot's body was a constant reminder of death, of how close it was, and she tried to avoid looking at her. But she had to step over her from time to time to get more of the beams.

She watched Carver, who seemed oblivious of their predicament, as though this were only some kind of test that he had to pass. Damn! He must see that this was a death sentence. That someone had deliberately tried to blow them to bits. The thought made her head swim. She took raggedy breaths and managed to get herself under control.

Carver looked at their handiwork. The whole thing was a messy design, with one large timber as an overhead crossbeam, braced into place at both ends by many shorter pieces. Carver glanced often at the blue spot far overhead; it was a goal that kept him moving.

Using a leaning timber, Carver shinnied up to the braced horizontal beam. Carefully he crawled onto the crossbeam. Sharon wrestled another timber to him. He leaned it against the narrowing wall. She passed up more pieces, and he braced the leaning beam. He shinnied up; he was only a few feet from the hole they had fallen through.

They repeated the process, with shorter and shorter pieces of timber, some of them no bigger than tree branches. Carver moved slowly; he didn't want the whole thing to collapse. He didn't think he had the strength to do it all over again.

"Is there one more piece," he called down to Sharon, "about four or five feet long?"

She looked on the floor.

"No. We've used the last piece."

He sighed. He feared that his strength would fail him. He wanted to climb down and rest. But . . . He gritted his teeth and leaned across, his hands touching the dirt wall. Slowly he turned himself around and used his knees and legs as braces, holding himself in position.

His elbows and palms and knees were raw. His shirt was nothing more than a couple of torn sleeves held together by threads and scraps. He inched himself upward toward the tunnel floor where they had fallen through. He was close enough—he swung one leg up and hooked it over a sagging rail track. He scraped his knee on a shattered railway tie.

In less than a minute, Carver was once again in the tunnel. He called down to Sharon that he had made it. He kept the flashlight lit and dropped it to her. He made sure he still had the painted lead object in his pocket.

He poked around the wide area, avoiding the gaping hole in the floor. Several old boxes yielded picks, axes, and coils of rope. He dropped them to Sharon. He called to her to tie a sling around Tilly Lot's shoulders. When she called to him that she had, he asked her to tie another rope around herself.

Shortly, Sharon was beside him. She slumped and rested on the dirt floor. He also rested, and neither of them spoke. He looked up at the crevice that led to daylight. Yeah, he thought, the explosion had made it a hell of a lot wider. It had to be wide enough.

After a while Carver struggled to his feet. Oh, he was sore!

Stiff all over. They spent the next minutes hauling up the dead woman.

His next climb took about ten minutes. Again, with his back to the crevice walls, he used his knees and legs as braces. Sweat poured from every pore as Carver levered himself up painfully. Then he was out, his eyes blinking against the sunlight.

He dropped the rope and called to Sharon. When she was out, they lay back on the ground and stared at the sky. Following Carver's instructions, she had brought up the other rope connected to Tilly Lot. She looked at Carver, wondering if Tom could have done as well. But there was no escaping the fact: Carver had saved their lives.

After a while they became aware of voices, not far off. Carver stood and looked down the mountain, toward the mine entrance. From this angle he saw nothing. He urged Sharon to her feet and led her down. In minutes they saw a group of men at the entrance to the mine. Carver waved to them, not trusting his voice for shouting.

They must look a sight, he thought, all tatters and covered with sweat, blood, dirt, and mud-spattered from head to shoes.

TWENTY-TWO

"Thank you, Sheriff," Carver said.

"Did damn little," Sheriff Clay replied.

Two hours after climbing out of the crevice, Carver and Sharon were in Sheriff Clay's office. The rented truck had been returned and they had showered in the jail. Sheriff Clay had brought them denim pants and khaki shirts. Carver transferred the black stone (as he still thought of it) to his denims. Sharon looked gaminlike, with her pants and shirt about two sizes too big.

Tilly Lot's body had been hauled up and sent to the local mortuary in Placerville. Sheriff Clay felt the loss of his friend, and cursed silently and loudly.

"What I want to know," Sheriff Clay said, "is how that bastard came to dynamite the mine. How did he know you were going inside?"

"It was a target of opportunity," Carver said. "He was going to use the dynamite one way or another. He might've blown up the cabin or he might've wired up our cars. As for why . . . he probably thinks I know something or that I might learn something.''

"Wonder where the guy got the blasting stuff?"

"I have no idea, Sheriff," Carver said.

"Don't make sense. The city cops're looking into this case, too. This son of a bitch gonna go around blowing up all the cops?"

"He seems only concerned with me—or Sharon."

"Yeah, but the son of a bitch was ready for anything. Might have blown up a mountain pass down on top of us or something. Son of a bitch!"

Bitter anger filled the air of the office. He had Carver's sworn promise to keep him informed. The sheriff was another who wanted to see the killer brought to justice.

Carver and Sharon shook hands with Sheriff Clay and then drove out of Execution City. For the first few minutes of driving, Carver said nothing. His racing thoughts pursued a thread. He had been sifting through everything he had seen, heard, and learned. Around and around in his mind went the black-painted object made of lead. Was it at the core of Ferrik's disappearance? Or something else? Who wanted the other stones desperately enough to send those two hoods to get them?

Slowly, oh, so slowly, a motive formed. And the face of a killer.

"You haven't said much," Sharon said. "You have an idea, don't you? Don't you, Carver?"

"Yeah, maybe. Just let me think."

"You could do better if you weren't driving."

They stopped for coffee and sandwiches in Placerville. Sharon took over the driving for the last leg of the trip. Carver slumped in the passenger seat, his thoughts far from the heat of the day or the vista of the Sacramento Valley before them.

What about those timetables and maps he had found in

Ferrik's cabin? Weren't they the same as the ones he had seen in Frank Argent's apartment? Carver was sure of their significance. And there was something someone had said . . . something that didn't sound right. Someone had said—what? Then he remembered. The lie. Someone had lied. Yeah, that was it.

The knowledge made him shudder—but it finally made some sense.

He had a lot to do.

The return trip took about two hours, and shortly after sunset Carver had parked at the Hi-Valu service station.

"Now what?" Sharon asked as Carver opened the door to his office.

"Change out of these clothes, for one thing," Carver said. He pinned the timetable to the corkboard. He looked into Rose's office and saw several letters on the floor near the mail slot. He ignored them; no time for that.

"You know what I mean," she said harshly.

"Yeah," he said, and settled into his desk chair in his office.

"Well?"

"You're out of it," he said. He faced her, his hands flat on the desk. "Don't get cute and make all kinds of demands. You're out of it. I didn't find Tom Ferrik. He doesn't want to be found. And that's the end."

"Is that what you're going to tell Amber?"

"Not yet." He rummaged in his desk and took out Sharon's distributor rotor. "I'll take you back to your car."

"I want to go with you to see Amber."

"Goddammit!" Carver shouted. "Don't you listen? I'm not going near Amber or anyone else." He knew he was letting his fear get the best of him. Had to get himself under control. "You were almost killed today. So was I. Tilly Lot *was* killed. Just as easily, it could've been us."

Sharon stepped back from his outburst. She sat in a chair, gripping the arms.

"No," she whispered, "I haven't forgotten. I'll never forget it. But, Carver . . ."

"Don't say one word!" he ordered. "Just shut up. Sit there if you want, but don't expect me to jump any time you want something."

"You don't know what you're saying."

"Maybe not. But I know when to be scared. Someone doesn't want Tom Ferrik found. And they don't want me poking around—finding anything—or figuring out what any of it means."

"What have you found, Carver?"

"This for one."

He threw the lump of black-painted lead onto the desk. She came to the desk and picked it up.

"This?" she asked.

"And those," he said, biting down on the words and pointing to the timetable on the corkboard.

She looked at them, but they meant nothing to her. Sharon picked up the black-painted object and looked at where Tilly Lot had scraped away some of the paint. "What is it?" she asked.

"A trial run," he answered.

"A what?"

"A test to see if it would work. I'm sure of it. I've found others, but they were taken from me."

"What kind of a test?"

Carver shook his head. He looked at her and then went into his apartment and changed into clean slacks and a shirt. He picked out a lightweight jacket and brought it with him into the office.

"Accept it," he said. "I'm taking you to your car."

"And then what?"

"I'm going to come back here and get a good night's sleep."

"What?"

Carver shrugged.

"You don't give away much, do you?" Sharon said.

"Only what I have to."

He opened the office door and gestured for her to leave. They walked to the Hi-Valu and Carver drove Sharon to her car. Two parking tickets fluttered under the windshield wiper. Carver put them in his pocket.

"I can't stop you from tailing me," Carver said as he replaced the rotor into the distributor cap, "but I meant what I said. I'm taking a shower and getting a good night's sleep."

"But—"

"I'll say this once, Sharon. You were almost killed today, and all because your brother got greedy."

"No! Frank wasn't like that. I knew him. I know he wouldn't do anything like that."

"What you believe and what actually happened . . . two different things. Don't interrupt. He got in with some rotten characters. They killed him. Whatever they wanted to get out of Frank didn't keep him from getting killed."

"I don't believe you about Frank—"

"I don't give a damn what you believe. It's all going to come out in the end. I don't want you dead. You know how I feel about you."

"I think . . . that you think you're in love with me. But you know I'm in love with Tom."

"Yeah, who is—" He stopped.

He was about to say that Tom Ferrik was white, that Sharon would do better with her own kind. Was he actually going to say that? That's the kind of dumb thing Ernie Ludlow would say. Carver shook his head; he would never say it—but he thought it.

At that moment he didn't like himself much.

"You started to say Tom is what," Sharon said. "He's what?"

"Tom might . . ." Carver said slowly, ". . . might be up to his eyeballs in this."

Why had he told her that? Was he that jealous that he would lie to discredit Tom Ferrik? Wasn't he convinced yet that Ferrik was out of all this? That Ferrik had his own reasons for keeping out of sight? Why bother to heap suspicions on him?

Carver still didn't like himself at that moment.

"Then you know what this is—"

"I have a good idea."

"What are you going to do with it?"

"I'm going to think about it," Carver said.

She looked at him as she slid behind the wheel of her car. She started the ignition, still gazing steadily at Carver.

"You're not as scared as you say," she said flatly.

Carver didn't reply.

"You like this, Carver. Being a detective. I said once I didn't think I could understand a job where you distrusted everyone, never assuming a person is telling you the truth. I think something like that could destroy you. But you like it, don't you, Carver?"

"I'm good at it," he said.

"No, there's more to it. There's something inside . . . some drive, some kind of need . . . I guess I'll never understand it."

Carver nodded, not in agreement but in acknowledgment of her attempt to understand. He turned and went to his own car. He drove back to his office.

All right, Sharon could do anything, even trail him back to the office. It didn't matter. Had he warned her off strongly enough? Or was she the type who got her back up and did exactly the wrong thing? No sense of survival? Carver hoped she had gone home.

He rummaged in the refrigerator and fixed himself a cold salad and opened a bottle of chilled white wine. He sat at his desk and ate, his thoughts on Sharon, the black rocks, and the timetable. He was sure everything was going to happen in the morning. Or the morning after that.

For a long while, he stood by the open window and watched the traffic below. He listened to Sibelius's *Carelia Suite* and watched the sky turn dark. The city lights turned on, one after the other, like regimental fireflies.

He turned on the desk lamp and then went to the file cabinet. He took out the .357 Colt Python and spent some time oiling and cleaning the weapon. Finally he called Rose Weinbaum.

"Amber is fine," Rose said after Carver had asked her. "And the police still come by about every half hour or so."

"Have you heard from Ludlow?"

"About what?"

"Anything."

"No, he hasn't been here and he hasn't called. Should he have?"

"I was hoping he might want to check on you and Amber."

"Are you kidding, boss?"

"No. But then you know me, the eternal optimist."

Rose laughed. She asked him how things went in Execution City and he gave her a brief telling. She told him Mike Tettsui was still on duty. Did Carver want to talk to him?

"No, there's nothing yet," he said. "I'll call in the morning."

Carver hung up. He was ashamed to admit to himself that he didn't have the courage to tell Amber he had failed to find her daddy. He shrugged, attempting a futile indifferent state of mind. He finally went into the outer office and picked the mail off the floor. He sighed. Nothing from Sacramento.

He hated failure—and he had failed Amber Ferrik. She wanted him to find her father and he had failed at that. But he had another idea that might bring Tom Ferrik out of hiding. Sure, it was easy. Just find out who had killed Lou Piombo and who had tried to dynamite himself and Sharon Argent. Carver had an idea who was who and how to settle the whole case. If the cops didn't have it wrapped up.

He was tired. God, he ached all over. Every bone seemed to have been struck with a sculptor's mallet. Carver took a shower and then went to bed. For much of the night, he thrashed and turned, twisting himself into the single sheet he slept under. His dreams were chaotic, often of himself in some kind of deep, deep blackness he could not climb out of.

TWENTY-THREE

The ashtray jumped when Carver's fist slammed down onto the desktop.

"Dammit," Carver said. "This is no time to be cautious."

Bob Hutte wiped his brow.

"I think you're wrong, Carver," he said, "and even if you're right, there's nothing we can do now. We could call the police—"

"Tell me."

"I can't," Hutte said. "I just can't."

The two men were in one of the offices on the mezzanine of the foundry. The room was simply furnished: a couple of wooden desks, wooden filing cabinets, several straight-backed chairs. One telephone on the desk at which Bob Hutte sat. Light fought its way past dusty windows.

"Once in a while there's a point . . ." Carver said, hitting each word hard, ". . . a point when you've got to talk. If not me, then the police."

"I—"

"Tell me, goddammit."

The door opened and Karl Hutte stomped into the room. His thick eyebrows were twisted in anger, his hands knotted into fists.

"What is this?" he asked, his voice booming. "I could hear you from several . . . Why has this *schwarzer* returned? I do not want him here. *Nein*."

"You're going to be robbed, Mr. Hutte," Carver said.

"Robbed? Of what?"

"Dad—" Bob Hutte began.

"Gold," Carver said. "Gold that you're shipping to your jewelry foundry on the peninsula."

Karl Hutte stood, breathing hard. He looked at his son and then shifted his knobby stare to Carver Bascombe. He turned his eyes again on his son.

"How does he know this?"

"Dad, I didn't tell him, I swear."

"This is my business and I take the precautions."

"Yes, Dad, but this man, he's a detective and he knows."

"He is not a real *polizei*. So you tell me. He is a confidential agent. He cannot know. Impossible."

"Tell me, goddammit!" Carver demanded.

"You know how," Hutte began hesitantly, "some diamond merchants ship gems?"

Carver nodded and wiped his brow.

"They just put them in their pockets," Hutte explained, "and drive or take a taxi to the buyer. Or if they're going cross-country, they'll just put the stones in an attaché case and fly the airlines. No guards, no security, nothing like that. They don't want to attract attention. Sometimes the diamonds are in lunch bags. Very innocuous, you understand?"

"Yes, Mr. Hutte," Carver said impatiently, "I know about that."

Karl Hutte interrupted. "Do not tell him one thing more. Not one more word."

"Tell me about the gold," Carver demanded. "You don't ship gold in your pocket."

"Of course not," Bob Hutte said. "Our gold bars weigh twenty-five actual pounds. In gold troy weight, that's about four-hundred-forty troy ounces. We send two men, security men from a shipping firm, and they carry the gold in two reinforced attaché cases."

"How many bars?"

"Four. Two to each man. Over half a million dollars. They take it on board a train to the jewelry foundry in Atherton."

"I figured it had to be a train," Carver said. "Just whose crazy idea was this?"

"Nein!" Karl Hutte said loudly. "It is not a crazy idea. It is my idea, and I say it is so. My son thinks he runs things here, but this time I have my way. It is not crazy."

"Why use a train? That's what's so crazy."

"Because I say it is safe. *Ja.* We only have to ship about once a year. On a train two men can both be alert, not having to worry or concern themselves with driving. There are lots of people aboard. And of course a train cannot be forced off the road."

"All right, here's the jackpot question. When?"

"You mean," Bob Hutte said, "when do the couriers take the gold."

"Yes, dammit, when."

"Today. The couriers just left for the depot, about twenty minutes ago."

"Ja," Karl Hutte said smugly. "We have a little celebration, as we often do, a cup of strong German coffee, and they take the cases and walk to the depot."

"The station is only a couple of blocks—"

"I know," Carver said. He moved quickly to the door. "Call the police," he ordered.

He ran from the office, down the staircase, and out of the foundry. He had been right. This morning. Not tomorrow morning or the morning after. He drove the few blocks to the Townsend Street depot and jumped out. The ticket seller told him that the train had just pulled out. Carver ran back to the Jaguar. He pulled the timetable from his jacket pocket. The next station he might catch the train was at San Bruno. Carver flipped on the ignition, jammed the car into gear, and floored the accelerator.

He followed the line of least resistance, taking the 280 freeway south. He had less than eighteen minutes to beat the train. There were several stops before San Bruno, but they were only three minutes apart and there were many tunnels. He didn't think the hijacking would take place until farther along the route.

Sixteen minutes later he pulled into the San Bruno station. The train was just pulling out and Carver raced along the tracks, his feet slamming on the gravel. He caught the last car and swung himself on board.

The dusty, gray cars swayed, and Carver spent a moment getting his balance. Before crossing the connecting vestibule, he made certain his revolver was secure in its shoulder holster. He was sweating, even in a lightweight pale beige seersucker jacket. He removed a five from his wallet and held it in his hand. He didn't want to take a chance on letting a conductor see the gun.

Carver began methodically searching each car. He didn't know what the two couriers looked like, so he'd just have to keep his eyes open. He couldn't skip any of the cars since he was also looking for someone who was going to hijack the gold. And Carver was fairly certain who it was going to be.

The first car was a zero. There were few passengers since the morning commute was in the other direction. The carriages were double-deckers, with narrow metal steps to the upper deck. The second car was only half filled. Carver moved carefully, scanning each face, waiting for a face hidden behind a newspaper to come into view. The air inside was stuffy, even with many of the windows opened. The smell of stale cigarette and cigar smoke seemed to hang in the air.

A conductor wearing a black wicker cap stopped him. Carver paid for a ticket to the end of the line. He continued on to the next car.

The next stations were Millbrae, Burlingame, San Mateo, Hayward Park, and about a half-dozen after that to Atherton. He paid little attention to the passing view. Alongside the tracks, weeping willows drooped in the heat, eucalyptus trees gave little shade, and acacia trees were more like dead, dusty bumblebees. In between the small towns were streets lined with used-car lots, industrial parks, ready-mix gravel works, and banks, lots of banks.

Carver slid open the doors to the next vestibule—and a man came down the metal steps.

"Freeze, Bascombe," a voice said.

Carver recognized it.

"Sure," Zinn said, moving up close, pressing the twin muzzles of a sawed-off shotgun into Carver's back, "this is when. You knew it all along."

"No," Carver said, keeping his eyes to the front, "I didn't know."

"Shut up," Zinn said, and pulled a nylon stocking over his face. "Move along. It's the next car. Go in and keep walking."

Carver did as he was told and went into the next car. A conductor sat near the door counting tickets. The man looked up and froze when he saw Zinn enter with the shotgun. Farther along the carriage Carver saw two men who might be the two couriers sitting together. One man, solidly built and middle-aged, had dozed off.

"All right, everyone," Zinn called out, "just stay put. Stay mellow. Nobody gets hurt."

The conductor looked angry and began to rise. Zinn struck him hard between the eyes with the butt.

"Except him," Zinn said.

No further explanation was necessary.

He stood at the far end of the carriage, his shotgun leveled down the aisle separating the seats. The passengers looked in surprise, with several starting to stand; others told them to sit. All the voices were shocked and murmuring. Zinn told everyone to shut up. He walked over to the two couriers.

Zinn waved the shotgun in a gesture for them to stand. The taller man started to get up, swayed, then clutched the seat ahead of him for support. Zinn slammed the shotgun barrel against the man's head. The courier fell back, unconscious. Zinn looked around fast, swinging the shotgun in an arc. Menacing. Eager. The other courier didn't move; he seemed drunk.

The train's air horn honked loudly, and the train pulled into Hayward Park. Carver stood near the vestibule doors, wondering if he'd be able to pull off a shot. Not unless he could do it without hitting anyone else. Had to wait.

An automobile horn honked alongside the carriage.

Zinn picked up the two attaché cases the couriers had carried, the shotgun tucked under his arm. He grunted with the effort, but that merely made him smile. He backed out of the carriage. He dropped the two cases on the ground outside. A car was parked near a row of eucalyptus trees. Zinn stepped off the train just as it blew its horn and began to move.

Carver glanced out the window and saw a fat man behind the wheel of the sedan. The same man who had tried to snatch Amber Ferrik. Carver pulled open the sliding doors of the next vestibule and plucked his .357 from the shoulder holster.

Zinn manhandled the cases to the car as Cholly pushed open the rear door. They worked quickly. Zinn put the cases in the backseat.

Well done, Carver thought, but you're not really going anywhere.

As the airhorn signaled the train's imminent departure, Carver leveled his revolver at the engine of the sedan. His finger squeezed the trigger. Suddenly, just as he was about to fire, a figure stepped out of the last carriage. A black pistol seemed to be an extension of the figure's hand. The figure's arm was raised fast. Aiming. At Ed Zinn.

Two shots exploded rapidly. Two closely spaced shots tugged violently at Zinn's back. He jerked forward, clawing at his back. Startled by the gunfire, a flock of birds burst from a row of acacia trees. Blood stained Zinn's fingers, which were clutching at his wounds. He slumped forward, clawing at the roof, then slid onto the wood. He twitched several times, then fell to the ground.

The birds whistled and squawked loudly.

The train rolled faster, and Carver watched as the figure moved toward the parked car. The distant figure was a woman with gray hair, bulky sweater, and dark trousers. The mouth was a red slash of lipstick, and dark footballs of eyeliner ringed her eyes. Despite the disguise of heavy makeup and gray hair, Carver was sure who it was.

The woman stood about fifteen feet from the sedan, and before Cholly Lehm could collect his wits and get the car into reverse gear, she put three bullets through the windshield. Three bullet cases flew from the automatic, glittering in the sun. The entire shooting had taken less than ten seconds.

Carver could have jumped off, but he watched the woman in morbid fascination. She hurried to the sedan and pulled Cholly out of the driver's seat. Cholly just flopped onto the ground, not moving. Even at that distance, Carver could see bright red blotches masking his face. The woman got in and drove off. With the attaché cases. With the gold.

TWENTY-FOUR

The train gathered speed. Carver put his revolver back into his shoulder holster. He was certain what the woman would do next. All part of the thread stitched through the case. Swaying with the fast-rolling train, he strolled back into the carriage. The passengers were crowded around the windows, chattering away and pointing. The two dead men were mere dots in the background and getting smaller. Carver paid little attention to the passengers' excited talk. He was more interested in the two couriers.

Several of the more compassionate passengers attended to the two unconscious couriers and the conductor. One woman dabbed water-soaked handkerchiefs on the conductor's brow.

An overweight young man and a well-dressed woman were trying to wake the tall courier who had been slugged. The courier slumped awkwardly. The woman patted a wet handkerchief against his bloody temple. The woman snapped an order and the young man ran to the water fountain for a paper cup of water.

Carver sat with the woman and the couriers. He looked at the two men, and the woman looked at Carver.

"I can't seem to wake him," she said worriedly. "Do you think he's dead?"

"No," Carver answered, putting a hand under the man's nose. "He's breathing. Raggedly, but he's breathing." He reached over and rolled up the eyelids of the other courier.

The other was dead to the world. Unconscious. Carver could not wake either man.

Minutes later, the train hooted its way into Hillsdale. Carver got off before the local police swarmed aboard. There was no hurry; the next returning train would come through in about ten minutes.

Time was on his side. Carver was relaxed, although his thoughts ticked over, a machine idling, ready to accelerate. One thought brushed across his memory: The ancient alchemists searched for the philosopher's stone, to turn lead into gold. Yeah, he knew what would happen to the hijacked gold. So there was no hurry.

Should he call Sergeant Ludlow? Carver thought about that for less than ten seconds. No. He wanted this one all to himself. If any rationalization was needed, Carver had to know if his own deductions were correct. He knew—was sure—who had stolen the gold and who was the one other person involved, the one person who had stepped out of character and betrayed himself, revealed himself as the killer.

He smiled to himself as he swung aboard the train for the return trip. The huntsman had to have his quarry.

The trip took about half an hour. At the San Bruno station Carver climbed into his Jaguar and drove back to the foundry. He saw Sharon's blue car parked nearby. That was okay, Carver thought. Might make it simpler. He walked the short distance to Hutte and Son.

*　　*　　*

Many miles south, at the Hayward Park depot, a deputy sheriff moved away from the two covered corpses. He pushed his way through a crowd of sweating reporters, photographers, and county sheriff's department forensic technicians. The reporters threw questions at the deputy sheriff, but he brushed them aside. He headed for a patrol car.

A half-dozen uniformed officers kept the local citizens behind sawhorse barriers. The deputy sheriff picked up the microphone from his automobile dash and made a call.

Sgt. Ernie Ludlow answered and identified himself.

"This is Deputy Sheriff Argilla," the sheriff said, "and we got a couple of bodies here in San Mateo County. They could be the guys you put out a bulletin on."

"Yeah?" Ludlow asked. "Who?"

"One guy, shot in the back twice, has a wallet and the driver's license says his name is Edward Zinn."

"Okay, that's one," Ludlow replied, keeping his voice steady. Excitement bubbled inside, and Ludlow rubbed his stomach.

"The other dead man is a real fat guy. No identification on him."

"Probably Cholly Lehm."

The deputy sheriff gave Ludlow a brief recital of what had happened, as far as could be gathered from the passengers on the train.

"Now, there're two men," the deputy sheriff said, "who say they're couriers and they were carrying over half-a-million dollars in gold. I had them brought here. You wanna talk to them?"

"Fuckin' right."

TWENTY-FIVE

Carver felt bone-weary. He ached all over. His ribs were a constant pain, and his arm felt hot where he had pulled out the splinter. Probably festering. Carver made a mental reminder to himself to see a doctor the next morning.

Outside the foundry he paused, then tried the closed door. Locked. Of course; it had to be locked. That was part of it, too. He could pick it open, but that might take a few minutes or longer.

Make it easy, he told himself. He'd get into the foundry through Sharon's studio. Carver entered the street door to the studio. Sharon was hunched over a drawing board, working on a drawing. A radio played classical music, and she didn't hear Carver.

"Sharon," Carver said quietly.

"Carver!" she exclaimed as she turned around.

"I'm just passing through," Carver explained. He put his finger to his lips. "The foundry is locked."

"There's no one there today," Sharon said. "Karl Hutte

sent them all home. Said there was little work to be done.'' She looked at him and realized that he was tense, his eyes narrowed into hard slits. ''Is there something the matter, Carver? Is it about Tom? Have you heard from—''

His stare silenced Sharon, and again Carver put a finger to his lips. A slight reassuring smile flickered over his face.

He opened the side door, and moments later he stood in the dark and shadowy—and almost empty—foundry. Carver stood by the wall, his eyes slowly getting accustomed to the gloom. The hush of the foundry was eerie, as though an unseen danger slumbered.

The sunlight barely pushed its way past the dirty clerestory windows. The foot-thick posts were like obstacles in a murky maze. The overhead winches and hoist chains caught stray gleams of light. The black, monolithic crucibles seemed ominous.

Carver stayed in the shadows, moving cautiously. He stopped and slid the Python from under his arm. He touched his pocket to be sure he had at least one speed-loader.

The sand and clay floor felt gritty underfoot. The smells of burnt wax and scorched sand filled the air. Most of the fire pits were banked, just glowing coals. They added little additional light to the dim interior.

In the far corner was a single glowing crucible, and two workers stood nearby, close to a fire pit and a casting pit. Both wore heavy gloves, leather aprons, and eye shields. They were reflected in the sunset glow of the heated crucible balanced on a pair of heavy tongs and a chain hoist.

This is where the thread ends, Carver thought. Where Frank Argent's crazy idea would be almost complete. Where stolen gold would be cast into counterfeit nuggets. He fingered the stone in his pocket. The stones were a prototype, a test that foolproof nuggets could be created.

Nuggets can be found in rivers or mines. No purchase records—finders keepers. Easy enough to plant counterfeit nuggets in the river in front of Tom Ferrik's cabin. But it would only work if it were possible to make foolproof nuggets, even to introducing foreign minerals into a nugget casting. So Piombo was used.

Carver shook his head. He had a twinge of admiration for the whole idea. Again he fingered the stone.

The way he figured it, Piombo had made a series of trial casting, using lead instead of gold. It had worked. And Piombo had painted them black to disguise them.

Carver moved carefully, one drifting shadow among many. He held his revolver loosely. So far neither person at the working fire pit had seen him. Carver worked his way past hanging crucibles. His shoulder grazed a chain hoist, rattling the links. The two people heard the clinking and turned around.

They spotted Carver and both of them reacted. One went into a crouch and rolled off into the darkness behind. The other snatched off his safety goggles and stepped behind the nearest beam. Carver crouched and cocked his revolver. He sidled sideways quickly and stood behind a foot-thick beam.

"What do you want?" one of them asked.

Carver didn't answer.

Then the gunfire erupted. Shots ricocheted off crucibles or struck wooden walls and posts.

"That won't do any good," Carver said when the noise stopped.

A gunshot banged and the slug whined off the crucible into the darkness.

Carver dropped into a crouch and moved behind a crucible. He didn't believe in staying in one place too long. They might try to outflank him. But there might be a way to turn them against each other.

A time span of strained silence hovered in the air like a deathwatch.

"Hutte," Carver called, "you don't have the time now to

cast that gold into nuggets.'' The hunting instinct told Carver not to talk, but this was the chance to divide and conquer. ''And, Bob, I know you were the one who tried to shoot Amber Ferrik.''

''You're a liar, Bascombe,'' Bob Hutte said, almost in a whisper.

Above him, Carver heard an office door slam open and closed, and then the stomping of heavy feet down the stairs.

''What is this?'' demanded Karl Hutte. ''Who is it that is shooting in my foundry?''

''Get down, Mr. Hutte,'' Carver yelled.

''*Nein!* This is my business, and you do not have the right—''

A gunshot chipped a crucible near where the old man walked. Karl Hutte didn't hesitate; he kept on coming. Carver wondered if the son had fired the shot.

''Go away, Dad,'' Hutte yelled.

Carver turned, keeping his back protected by the crucible, and faced the older man some yards away.

''Your son stole the gold you shipped.''

''*Nein*, you lie!''

Carver shrugged and turned back to the two people crouching near the gold-laden crucible. The old bastard had more faith in his son than Carver did.

''Robert!'' Karl Hutte said loudly, and moved forward toward his son. ''Do not do this. I am your father, and I tell you—''

''Shut up, Pop,'' another voice said, and a shadow moved from the side door toward Karl Hutte.

Goddammit, Carver thought. How did Ludlow get here?

Karl Hutte moved toward his son, and Carver watched as Ludlow stepped in front of him. The homicide detective kept an eye on the two gold thieves. The old man just kept on coming, and Ludlow grabbed him. With a grunt, Karl Hutte backhanded Ludlow and kept on walking toward his son.

Ludlow tackled the old man, and the two of them wrestled on the floor. Ludlow finally managed to get Karl Hutte's hand behind his back and held him in an armlock. Ludlow breathed hard and pulled his short-barreled revolver. He shoved the weapon into the old man's back.

"Easy, Pop," Ludlow said from between clenched teeth.

The side door opened, and Sharon Argent stepped in, her face puzzled. Carver swore under his breath.

"Hey, stupid!" Ludlow yelled from the floor. "Get the fuck outta the doorway."

As if to punctuate his warning, a shot tore a piece of wood from the door frame. Sharon ducked and crawled into the shadows.

"Okay, Bascombe," Ludlow said, "I got this . . . wiggling old fart . . . stay still, damn it, Pop . . . and the dame is okay. It's your show."

"Barbara, listen to me," Carver called. "I was on the train. You must've seen me. It must've come as quite a shock when those two men grabbed the gold before you could. Did you believe one of them tried to shoot Amber?"

More silence.

"It wasn't either of them," Carver called. "It was Bob Hutte."

Barbara Stahl snapped a shot at him, and Carver heard the slug rip the air inches from his face. He crouched and moved sideways to another beam.

"Barbara," he called, "Hutte was going to double-cross you."

He hoped his words masked his movement. He had a clear shot behind the beam where Barbara had hidden. But she wasn't there.

"Shut up, Bascombe," Bob Hutte ordered harshly. "You don't know what you're talking about. Don't listen to him, Barbara. It's a trick."

Carver wondered where Barbara had gone. He scanned the

darkness . . . and out of the corner of his eye he saw a pale oval face. Barbara. She had outflanked him and was aiming her pistol straight at him. Aimed at him. Pulling the trigger.

And Sergeant Ludlow saw her.

She fired one shot—and Ludlow fired two.

The two slugs kicked her backward. Barbara Stahl sat down hard, her eyes glittering for a moment in the glow of coals in a fire pit. Two mottled holes covered her chest. Then Barbara slumped over.

Bob Hutte moved closer, ducking between a crucible and another beam.

"Watch it, Bascombe," Ludlow called, still struggling on the floor with Karl Hutte, "he's working his way toward you. What, I gotta do all your work?"

Carver sidled sideways like a crab, in the space between a beam and crucible. In the open.

Bob Hutte stepped out from concealment and fired. Carver fired once.

The bullet caught Hutte high in the chest and tossed him back. He struck the heated crucible and fell under it. The crucible swung wildly and then tilted. A stream of fiery gold poured onto Hutte's face.

A scream started but was cut off suddenly. Only the sounds of sizzling and crinkling were left as the molten metal splashed over Bob Hutte.

Carver turned his face away.

Karl Hutte wrestled easily away from Ludlow and moved like a sleepwalker to his dead son. He stood stiffly by the swinging crucible, a dark silhouette with head bowed. He fell to his knees.

Dusting off his trousers, Sergeant Ludlow joined Carver. Sharon Argent came out of the shadows, walking strangely, as though hypnotized. She stood a few yards from Carver and looked at him as though she had never seen him before. She refused to look at the tableau of Hutte and son.

"You oughtta be grateful, Bascombe," Ludlow said. "I don't think you coulda handled those two and the old bastard. Good thing I heard from the two couriers and put two and two together. They were still groggy, but I got the idea about the gold real fast."

Carver nodded and shoved his revolver back into the holster.

"Okay, don't thank me." Ludlow grunted. "I'm used to it. Part of the job."

Sharon continued to look at Carver for a few seconds, like a person who had been given a puzzle to decipher. She tried to see him as she had known him in the past days. The memory was distorted, filled with fear and bewilderment.

Still kneeling by his dead son, muttered curses spilled from Karl Hutte's lips. He slowly turned to Carver and to Ludlow. His eyes glittered redly in the glow from the fire pit.

All he saw were three black people standing in the gloom of the foundry. He rose from his knees and supported his swaying body against a beam. He pointed a finger at them, his face twisted with anger.

"You *schwarzers,* you filth, you damned ones." His eyes blazed. "You have killed my son. You could not take him alive. No, you had to kill him. You and all your kind, you are only good for killing. You can only destroy. *Schwarzers!*"

TWENTY-SIX

The next day Carver had a doctor check him over. With his ribs freshly wrapped, he spent several hours at the Hall of Justice giving his deposition. From there he drove to Sharon's apartment. Her blue car was parked nearby, and he stopped and parked. He got out, walked a few yards—and paused in midstride. No, there wasn't much point, he thought. Maybe it's too soon to see her. He thought about telephoning her later that evening, but decided against it.

No, if he was going to see her, it had to be now. He walked up the stairs and pushed the bell button.

"Hello," Sharon said when she opened the door. The word was flat and hollow.

"Could I come in?"

"No. There's really no point. Is there?" Sharon said. Her voice had regret and disappointment smeared through it.

"I talk better inside," Carver said.

"No, I don't think so. Maybe we could've been friends

. . . once. But that's all we could have been. But after yesterday, I need—I need time to think.''

"About yesterday . . ."

Sharon held up her palm, shaking her head. "Don't, Carver I saw you destroy a human being. Saw Barbara Stahl killed I'm still . . . Oh, I don't know! But I'm a creator. And Tom is a creator, too. I know his faults—he's arrogant, temperamental, and I suppose very highhanded. But he believes as I do.''

"Sharon, I'm sorry. . . ."

"That's not very good, Carver. I believe in building things, making things. With my imagination. It's what I want the whole world to be. Creators, not destroyers." She paused and ran a hand over her face. "It's everything I believe in, and I . . ."

She looked at him, her cheeks wet with tears. Sharon Argent turned away from Carver and closed the door.

He returned to his office, where Rose poured him a tall glass of iced tea. Carver slipped off his shoes and rubbed his feet together. His mood was gray, depressed. He had not felt himself in the midst of such failures for quite some time. He had failed to accomplish the task he had promised Amber, to find her father.

He had failed to prevent Zinn and Lehm from grabbing Amber in the park. Rose had accomplished that. He hadn't seen Zinn following them into the Sierras. Failed to keep Tilly Lot alive. And certainly had failed to take Barbara Stahl and Bob Hutte alive. Failed to keep De Anza and Ludlow informed every step of the way.

And had failed to keep his heart out of the case. Failed with Sharon.

"You'll get over it, boss," Rose said.

Carver looked out the window and put aside the tea. For a few minutes he listened to the fan clattering. He took a bottle and a glass from the desk and poured himself several ounces of Wild Turkey bourbon.

* * *

Ah, there's nothing like a cigarette, Sgt. Ernie Ludlow thought to himself. A dedicated smoker. He relaxed in a chair that Rose Weinbaum had brought in from her office.

Tom Ferrik and Amber looked expectantly at the homicide detective.

Sergeant Ludlow looked at Tom Ferrik; he didn't like the man. Too goddamn much of an artsy-fartsy type. Grown men wearing headbands with their long hair in ponytails—fuck 'em. But he liked the little girl; Amber was excited about going to see the harbor seals at the aquarium in Golden Gate Park.

So ignore Ferrik. Could be worse, he could have sported studded leather and his hair could have been purple with chartreuse spikes.

Tom Ferrik sat facing Carver. He was a pleasant man, not quite as arrogant as Carver had thought him. Ferrik sat erect, as though he had been admonished for bad posture. He swept one hand over his hair, pulling on his ponytail. His Navajo-design headband was dark with perspiration.

Amber stood next to her father with one arm through his. She smiled at him, without resentment, totally loving him. She chattered away, telling Ferrik all about Rose and Mike Tettsui, and the excitement in Golden Gate Park, and that Rose had a gun she kept in her purse.

Ferrik shushed her with a grin.

"All right, Sergeant," Carver Bascombe said. "What's on your mind? Tom Ferrik has promised Amber to take her to the aquarium."

"This won't take long," Ludlow said. "We got the official stuff. The bare bones. Hutte wanted to keep his father's business financially solvent, collect the insurance from the gold theft, and still have the gold to sell." He dragged on his cigarette. "You know me, I like to know all the little details." He tapped his forehead.

Yeah, Carver thought, he knew. Ludlow's photographic and retentive memory, everything filed away in the gray matter.

"Please, since you've asked me here," Tom Ferrik said, "let me tell part of it, the beginning. I knew Barbara and her moods better than anyone."

"Go ahead," Ludlow said.

"Before our divorce, Barbara and I were not well off, and afterward—even though Amber was in my custody—Barbara believed she could still get her away from me. But once I began to make a lot of money . . ." He shook his head, his ponytail whisking against his shoulders. "She could never afford a court fight. Barbara believed desperately that if she had plenty of money, lots of money, she could just take Amber—kidnap her, if you will—and go anywhere in the world, out of my reach. So getting money was an obsession. Barbara was never the most mentally stable person."

"Okay, so Argent met Barbara. How?"

"In Sharon's studio, of course," Carver said. "Sharon told me that Barbara came there to warn her off Tom. Frank was there, and they talked. They ran into each other a few more times in North Beach. He listened to Barbara's problem, and maybe he suggested this idea he had."

"Was my mommy a bad woman?" Amber asked Carver.

"Not really, Amber. She just didn't know what she was doing."

"So the idea was Argent's?" Ludlow said.

"I'm not sure," Carver said, "that he meant it to be taken seriously."

Carver wanted to believe that Frank Argent's proposal was more in the nature of an intellectual problem, not something to be carried out in reality. But did he want to believe that because of his feelings for Sharon? He wasn't sure. Maybe Frank had wanted to back out—but was in it too deep. Maybe.

"Why cast fake nuggets?" Ludlow asked. "Why not just sell the stolen gold on the open market?"

"Too easy to trace," Carver said, "too conspicuous. Especially after a hijacking."

"Christ, there're easier ways. They could've cast counterfeit Krugerrands or other gold coins. Piombo could've done that easy."

"I wouldn't be surprised if they thought of that. But that would require purchase records. No, they had to have found the nuggets. But it would work—only if it were possible to make foolproof nuggets."

"So Argent went to his old buddy, Lou Piombo," Ludlow said.

"Right," Carver replied. "A sculptor who didn't mind a bit of thievery and trickery. A good con."

"And Frank Argent knew about the couriers. He used to work for the shipping firm that supplied them."

"Yeah, Frank knew. He told Barbara, and that the foundry was in financial trouble."

"My wife," Tom Ferrik began, then paused and amended himself, "my ex-wife, knew Bob Hutte from when I used the foundry to have castings made. It must have been easy to sell Hutte the idea to hijack himself; it would certainly keep the foundry financially solvent."

"But Piombo got curious," Carver said. "It didn't take long for him to figure out what they were up to."

"Enter Ed Zinn and Cholly," Ludlow said.

"Unfortunately, yes," Carver said. "Piombo didn't know where the gold was coming from or when it was it going to be shipped. And, remember, Piombo didn't know about Barbara's part in all that."

"One more reason for calling in Ed Zinn," Ludlow said harshly. "Piombo needed muscle to keep tabs on Argent. Follow him around. Even beat the information out of him, if necessary. But they killed him before he could talk. Argent didn't know the shipping date. Barbara was keeping him on a tight string." Ludlow shook his head. "Some tough bitch."

"Yeah, and she killed Piombo when she realized he was going to steal the gold for himself. After all, he figured, why go for some convoluted scheme involving fake gold nuggets when he and Zinn could take the whole shipment for themselves."

Ludlow turned to Ferrik, barely concealing his dislike of the man.

"So Barbara took a shot at you in your studio, and you ran."

"That's correct. I was truly terrified. I ran—and that's where Barbara picked up my jacket and my wallet. She knew I had heard Frank's crazy schemes in the past and figured I'd know what was going on with the gold nugget scheme. And of course she was correct. I knew, and I knew she'd have no second thoughts about killing me. With me dead, she'd have Amber and a lot of money from the sale of the nuggets."

"I suppose she put your coat on Piombo to muddy the waters, or maybe to warn you off."

"Yes, I suppose so," Ferrik said, holding Amber and mussing her hair. "But it was probably both, all mixed up in her mind."

"But it was Bob Hutte who took a shot at Amber?"

"Yeah," Carver said. "He didn't want to kill her. Just wound her. He was a good shot. The shooting was another vicious warning to Tom to stay hidden until everything was completed."

"Actually I was glad to oblige," Ferrik said. "I understood very well the messages they were sending. But I didn't care one way or the other if Hutte stole from himself, or even if they could make the nugget scheme work. As long as they left me and Amber alone. I'd take my chances with Barbara later."

Ludlow mused, taking a drag on his cigarette. He wiped his brow, deep in thought.

"When he realized," he said more to himself, "that Bascombe was butting in, Hutte went off the deep end. He sent a couple of tough street guys to grab all those black stones from Piombo's studio. Then later, he stole the dynamite and tried to kill Bascombe—without any concern for anyone with him. A real nut case."

"Barbara and Hutte didn't know Zinn and Lehm," Carver explained, "but they knew Piombo's buddies were looking for the gold. Somehow Zinn figured out that Hutte was the shipper, and he followed the couriers onto the train. I guess he told the fat guy to meet him at the Hayward Park depot with a car."

"Okay, Jack," Ludlow said to Carver, "how did you know to return to the foundry? There were other places Barbara Stahl might have been taking the hijacked gold."

"Because Bob Hutte stepped out of character. He didn't go against his father's plan using the couriers to carry the gold. And he didn't apologize for his father's idea. Why should he? It fitted his and Barbara's scheme just fine."

Amber looked at Carver and then at the others.

"I want to go to the aquarium," she said. "My daddy promised."

"Yes, dear," Ferrik said, and laughed. "We'll meet Sharon there." He looked at Ludlow. "I guess that's about all. We can leave now, I presume."

"Sure, Jack," Ludlow said. "This wasn't official. We got all the important stuff on file already. Sure, take off."

Rose Weinbaum had been standing in the doorway, fanning herself with a batch of just-delivered letters. She waited until Ferrik and Amber had left, then put one long envelope on Carver's desk. The envelope had an official seal in one corner.

"That's my cue," Ludlow said, and put on his hat. "I'm meeting Raf later."

"Celebrating his promotion?" Carver asked.

"He didn't get it," Ludlow said.

"What?"

"Nah, like I told you he wouldn't. He's a Mex. No way he's going to get to be captain of detectives. Guy named Callahan got the job."

"I don't know him," Carver said. "Was Callahan really more qualified?"

"I'll say," Ludlow said, and laughed hoarsely. "He's Irish."

He went out the door.

"I don't think I like him," Rose said.

"He's all right. Sometimes."

Carver played with the envelope, turning it over and over on the desk.

Even De Anza had failed. What next?

"Carver, aren't you going to open that letter?" Rose asked, indicating the envelope in his hand. "You've been waiting for it."

Carver nodded slowly and carefully slit the envelope with a pocketknife. He read the contents from the State Bar.

"Well, dammit?" Rose said.

A slow grin parted Carver Bascombe's lips.

"I made it."

By the year 2000, 2 out of 3 Americans could be illiterate.

It's true.

Today, 75 million adults...about one American in three, can't read adequately. And by the year 2000, U.S. News & World Report envisions an America with a literacy rate of only 30%.

Before that America comes to be, you can stop it...by joining the fight against illiteracy today.

Call the Coalition for Literacy at toll-free **1-800-228-8813** and volunteer.

**Volunteer
Against Illiteracy.
The only degree you need
is a degree of caring.**

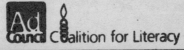

Ad Council   Coalition for Literacy

LV-2